I0727726

also by Michael Hopping

Meet Me in Paradise

MacTiernan's Bottle

Rhythms on a Flaming Drum

MICHAEL HOPPING

Pisgah Press
Candler, NC

Pisgah Press

Pisgah Press was established in 2011 to publish and promote works of quality offering original ideas and insight into the human condition, the realm of knowledge, and the world around us.

Printed in the United States of America

Published by Pisgah Press, LLC
PO Box 1427, Candler, NC 28715
www.pisgahpress.com
pisgahpress@gmail.com

Cover design by David Lynch, www.lynchgraphics.com
Phoenician charm by Amy Brandenburg
www.amybrandenburg.com

Library of Congress Cataloging-in-Publication Data
Hopping, Michael
Rhythms on a Flaming Drum/Hopping

Library of Congress Control Number: 2014949492

ISBN-13: 9781942016014
ISBN-10: 1942016018

First Edition
January 2015

acknowledgements

I don't primarily identify as an activist but have been privileged over the years to work on several projects alongside people dedicated to propositions of peace, social justice, and environmental sanity. Ned Doyle champions sustainable energy solutions. Mary Olson of the Nuclear Information and Resource Service and Dr. Lew Patrie have focused on dangerous nuclear technologies. Bob White started a community garden. Wally Bowen pioneered digital community media in Western North Carolina. There was a mad poet/journalist. And the ubiquitous Jim Brown, networker and master of logistics. Clare Hanrahan, who tirelessly puts herself on the line for human rights. The list goes on. They and tens of thousands of unsung others are due a thanks most too seldom hear.

As this novel took shape, participants in the Wednesday Afternoon Writers' Group and the Great Smokies Writing Program offered valuable feedback. Radical Fringe Writers helped with the polishing. Ray Russell explained points of law. Fred Hansen advised on IT issues. Laurel Reinhardt reviewed passages concerning alternative belief systems. Theater questions were fielded by Maryedith Burrell. They did their best. If there are errors, the fault is mine. I'm grateful to Maryedith, Mitch Hopping, Clare Hanrahan, Jerry Stubblefield, Ellen Thomas, and Sarah-Ann Smith for soldiering through drafts of the text. And thanks to A. D. Reed of Pisgah Press for believing in the book.

Finally, I suppose I should "thank" the global tilt toward authoritarianism and inequity for inspiring the questions raised in these pages. Shifting conditions force uncomfortable choices between stability and change. American history can be read as a record of adaptive change that has often pitted aspirations for domination against demands for greater social justice and the common good. While it has seldom been more evident that he who has the gold makes the rules, progressive movements have won several major battles across the centuries. Despite the generally bleak trend at present, this country may yet again rise to the challenge of the original golden rule. But regardless, down in the trenches the work goes on….

for the agents of progressive change and those who care about them

Rhythms on a Flaming Drum

rhythms on a flaming drum

The crow plucks its gobbet and flaps away, a blue-black horror beating like a heart through trees endlessly done for the season. Wing and branch, weft and warp. Now you see it; now you don't. Illusions are eternity's stock in trade. Jump forward, back, up, down or sideways. Call the search for other possibilities free will. But the pattern is indifferent to justifications, deaf to begging, already complete. Only the eye is moving.

rhythms on a flaming drum

Caitlin Schmidt's attention bounces around the display in the window of an antique store, from the WHITES ONLY sign propped in the corner, to a pink music box with a ballerina on top, a frosted perfume bottle, a tassel-shaded lamp, the bottle again. She's telling herself a story of their connection. A dreamy girl trades her innocence for money. Had Caitlin noticed the lamp first it might have colored the ballerina's tinkling performance of "Dance of the Sugar Plum Fairy" with a dowager's sepia-toned nostalgia. Maybe next time. Changeability is the point of Caitlin's game. At stressful moments she's comforted to rediscover the explanatory power of context. No interpretation is The Truth. Framed differently, a scary scenario becomes something else.

She refocuses to her reflection in the window glass. Who is *this* fair-skinned young woman? The Italian sunglasses and floppy hat obscure a face you wonder if you'd recognize. Some starlet perhaps. Under the conservative casual outfit she's got the body for it; you know she has. Her boutique shopping bag confirms your suspicion that she's a titan, into expensive clothes. Two cops, not the usual single, stroll along the other side of Carolina Lane. They glance in her direction. It's over almost before it begins; she's out of their league. The actor in her notes the angle of the heads as the blue shirts listen to old-fashioned radios clipped to epaulettes. Bunches of plastic handcuffs dangle from their belts, behind, where it's less obvious.

When they round the corner at the end of the block she's transformed again: just another consumer eager for the Lane's temptations. She drifts past shops selling Appalachian knick-knacks, Celtic woolens. Smells of onion, kraut and grease advertise a hotdog cart boasting an umbrella paneled in ketchup-and-mustard-colored triangles. SAUSAGE DOG, ALL THE WAY: $4.95. The doorway of MANIFEST WORD CHRISTIAN BOOKS is fragrant with sandalwood. Not even children wild with July freedom pause at the recessed loading dock where a riot wagon waits discreetly. The headline of the *Calhoun Journal* in the vending box reads "Brazil Elects Bolivarian President." Only leftist radicals would connect this latest rejection of free-market coercion in Latin America to the presence of a riot wagon in North Carolina. Caitlin drops a buck into the guitar case of a handsome African-American busker singing Woody Guthrie. They nod to each other. *Any time now.*

City Administrator Bryce Hufnagel chose not to spook the cash cows this morning. The dismissal of the Sawligoochee Riverwatch lawsuit attracted scant media attention. To no one's surprise Palomar Coatings wasn't required to produce documents that might link its wastewater discharges to high rates of birth defects and cancer. Municipal Water Services, LLC, was granted immunity outright. Law enforcement must have cheered the Riverwatch announcement of a protest action in the rural privacy of the Palomar campus on Lake Hollister. If heads need busting, what better place? But the blue shirts patrolling City Center are on high alert as well. Experience has taught Admin to be wary of misdirection.

Caitlin is mindful of the closed circuit cameras overhead. She keeps her hat brim between them and her face. Her coppery hair is tucked up. Too warm today for a wig. Where Carolina Lane ends at Burnside, she stops to inspect the wooden masks in a gallery window. They were carved by Vietnamese peasants living in a region still too radioactive to farm sixty years after President Goldwater convinced the world that U.S. nuclear weapons are no joke. The masks also attract an older couple weighed down with booty. The three exchange information on police activities. None stares as the riot wagon emerges from Carolina Lane and turns east toward Palomar. No lights or siren. "We're on," Caitlin says. "Let's make some TV. But no mugging for the cameras."

rhythms on a flaming drum

bad water

Calhoun News2's evening report of progress in America's global police actions and a State Department denunciation of Humberto Chagas's election in Brazil is followed by images of protesters being pulled off the security fence at Palomar Coatings. A voice-over informs viewers that four deputies and one federal agent were injured in the melee. The scene shifts to a press briefing. Backed by Lumet County Sheriff's Department and Calhoun PD officials, an Integrated Security Authority spokeswoman declines to estimate the size of the mob. There were several arrests. Detainees face multiple felony counts including attempted murder. The studio anchor adds that former Palomar employee and gadfly Theodore "Teddy" Arnold is among the detained. Arnold, a paraplegic, allegedly assaulted a deputy with a can containing an unknown toxic substance. The stricken officer was taken to Lumet Regional Medical Center for treatment. Further word on his condition is not available.

Caitlin watches the broadcast at her dad's vacation home in Laurel Ridge, a private mountaintop village north of town. She humors his dinner invitations—unsubtle excuses for parental nosiness—in return for vegetarian fare, a condition her stepmother, Leilani, finds galling. Leilani is a believer in traditional values, such as meat and Dominion Party politics. At thirty-six, she's only eight years Caitlin's senior. Caitlin tries not to imagine the appeal Leilani's Hawaiian-Chinese intensity holds for her introverted father, a Republican who might almost be a Democrat if that party still existed. He's out on the patio grilling steaks and slabs of veggies, leaving the women to their own devices in the family room.

"If we had a Dominionist president, that sponger's citizenship would be revoked, praise God," Leilani proclaims. "And the rest of them too. Examples must be made."

"Why not just microwave them with a Hellfire Armored Vehicle? Surely, they have one. Less muss and fuss."

"You'll regret your jokes."

"No doubt. What's this?"

On the steps of police headquarters a News2 reporter displays a piece of paper. "Hundreds of these fliers appeared today in the City Center commercial district."

water advisory

local rates of cancer, birth defects and miscarriages are rising. industrial discharges upstream from lumet county's water source are suspected but the courts don't want you to know what toxic crap palomar coatings dumps in lake hollister.

tap water may be hazardous to your health. titans don't care. they have private filtration systems. guess again, titans. we switched a few feed lines. your lawns love us for it. drink up!

ps. locally brewed beer is safe.

"ISA and Calhoun police officials tell News2 that the investigation is ongoing. In the words of Lt. Roger Dillingham of the Calhoun PD, 'We take all terrorist threats seriously.' Building managers and restaurateurs say private water systems remain safe. But some City Center residents aren't so sure."

Leilani calls through the open sliding door onto the patio, "Wally, dear, you'd better see this. Hurry."

He dawdles at the grill, missing the person-on-the-street interviews. Leilani reloads the segment for him. At the end of it, he sighs. "This is a hoax. Somebody's pissed at losing the court case."

Caitlin agrees. "Besides, isn't municipal water tested?"

"Wally, have the maintenance man check ours."

"The backup filter in the mechanical room has us covered," he says. "Ready to eat? Turn that off. Caitlin, will you set a table for us outside?"

Laurel Knob drops steeply away from the patio railing. Wally and Leilani's view ranges southward, beyond Calhoun to Big Nebo Mountain, halfway to South Carolina. This evening Caitlin sees little out there but summer haze. Her dad's eyrie feels detached, a floating reality. She wipes down a marble-topped café table. She'll sit at Wally's right hand, Leilani to his left. No harm in a private joke.

Dinner conversation turns, as it often does on these occasions, to Caitlin's membership in Collective Harlequin, an alternative theater company with a following in the community of discontent that consumers slur as spongers. The Harlequins' current production is a high-energy revue, *on 2nd thot*. Wally and Leilani attended a performance in Chapel Hill. Between having to mingle with a sponger crowd and fearing that someone would recognize her husband, Leilani had been ready to walk out even before audience members were invited to join in improvisational sketches bristling with subversive wit.

Leilani suspects aloud that the troupe freeloads on Caitlin's money. Although the trust fund has, in fact, underwritten some Harlequin expenses, Caitlin doesn't believe her financial affairs are her stepmother's business and says so.

Wally changes the subject. "Still going out with Chan?"

He has mispronounced the name again. "Not 'Chan.' Xan, as in Alex*ander*."

"If his name is Alexander," Leilani interjects, "why does he call himself a nonsense word? Wally, this is what comes of allowing your daughter to waste her education and … and … consort with spongers."

"Alexander isn't his name," Caitlin says.

"So," her dad persists, "are you two still an item?"

If only you knew. To everyone but her, Xan Hicks is simply Collective Harlequin's new percussionist. "He's good, Dad. Really good. You should hear him play. He gets the most amazing sounds from random junk."

The Chardonnay bottle rides high in the ice bucket. Leilani, the dutiful help meet, clears dishes and offers to bring more wine.

"No thanks," Caitlin says. "I'm leaving soon."

"What's the hurry?"

"Rehearsal. Could I have a glass of water?"

"Water?" Leilani is aghast. "After that news report? No woman of childbearing age has the right to take such a risk, no matter how much she disrespects herself."

So routine is Leilani's sniping that Caitlin hardly registers it. What she does hear surprises her. Leilani plays the role of her dad's sexy thing but hasn't come across as a nesting type. "Dad, is there anything you've been meaning to share with me?"

Wally's brows knit.

"Like maybe you're trying to get pregnant?"

"Would it upset you?" Leilani asks, stooping to nuzzle his neck.

Of course it would, though not because of him. Her dad is a titan, a wealthy and powerful man with impeccable connections. Any child of his could consider herself lucky. He'd pulled the strings to quash the stupid sedition inquiry after her expulsion from Ruskin University six years ago. Had he not been the newly appointed Director of Program Development at OstarFX, the nation's leading source for intelligence services to government and industry, she might still be serving a forced labor sentence. *No, Wally Schmidt is not the problem, Leilani. It's you.*

"Don't worry, Caitlin," Wally says. "One uncontrolled variable in my life is plenty."

rhythms on a flaming drum

For the crime of advocating female contraceptive rights at Ruskin, ISA pressured Caitlin to confess to being a Digger. It wasn't true. It wasn't—not then. To the best of her knowledge she'd never met a member of that fringe anti-capitalist movement. At the earliest opportunity she fled to her dad's new home in Arlington. Only months later, with Leilani's appearance on his radar, did Caitlin regain the confidence to return to her hometown in North Carolina to take courses and audition for parts in theater productions. Memories of her brush with the secret police deterred her from social activism until the Great Memphis Quake.

Initial reports are of a magnitude-7.9 shock, city-wide devastation and mass casualties. This isn't a politically fraught issue. She fills her car with emergency supplies, sleeps a few hours and drives west before dawn. She doesn't think to leave a message for her dad until Knoxville is in the rearview mirror. Near Memphis a National Guard checkpoint turns her back. She exits the interstate and tries alternate routes. Her onboard navigation system is patient with crevassed pavement and bridges knocked off their supports.

Homes on the outskirts are relatively intact. Crashed vehicles and broken pavement become more frequent as she approaches downtown. People roam the streets. Zigzag cracks threaten the stability of commercial buildings. Sidewalks are littered with glass and fallen awnings. Looters crossing the street in front of her drop a giant TV during an aftershock. She slams on her brakes. The looters stop yelling at each other and look in her direction. She hits the gas.

When her fright subsides she turns onto a boulevard closed by a fallen overpass, makes a u-turn and parks. The sun, low over the river, silhouettes a snaggle-toothed skyline. She fears for the historic buildings. Normal cell communications are down but her satellite phone has signal. There are reports of NGO relief teams in areas ignored by Search & Rescue contractors. Direct Aid Now is establishing a camp in a housing project less than a mile from her location.

The apartment buildings there are badly damaged. Wall tents have already been erected in commons areas. A member of the DAN staff asks if she brought camping gear. She did. He welcomes her to the team. Adrenaline sustains her through the next few hours. Before sleep she returns a call from her dad. He's mad but that can't be helped. She passes out, bone-tired.

Relief efforts center on organizing basic life-support in a resource-poor community. Though the quake didn't kill anyone here outright, medical issues vie with food and water in importance. Caitlin serves as ambulance driver. Validated by DAN's distinctive blue-and-white cap and windbreaker, she shuttles emergencies to a hospital where the computers are running too sluggishly to dispute lies about lost health insurance cards.

She hears rumors of rescue efforts in the vicinity but her satellite phone provides the first specifics. Cable news reports that a producer on Linden Avenue observed a white man with a flashlight, backpack and sledgehammer enter the partially collapsed Barboro Hotel. Sonia Crockett's crew—which will share a Peabody Award for this innovation—monitors his progress with listening devices in the wreckage. The mood at Caitlin's camp is skeptical. When the would-be rescuer's shouts are swallowed by the rumble of a severe aftershock and don't resume, Sonia speculates that he may have been lost.

But then her network goes live with breaking news. Technicians detect rhythmic pounding inside the Barboro. Caitlin and the nation tune in, buoyed by a pulse of hope from the depths of calamity. Then nothing again. Hope curdles to fear until the hammering begins anew, accompanied by chanting. A prison work song? How insensitive would *that* be? Crockett compounds the racist undertones by dubbing the man with the hammer John Henry.

Caitlin and three others are dispatched to the scene bearing water, food and first aid supplies. The eight-story flophouse hotel covers a city block. Only the far side of the structure is standing. Elsewhere the upper stories slid off, or in. The parking garage in the open end of the horseshoe-shaped building pancaked. Odors of gasoline and rot seep from it. Heaps of brick and roofing material have closed the side street. On Linden, near the intact section of the hotel, a cameraman records men tossing bricks from one irrelevant pile of rubble to another. Around the corner, past a bus stop, Sonia Crockett has staked out the hotel entrance. It's a cloudy evening. An electrician runs an extension cord from the truck to power flag lights.

Caitlin and the DAN team scarcely have an opportunity to introduce themselves before the lights are switched on. Sonia strikes her pose and speaks excitedly into a camera. A white man steps out of the doorway behind her, followed by two little black girls and a man who is evidently their father. The four huddle on the sidewalk and drop to their knees, singing the song heard inside the hotel. They're swarmed.

Caitlin is too busy phoning her report to catch the brief

interview John Henry grants the network. She'll hear it later, a thousand times. He distills youthful fatalism to its liberating essence. "I'm not here to be exploited," he tells Sonia, refusing to identify himself. "All is lost; can't you see that?" She's flummoxed. Hasn't he just rescued three people? How does it feel to be a hero? "Got to go," he says. He enters the gaggle of onlookers and isn't seen again.

John Henry disappears but doesn't go away. His heroism and contempt are seared into the soul of a generation. The song he sang in those dark hours, titled "Let Your Hammer Ring" by the first kids to upload versions to YouTube, is a viral sensation. Social change movements, including the Diggers, adopt it as an anthem. His retorts become catechism among the dispossessed. A screen grab of John Henry's wild hair and skinny, sledge-toting profile glowers from t-shirts coast-to-coast. He's marketable as all get out but his influence foments so much resistance that the free market sours on him. By then, however, not even OstarFX software can purge John Henry from cyberspace. Caitlin won't forget his impish face and luxurious baritone voice.

beyond the pillars

Xan arrives in Calhoun on the first warm weekend of the year. He's new in town, scouting places to earn Xchange credits, or dollars if need be, by playing music. He sees an Xchange mart in a vacant gravel lot and decides to check it out. The people are all ages, from infants in slings to elders acting as safe bases for toddlers playing chase. Locally produced or recycled goods dominate the display tables. Behind one of them, a fat man in a wheelchair dozes with a Chihuahua in his lap. It yips at Xan's interest in a display case where pendants like old coins dangle on cords.

The man snorts, wakes and wheels over. "You like charms?" he asks. "They're Phoenician, 600 BC. Take a closer look." He opens the case and extracts a pendant.

Heavier than it appears, Xan thinks. *Real silver?* It has an irregular shape and off-center rim. One face crudely depicts an apparent warship at sea. The other features a triangular symbol with projecting rays.

The dog leaps onto the table, growling.

"Let him live, Peaches," the man says.

Xan is unable to decipher the design. "No wonder these never caught on," he jokes.

"Oh, but they did," the man gurgles. "You'll find them in archaeological sites up and down the coast of Europe and Africa. People don't believe me when I say I found these on a Georgia sea island." He clears his throat with a juicy cough, spits into a coffee can wedged between his legs. "I'll tell you a story. Back in the day, Egypt was coming out from under Assyrian occupation. Pharaoh rebuilt his navy and thought he'd fill some coffers by horning in on the Phoenician sea trade. The Phoenicians didn't argue; they sold him as many charms as he wanted. Guaranteed to see a ship safe from Alexandria to the Pillars of Herakles, the gateway to exotic lands. And it wasn't a lie. What the Phoenicians *didn't* mention was the ocean beyond the Pillars. Whole different category of water in the Atlantic. Necho II lost a bunch of ships and had some choice words about Phoenicians carved in stone at Karnak."

"You sure this is antique?"

"Not hardly. Made it myself." He pulls down the neck of his sweatshirt. Resting on a mat of gray chest fuzz is a piece identical to the one Xan holds. "There's still a few with a knack for these things," he says. "Not many. World's full of Egyptians." His fat jiggles with croupy laughter. "You an Egyptian?" He pats his dead legs. The dog jumps down into his lap.

Xan enjoys the guy's sass. "I've been tossing around a few years. Washed up here yesterday. Good design on this. Very cool."

"Before my accident I was a machinist. Fuckers at Palomar dumped me like trash." The story is no less disgusting for being common. "I don't let them forget."

"Glad to hear it." Xan hefts the pendant again. What it's heavy with is attitude. "What'll you take for this?"

"Xchange credits?"

"Some. Not from here."

"A credit is a credit. I'll take four."

"I'll give you five."

Dog and man cock their heads. The man's eyes narrow. "Why, sure," he says.

"Maybe you can answer a question for me. I play music, percussion mainly, steel drum, homemade instruments, sing. Thought I might busk here this afternoon, if that's cool. Who do I see?"

"Me, I guess. I'm Teddy Arnold." The man extends his hand. "We might have room if you aren't too loud."

"Not loud, just good."

"Stop by later and show me the vote on that. I get ten percent."

For a first gig in town, Xan is pleased. He collects 11.5 credits, $32 and a ticket to a theater performance from a redhead who understands how to shake it. She stays a long while. Her dancing contributes mightily to the take. It would be ungentlemanly to decline the invitation.

rhythms on a flaming drum

Caitlin is drawn to the beats in the far corner of the mart. The player is some kind of rhythm magician. Under his sticks, miscellaneous pieces of wood, hubcaps, buckets and pipes come alive. She shimmies in his direction, distributing handbills for *on 2nd thot* as she goes. The sound blurs her vision; she can think of no other explanation for why it takes her so long to *see* him. The delicate facial features and wiry frame match those in her memory. Wasn't he taller? No; as she reluctantly assisted his escape from the national spotlight, her DAN windbreaker had fit him. His hair was darker then. Now it's clean and pulled back in a ponytail. Can she picture John Henry with a neatly trimmed beard? She believes she can. How many years has it been, four, five? She attempts to catch his eye but he's tranced out. The music takes her again. She dances.

Tonight is opening night. The Harlequins built *on 2nd thot* from the ground up: script, stage and sets, promotion, the arrangement of folding chairs to allow free movement in the warehouse theater. All the while honing set-pieces and begging the muse for the presence of mind to take advantage of improv possibilities with the audience. If there is an audience.

She doesn't spot him in the rear of the house until a metallic riff complements the lines of a rowdy Top-40 parody. He's drumming on an empty chair. Other audience members take his lead. From then on, the clapping and harmonizing occur at all the right places. *This is like having a backup band*, she thinks. Her performance jitters evaporate. The show begins to rock.

Toward the finale, actors circulate between stage and house to deliver lines or incite response. Caitlin, costumed as Rosie the Riveter, two-steps down his aisle, unhappily partnered by a domineering mop. At his row she tosses her oppressor into the audience. It's crowd-surfed away. She kneels at his feet and ties the laces of his shoes. "Tell me, don't I know your name?" she sings. "I've been tangled up in you."

Xan is marooned in the living room of Caitlin's apartment. "Don't go," she says. "I'll be right back." She follows the Steins, the last of the Harlequins at the after-party, out onto the former textile mill's third floor landing. The Steins, an older couple, balance free market jobs with nights in alternative theater.

The play was the bomb and the party a blast, Xan tells himself, *an interesting group of folks*. But it's late. His shoes wait by the door.

It opens. Caitlin spins through and clicks it closed with a flick of the hip. She shoots him a thousand-watt smile. "You a friend of Teddy's, Xan?"

"Never heard of him until today."

"You're wearing one of his charms."

"I liked his dog."

She shows him the pendant around her neck. "I have one too, see? Peaches is all bark. Teddy's another matter. But he's not what I wanted to talk about. I know you."

"That so? Who am I?"

"Hairstyles don't fool an actor. John Henry wore his loose, but they say he doesn't like to be recognized." She pads toward him on bare feet.

"Who?"

"John Henry."

"The black dude?"

"He wasn't when I met him in Memphis. He borrowed my jacket. Inconsiderate of him not to return it, don't you think?"

Face to face now, green eyes full of mischief, she undoes the band holding his ponytail.

He eases her wrists down to his chest. "I think you're maybe confusing me with somebody else."

That voice again, purring up from the depths. She didn't get to hear it much at the party. He'd circulated, listening mainly, revealing little. Her finger traces the outline of his silver disc. "I'm just saying you don't need to hide from me."

"Why would I want to?"

"I don't know. All is lost. Or was that just a line?" Desire and disdain flicker at the corners of her mouth. She allows his thumbs to trace the wings of her collarbones. Fingers trail lightly down the nubby silk at her back. Others knot in the waves of her hair. The kiss is a high dive into deep water. Nothing to do but hold on.

When they come up for air she whispers, "I think I'd like to drown."

All is lost.

Clothing floats away on the waterless sea of her couch. Xan meets his share of women on the road and travels prepared. He finds what he needs before his wallet is out of reach. But he's awkward tonight, off balance. Since the day that TV lady measured him for a brass plaque he's lived as though Memphis never happened. America was happy to settle for a blur who stopped talking back. Everybody, from cop to street kid, colludes with his anonymity. Until tonight. He's been blindsided, stripped of his disguise by a woman too tempting to refuse.

Sensing the apprehension Caitlin slows down, soothing, cradling, answering the questions his fingers ask with kisses, warming his hands with her own. *I'll guard your secret. The strength is in me; feel it here, and here, and here. Beyond this single fact I'm as uncertain as you. Feel that too.*

His touch says that he does, and more. She's claimed, challenged to join in surrendering control. Her body accepts. *If this is to be, this is how.*

Strength to strength, they sink. The salt skin of the world rolls over them. Contorted in the currents, they are reduced to swirling parts. Here a throat; there a leg sweeps by, a fullness. Bellies tighten, shot through with sparkling paroxysms. Nails carve flesh. Somewhere softness is riven and gasps. As one they wake to uncharted vastness. No monster, no edge, no fear, only exhilaration. Seaweed dances. Aerial currents swoop the birds. All that seemed separate now appears as endless variation on eternal rhythm, the tangible manifestation of invisible fire. Shells pulverized by the waves sand beaches where lovers venture, their tracks endlessly erased, moon by moon, generation upon generation. Wrenched and raw, caught in a vibrating crescendo, life clutches, its sole remaining defense against the final unmooring. But the power is too great. All is swept away.

A sea-green eye materializes behind wet strands of hair. The bearded man brushes them from her face. He smiles. Around their toes the tide is surging.

rhythms on a flaming drum

Caitlin leaves her dad's vacation estate pleased by Leilani's freak-out over the water news. *She'd felt vulnerable and well she should.* The Laurel Ridge water system must have been high on the Monkeywrench list of targets although Caitlin can't be sure. The decentralization and autonomy of Digger affinity groups has drawbacks but tight operational security is safer for everyone. She's due at the report-back meeting of her own group, the Street Artists, a covert Digger subset of Collective Harlequin.

Street Artist support for the Monkeywrench water project had been the first action Caitlin considered blocking. Leilani does, after all, raise an important point. Toxins are especially dangerous for kids. While titan parents richly deserve the straight-piped discharges of *laissez faire,* embryos and children are innocent, regardless of social class. The Steins and Mari Errandonea, who doubles as Street Artist and Monkeywrencher, countered by asking if the short-term exposure of titan kids outweighs the chronic harm Palomar inflicts on everybody else. Caitlin admitted it doesn't, not if the project has a realistic chance for success. But she remains uncomfortable.

This isn't the sort of question she can bounce off her dad. Wally's group designs the software OstarFX uses to monitor and disrupt terrorists and other banned groups, including Diggers.

He flourishes under corporate neo-feudalism. Titans are rarely inconvenienced by the restrictions imposed on consumers and alternative citizens. In Wally's mind stability is good; Diggers threaten it. She wishes he was more flexible. His advice is so logical and sometimes she needs that perspective.

Xan maintains that he's apolitical. She doesn't reveal Digger names or projects as such to him but they do discuss hypotheticals. He said powerful people benefit from an occasional taste of self-judgment. *As if the average titan is capable of it.* The complexities of his music coexist with surprising amounts of naïveté.

Ideologies aside, her conscience won't allow her to offer tap water to a child. If not for her dad's in-home filter would she have drunk any tonight? To inoculate herself against suspicion, probably. What if she wasn't using birth control?

The moral dilemma is shelved as she approaches the Laurel Ridge exit. Her not-so-new Civic is out of place here. Luckily the man at the gatehouse recognizes her. She flashes him a rich bitch smile. He raises the gate without the hassle of a vehicle inspection.

At the bottom of the mountain a billboard advertising the Joseph and Magdalene Homes for Children is a dreary reminder of everyday reality. "Tomorrow's workers start here!" *In training schools designed to instill mindless compliance.* Radio news teases an impending statement from the President. He's expected to say Bolivarian provocations to the free market will not be tolerated.

Caitlin parks two blocks from the Steins' home in Calhoun and disguises her appearance: jeans jacket, yellow do-rag and shooting glasses from her wardrobe department in the back seat. The floppy hat and Italian shades she borrowed from Reba Stein are there too, in a laundry bag. She slings it over her shoulder and locks the car.

Corporate sponsorships are revitalizing the College Hill campus of Carolina Highlands College—they've re-branded it the Carolina Highlands University of Applied Arts & Sciences but the new acronym is popular only among fans of opposing sports teams. Corporate money trickling down the hillside takes the form of tacky institutes where hand-picked students train for careers in sponsoring industries. Caitlin steps carefully along a broken sidewalk. The houses on this street have been converted to student ghetto apartments. Long evening shadows aren't kind to the peeling paint and ill-kept lawns.

Izzy and Reba Stein own a rare bungalow clinging to the memory of a brighter past. Warm pastels grace the woodwork. Above the front porch a pair of dormer windows stares onto the street, eyebrow rooflines raised in clownish amusement. Caitlin ascends the lolling tongue of porch steps. Tijon has his scooter chained to the railing. She presses the bell button and observes movement in the door's beveled glass panel.

Reba whisks her inside. "You looked *marvelous* this morning," the last faculty member—part-time—of the CHUAAS Dramatics Department exclaims.

Gertrude, the Steins' St. Bernard mix, is equally effusive. Caitlin, her cheek and arm dripping with slobber, deposits the laundry bag in the hall closet. "Thank the university for me."

Izzy thunders down the stairs. He's a psychotherapist who blames his gray hair and barrel-chested physique on a diet heavy with client sins. "Did you catch NewsStooge? That condo owner yelling how unconcerned she is?"

"My dad's wife had a fit," Caitlin says. "Are we all here?"

Reba directs them to the kitchen. "Denny and Tijon are upstairs. We're waiting for Mari. Gertrude, I think it's time for you to go to the bedroom."

"A beer?" Izzy asks, reaching into the fridge. He grabs two, opens them and hands her one.

They click bottles. "All is lost." Caitlin wouldn't have said it if Xan was around. He's uneasy with John Henry references. Izzy had picked up on that at the *on 2nd thot* after-party and took her out onto the landing to warn her that the drummer she invited might be ISA. She hopes Xan will eventually claim his past but he's not ready.

"Here's to titan paranoia," Izzy says. "Bring on the water tests."

"Leilani is demanding a full battery."

The doorbell buzzes. Without waiting to be let in, the Monkeywrench liaison to the Street Artists bursts into the kitchen, the sheath knife she always wears plainly visible at her side. So much for disguise. Despite the pronunciation of her name, Mari is no biblical madonna. She's Xena Warrior Princess to Caitlin's girly girl. Yang to Caitlin's yin. "Those pig bastards jerked Teddy out of his chair and beat the shit out of him. Then they disappeared him. Swear to goddess, it was a Black Mariah snatch." Mari is seldom in such a lather but she and Teddy are close.

"Let's go upstairs," Izzy says as Reba returns from the bedroom minus Gertrude. "Tijon and Denny need to hear this."

Under the lace-curtained window looking out from the dormer office, Tijon Porter, the Harlequins' most accomplished male actor, reclines with black cat dignity at the end of the futon couch. Denny slouches in a wing chair by the door, blond ponytail tucked under a NASCAR cap. The ebony plugs he usually wears in his earlobes have been replaced by a less obvious, flesh-colored pair. Denny's the Harlequin sound man and the computer whiz known in Digger chat rooms as Wraith. He retracts his gangly legs from the doorway. Mari sits at the computer hutch to download images from her camera.

The first of them, shot from high in a tree, reveal the deployment of the law enforcement combined task force. Demonstrators are boxed into an area between the plant's main gate, perimeter fence and a wall of portable barricades. Behind that are a Correctional Rehab bus, riot wagons, several black-and-white cruisers and two unmarked tan cars. A picture time-stamped 2:01 PM shows the protesters under attack from cops in riot gear. The mayhem plays out in subsequent frames. Protesters are beaten, pepper-sprayed and loaded for transport. By 3:10 the area is cleared of demonstrators. At 3:17, an unmarked black van with smoked windows appears. A fat man with his head in a bag is being dragged toward it. Six minutes later the van is seen leaving. The license plate looks federal.

Mari copies her images onto a thumb drive for Denny. In addition to Street Artist duties he's a NetBat, a member of the nationwide affinity group primarily responsible for digital networking and the Digger darknet. Most of his day was spent as an observer in a parking deck overlooking the rear of the federal building. He saw a black van depart the underground federal lot at 2:45. "It was still out at 6. I didn't see any prisoner transports."

Tijon, the busker Caitlin greeted this morning in Carolina Lane, has little to add. When flier distribution began he switched to the role of homeless Negro, prepared to distract attention from Caitlin and the Steins if necessary. Then he'd drifted over to the detention center, anticipating Palomar arrests. "They unloaded the bus and riot wagons at the prisoner entrance," he says, "but no van. Maybe they took Teddy to the hospital."

It's a doubtful prayer. Mari cycles back through her photos to one depicting a clubbing. "That's Teddy under there," she says. "Then I lost track of him until here," she skips ahead, "when he's unconscious and being dragged. I swear it's a snatch. That van is a Black Mariah."

The possibility that a Black Mariah might be active locally is awful news. Widely known but never acknowledged, snatch teams are ISA's bogeymen, operating free of judicial oversight. Izzy once treated a snatch victim who resurfaced too traumatized to function independently. She soon disappeared again; he never learned if it was by choice.

"This doesn't make sense," Caitlin says. "Sawligoochee

Riverwatch staged the demo. Teddy's group was only there in solidarity. Why snatch a loudmouth paraplegic?"

Izzy's dubious as well. "Since when do Black Mariahs disappear people in broad daylight? Teddy's arrest was announced. Who would he call from jail? Mari, who cares for his dog when he's not home?"

"Peaches stayed with me when I had the basement apartment at Teddy's place. I'll ask the new renters."

"I'll contact Lumet Regional," Tijon says. "Ah'm his sister from another mister."

Mari can't keep a straight face. "If Teddy hears *that* you won't need a hospital directory to know which room he's in."

After the laughter she says, "Another thing happened this afternoon. A weasely fisherman was watching the fire trail when I left the lake. He was all in camo, sitting on a log at least a hundred yards from water. I didn't spot him until too late. He wanted to know what I was doing. I told him, hunting mushrooms. He thought he should check my backpack for poisonous species but I gave him an eyeful of my knife and kept walking. The asshole didn't like that. He cast a spoon at me and snagged my shirt. I cut his line." She shows them a metal lure with red plastic eyes and a treble hook.

Reba's rouge accentuates the sudden pallor of her cheeks. "Did he chase you?"

"He'd have regretted it."

"Ah, the fearlessness of youth," Izzy declaims in Shakespearean throat.

Mari beams.

"Other comments or questions on this topic?" Reba asks, recovering her composure. There being none she says, "We must *all* be more cautious. That includes you, Izzy. You know how your heartburn acts up." She turns to Caitlin for sympathy. "Can you guess what he ate for lunch? You won't believe it. Street hot dogs.

With sauerkraut. We'll be up all night."

"…and the indignities of age," Izzy sighs, his Lear deflating to Walter Mitty. "I was hungry, dear."

rhythms on a flaming drum

Sieved through a canopy of trees, sunlight dances on the broad pool below Buckeye Falls. Tiny flies ply the air like dust motes. Out on the water a low-flier is dragged into the depths with a popping swirl. Wally swats at a buzz near his ear, recalling the Vermont ponds of his childhood. He was too busy shucking shoes back then to notice bugs. *When did it change?* He wipes his tassel loafer against a pant leg to dislodge a leaf. *That'll leave a stain. Wally, honey, did you remember your sunscreen?* He's being facetious now. It deadens the sting of becoming his own nagging mother.

He, Leilani and a dozen other potential donors are roughing it at the falls this afternoon courtesy of local hero Bobo Huskins, a business baron of the first magnitude. Bobo was Appalachian born and bred. To hear him tell it the years he spent globetrotting to build his empire were horrid. At present his goals are more personal. He wants to own the entirety of the West Fork watershed—to date he's locked up 3,800 acres of surplus federal land—and revive his cultural heritage. To that latter end he founded the Southern Mountain Alliance, the educational charity sponsoring this event.

Accepting the invitation was Leilani's idea. She's the social secretary in the Schmidt household; Wally appreciates that about her. Left to his own devices he burrows into his work. He's not a natural mixer but she's right; fresh air prevents brooding. They've been carried up here in glorified golf carts for drinks at Bobo's new waterside gazebo. Its timbers came from this land, as did the rock for the stonework. Under the shade of the green copper roof, ladies and gentlemen not interested in venturing further into nature chat on cushioned benches, canapés and drinks in hand. Wally gives Bobo credit. The man throws a first-rate fundraiser.

"Wally," Leilani trills behind him. "Isn't this wonderful?"

She's arm-in-arm with their host. Bobo towers over her, wearing his trademark Cheshire grin. It's the kind, as he admits himself, that causes a man to protect his wallet.

"Good to see you, Bobo," Wally says. "I was just thinking how much I miss the days of being wet and dirty and smelling like fish. Are those speckled trout I see in there?"

"Twelve inches and more, some of them. Finest natives in the Blue Ridge. My head groundskeeper spent the best part of two winters prospecting creeks for breeding stock. At least that's what he told me he was doing," Bobo winks. "Sometimes it doesn't pay to ask too many questions."

"Beautiful spot," Wally says. "Your gazebo is a work of art."

"The missus wanted a covered place to sit. My man Josh, the groundskeeper, oversaw construction. Nothing says Southern heritage like putting it to work." He holds up his drink. "Take the whiskey in this glass. Produced right here the old-fashioned way. Corn, sugar and branch water. All taxes paid, of course."

"It's so awful about the water," Leilani says.

Bobo is confused. "This water is pure as it comes. Percolates down through these rocks and I own them all. The only man pissing upstream is me."

"And you wonder why girls prefer wine? I meant the pollution and the terrorist sabotage."

"Not a thing wrong with municipal water," Bobo says.

"Anyway, we're on a well here. I like the taste better, no chlorine and whatnot."

"But when you go to town? Or the drinking fountain at church?"

"Doesn't bother me at all. I have men on the Palomar board. They'd tell me if there was anything amiss. Don't let the agitators get to you. I know that trick, use it myself. Start a rumor, then buy or sell before the suckers catch on."

"But the health risks…"

"That's the idea. Gin up a panic so folks don't use their heads. Truth is, Palomar could dump damn near anything into that big old lake without hurting anybody. I wouldn't eat fish out of Hollister, but water drawn miles downriver? Like they say, the solution for pollution is dilution."

"And the disease rates? Are the saboteurs inventing that too?"

"There's always disease. Remember, we're not talking you and me here. They don't say *who* gets these diseases, do they? Spongers don't take care of themselves, don't go to doctors, breed like rabbits. What do they expect?"

Wally watches Leilani's face tighten. She hates not being taken seriously. He says, "Speaking of that, Bobo, fill us in on your new Alliance project. It involves the training schools?"

"That's right. Education is the cornerstone of tomorrow. The Alliance can't bear the thought of training schools stunting bright Southern minds. It's not a kid's fault if his parents are unfit. Why should their crimes doom him to a lifetime as a menial? If he's got real talent he ought to have the opportunity to better himself, go to college. How many service and stoop laborers do we need, for Christ's sake?"

Wally says, "Thanks to the scarcity of immigrants, the Department of Labor projects shortages for years to come."

"Thanks to incompetent planning, you mean. One supply dries up, you tap another. I know neighborhoods you can't drive through without hitting a criminal. There's no excuse for Correctional Rehab to lack an adequate workforce. And, whatever your feeling on the Babies for America Act, nobody questions the importance of high sponger birth rates."

Leilani asks, "I thought the Alliance proposal was to take children *out* of hostels and training schools?"

"A select few. The Southern Mountain Alliance proposes to bring out the cream of the crop and raise them right. Grow them into good consumers."

Wally raises his voice as a 4x4 utility cart pulls up to the gazebo. "What have you got in mind?"

"A four-pronged approach." Bobo counts them off on his fingers. "Selection. Adoption. Scholarships. Employment. Employment in a managerial level, free market job. I've got a gal to explain the details later at the house."

The cart driver signals gingham-shirted wait staff to unload coolers from his vehicle.

"But enough of that," Bobo says. "Our next round of refreshments has arrived and I've asked Josh there," he indicates the driver, "to tell us about building the gazebo. Are you familiar with mortise-and-tenon joinery?"

Leilani says, "My glass is empty. Wally, may I bring you something?"

"A dose of Bobo's moonshine will be fine. Thank you, dear."

Huskins corrals the donors for the gazebo presentation. The glass Leilani hands Wally is pleasantly chilled. The liquor isn't bad either. Josh Rice has the weathered face of an outdoorsman; he might be anywhere from thirty to fifty. Affable, energetic and in command of his facts, he describes harvesting the logs, forming the green timbers and mating them with precision. It was the Tab A and Slot B technique on an adult scale, involving odd angles handcut into pieces sometimes weighing hundreds of pounds.

At the conclusion of the presentation, Bobo tells the donors.

"Friends, Josh here won't mind me saying that you've just witnessed a sample of what the Southern Mountain Alliance intends to accomplish. If training schools were the rule when he was a youngster he'd be nobody, not the overseer of this fine project. It's a fact. His momma was a sweet girl who couldn't stay out of trouble. Eventually landed her in prison. She signed him over to Lucy and me rather than give him to the state. That boy was a hellion." Bobo chuckles at Josh with what Wally suspects is envy. "Today he's an upstanding Christian with a wife and three darling daughters. Supervises a dozen men. We're proud of how he turned out, aren't you?"

Josh must be used to this sort of public humiliation. He eyes the ground as his rescue from nobody-hood is applauded.

"With your help, friends," Bobo continues, "the Rise Up Initiative will save the next generation of Josh Rices. They need someone to believe in them, to back them. I'm asking you to stand with the Alliance and make it so."

rhythms on a flaming drum

obituary

Mari calls as Xan is leaving for work. She tells Caitlin there's to be an emergency gathering at the Kava Bar tonight. Caitlin rushes to her computer. A terse notice in the *Calhoun Journal* confirms the news.

Theodore Duval Arnold

Theodore D. "Teddy" Arnold, 54, of Calhoun, died on July 29. Mr. Arnold was formerly employed at Palomar Coatings. He was a son of the late Errol J. and Mattie Nations Arnold. Mr. Arnold is survived by a brother, Levon A. Arnold, of Knoxville, TN. Funeral arrangements pending.

Caitlin reverts to the little girl who believes in the power of not knowing. Not knowing prevents a thing from being true. But she's made the mistake of reading Teddy's obituary. So now he's really dead.

Activists have been killed elsewhere, but this is Calhoun. She'll never be able to look at a cop without thinking of Teddy. She can't speak. Who would she tell anyway, except Xan, and he's not here. She retreats to bed and hides under the covers, where the smell of him and fabric softener gradually restores a measure of calm.

She'll get her act together and do her shift at the credit counseling center as scheduled. Sorting through the sketchy records of clients in money trouble should take her mind off Teddy.

babies for america

Mari's meeting is happening in the outdoor performance space of the Nirvana Teas & Kava Bar at the high end of the delightfully convoluted Peacock Courtyard, in City Center. The report on Teddy has swept town. More people know *of* Teddy than actually knew him. They may have been uncomfortable with his strident tactics but his heart was in the right place and his death in custody does not sit well. Caitlin estimates the turnout at a hundred plus. The courtyard echoes with angry murmurs. Teddy's friends are well-represented, as are Sawligoochee Riverwatch and other activist groups. Xan is far from the only non-Digger Harlequin in attendance. There's also a probable agent provocateur, a woman who encourages violent proposals and takes a lot of pictures at grassroots events.

Tijon has agreed to facilitate the meeting. No one is better at leavening debate with humor. Caitlin will take stack for him. She has the knack of remembering the order in which people signal a desire to speak. Tijon calls the assembly to order with a shout for the group to clap once.

"Now clap twice," he says. The two claps are louder and better coordinated. He asks if there's consensus on Caitlin and him serving as the facilitation team. The crowd wiggles skyward fingers, twinkling assent.

He begins with a moment of silent reflection on Teddy's passing. Many heads bow. Others stare defiantly ahead. Caitlin isn't religious but prays anyway.

An agenda is consensed upon. Mari recounts Teddy's disappearance at Palomar and the fruitless efforts to obtain information afterward. Teddy's brother didn't hear anything, she says, until ISA representatives personally informed him of the death. Levon refused to sign the papers they brought to his house, not understanding what they were for. It will cost $1,200 to claim Teddy's body. Otherwise Levon will receive his brother's ashes in due course. Levon doesn't have $1,200.

Mari hands the mic to a man named Steve who lives in Teddy's basement. He tells how ISA rousted him and his wife at home after Teddy disappeared. At gunpoint they were forced to lie face down while their baby screamed and agents ransacked the premises. Teddy's computer, file cabinet and other belongings were taken.

Tijon opens the floor to proposals. Six are offered. The two suggesting street actions draw support from the ISA plant. "Breaking a few pig windows will teach them a lesson," she insists. Her enthusiasm chills the contingent advocating a march and sit-in. Twinkles of support for either idea are far outnumbered by downward wiggling fingers of disapproval. Others in the crowd raise crossed forearms, blocks, signifying adamant objection. Caitlin's stack-taking skills are tested as the meeting works through the remaining ideas. It becomes necessary to physically line up those wishing to be heard.

The group negotiates consensus on combining the four proposals into a fundraising benefit to help with Teddy's expenses and the legal needs of arrested Palomar protesters. Courtyard merchants agree to Sunday afternoon, typically a slack time for business. Members of Collective Harlequin and The Blownglass Trio will headline the music.

Tijon often celebrates the completion of an agenda by inviting the assembly to give itself a cheer. Not tonight. He leads the group in singing "This Land is Your Land," complete with Woody Guthrie's politically unwise verses.

The apartment is stuffy when Caitlin and Xan finally get home. They open the window and crawl onto the fire escape to sit on the cool metal mesh. She lights a candle for Teddy—a hand-me-down gesture from her mother's Irish Catholic roots—and sets it on the railing. She leans on Xan's shoulder.

"It's so hard to believe," she says. Low clouds reflect the glow of Calhoun to infernal effect.

"Yeah." As a rowdy group passes by on the street below, Xan says, "Want to hear what happened to my folks?" She studies his face in the candlelight. Until now he has dodged her interest in them, other than to tell her he was eleven when they died. "They were schoolteachers. We moved to Haiti after Duvalier. The idea was to teach and bring democracy, you know? I thought Port-au-Prince sucked until I met a pack of boys my age. *Les Frères* were geniuses at turning nothing into something. They taught me to drum. Everything was cool from then on, until the *coup* rumors. Dad ignored them. But one day this rusty truck full of paramilitaries drives up to the school. They march in and, without a word to my parents, execute them. Mom across the hall; Dad in front of me. If a *Les Frères* kid hadn't pulled me out of there I'd be dead too."

"Oh my god," she whispers, straddling him and taking his head in her hands. "Why?"

"To show who's boss? Does it matter?"

"Of course it does." She kisses his forehead.

He shrugs under her. "I hated my parents for not getting out when they could."

"They didn't know what was going to happen."

"Idealists never do."

What a terrible thing to say. She sits back, her hands dropping to his shoulders.

"It's true, isn't it? But I forgave them after a while. If it wasn't the Tonton Macoutes it would have been a bus wreck in Little Rock or a falling piano. In this world, shit happens."

"That's so cold."

"Sorry," he says, leaning forward to kiss her. "My parents were good people. I loved them more than anything. They just guessed wrong one day too many."

"There was one night they guessed right." She snuggles close. "Do you ever think about it?"

"About what?"

"Kids. We can't let them kill us all."

"That's what we're supposed to think. The machine always needs fodder. Why cooperate?"

"I know; you're right." She fingers the charm on his chest. "But what if twenty or thirty years from now there's nobody like you for a lonely Digger to find? The world would be truly rotten then."

Setup for the Teddy Arnold benefit proceeds smoothly for Xan and Denny, Collective Harlequin's soundman. The outdoor stage at The Spouter Tavern, in the low end of the Peacock Courtyard, is an ideal venue. Acoustics and stage visibility are better in the pit than up at the Kava Bar, plus Denny has access to the soundboard. Xan's percussion kit for the event includes the tavern's dumpster, a monster bass. A stage-side dumpster might offend consumer patrons but this isn't their joint. The Brew & Spew, as it is known, serves gut bomb food and more PBR than Tire Iron Red or other craft beers. Regulars tend to be young, pierced, sick of kissing free market ass. Their music screams, hence the muscular sound system. Mari and some of Teddy's friends filter in. They'll be collecting donations, dollars only, no Xchange credits. Feds don't take Xchange; the work-based currency is technically illegal.

Denny stays for lunch but the musicians are gathering at the Kava Bar. It and the Udon Noodle Factory at mid-block are the only shops with outside, street frontage. Tourists pose in front of the Peacock Gate, the lower end showpiece of the three public accesses, never caring what lies behind the wrought iron. Chamber of Commerce guidebooks don't say and the courtyard is cool with that. The Kava Bar takes a refined approach to coping:

exotic teas, kava, couches and acoustic sounds.

Xan's in no hurry. The courtyard has a history he's only beginning to piece together. During the Jazz Age the Peacock Gate closed off the alley behind the tall hotels at the bottom of the block. The horse stables there were replaced by buildings now housing The Spouter—originally a speakeasy—and a tattoo parlor. But most of the courtyard's architectural features are older. Mortar oozes like fossilized frosting between the fire-blackened stones of rough-cut foundations. Inside the current perimeter of shops and art studios, remnant walls and stairways terrace the open space. Some stairs lead to dungeon apartments. Others climb toward Kava.

Caitlin greets him there with a swaying embrace. The Blownglass Trio is finishing a chorus of "I'll Fly Away." Scamp Wallace lays aside his guitar and reaches for the banjo. They ease into "Big Rock Candy Mountain"—Caitlin sings it in the first act of *on 2nd thot*. Scamp wants her to add the raunchy verse omitted in the theater production.

"Come on," he pleads. "They promise lemonade springs where the bluebird sings but all we get is pissed on. Try it with me."

> *The punk rolled up his big blue eyes*
> *And said to the jocker, "Sandy,*
> *I've hiked and hiked and wandered too,*
> *But I ain't seen any candy.*
> *I've hiked and hiked till my feet are sore*
> *And I'll be damned if I hike any more*
> *To be buggered sore like a hobo's whore*
> *In the Big Rock Candy Mountains."*

Xan's true love would have to be a whole lot drunker than he's ever seen her to wrap her lips around those lyrics on stage. "You're singing too," she tells Scamp. "Why don't *you* take that verse?"

Unfortunately he's up for it.

Both Tijon and Scamp lobby to close the show with "Let Your Hammer Ring." Prior to this moment Xan hasn't been confronted with the prospect of playing John Henry's song. Caitlin glances in his direction. She'll veto the idea if he needs her to. He answers with a resigned exhalation. *It had to happen sometime.*

He orders a double kava shot at the bar. His portion of calm and clarity is ladled into a plastic cup rather than the traditional bowl. With the first muddy-tasting sip tingling on his tongue he steps outside. The courtyard is filling. Mari and the others will be pleased.

He returns as the band decides to strip "Hammer" to voice and percussion. Xan has no problem with that. "It's a prison song," he says. "Anybody want to shake a log chain? County farm maracas, a rustle under the vocal?"

An admirer of Caitlin's buttonholes her and Xan on their drift toward The Spouter; "Teddy would have loved this!"

The lower half of the courtyard is packed. The Peacock Gate has been closed. New arrivals are entering from the upper end. People in lawn chairs occupy studio balconies. Xan and Caitlin debate pushing on to the tavern but decide to spectate a while.

Mari opens the proceedings with a Native American prayer. Then she brings the MC, popular internet radio personality Gil Punshon, to the stage to get the entertainment underway with The Blownglass Trio. They pump life into an audience flat with grief. "I'll Fly Away" becomes a rousing sing-along.

Caitlin and Xan go backstage during the speeches. There are testimonials from Teddy's friends, an International Workers Party call to action against ISA brutality, and an update on the remaining forty-six protest detainees. If convicted, some face Correctional Rehab internments of two years. A legal defense fund has been established.

"Please give generously," Punchon purrs in his cigarette drawl. "And now, let's welcome the man who's always beat. Never beat down. Our favorite performance poet, St. Dean!"

Xan has accompanied St. Dean before and does so now on selections from Ginsberg's "Kaddish" and "Howl." Dean's words twine around the spare scaffolding of the drums. The crowd digs it.

Next up is Sawligoochee Riverkeeper Brent McWhorter. His organization filed the Palomar lawsuit. He starts in to defend the plant demonstration but the paper he's reading from trembles so badly he gives up. "I'm sorry," he says. "We didn't intend… This wasn't Teddy Arnold's fight. He offered us bodies for the demo. Those were his words; 'Can we put some bodies on it for you?' I can't forgive myself. Thank you."

He departs the stage to shouts of, "Palomar is guilty, not you," and "Fuck you, ISA." Xan imagines a teargas reply from an overflying crowd-control drone.

Punshon must be thinking along similar lines. "That's right, folks," he shouts. "Put your hands together for Brent McWhorter. Let him hear how you feel about him."

Applause echoes off the bricks and sooty stones.

"And folks," Punchon says, "don't forget the vandals that stole the filter bypass handles and gave the titans a taste of dirty water. We don't condone illegality, but God bless our plumbers!" There is a cheer, another round of applause. "Look for the donation buckets coming around. The red ones are to bring Teddy home. Folks we've got to do this. The green ones are legal defense. We've got to do that too. Dollars only. And now, let's bring out Caitlin Schmidt and Tijon Porter!"

Tijon kicks off the set with Bob Dylan's comic "Talking World War III Blues." Scamp decides against buggering "Big Rock Candy Mountain" with his verse. The rambunctious vibe continues until Caitlin drenches it with a cover of "It Ain't the Wind, It's the Rain." The audience can't decide if clapping for this aching farewell to

Teddy would be respectful.

"We'll miss him," Tijon says. "Remember to donate. We have one more for you. You know this one. Join in as the spirit moves."

Xan watches himself lift the lids on the dumpster. He hits a booming shot with a bachi stick. And again.

Tijon moans,

Let your hammer ring
Let your hammer ring
Singing to the Lord
Let that hammer ring

Captain done gone
Let your hammer ring
Left us chained down here
Let your hammer ring

Images penetrate the dumpster thuds Xan's using as a mental shield.

Lord, my mouth is dry
Let your hammer ring
Won't be no more water
Hear that hammer sing

The face he sees is black, weary, crusted with debris.

Gonna break this old jail
Let your hammer ring
Breathe some fresh air
Hear that hammer ring

There'll be no fresh air, only oblivion.

Ain't nothing behind me
Let your hammer ring
Can't stop now
Hear your hammer sing

Is that daylight I see?
Let your hammer ring
Make a joyful noise
Walk on

The percussion solo begins low, shuffling and scratching. Xan plays broken echoes and tinkling glass, a rising murmur of settling debris. Without warning he freezes band-mates and audience alike with an earthquake aftershock, dumpster-style. He takes them to the deafening bowels of the Barboro.

The beat that emerges from the other side is a stately *thu-thump. Thu-thump.* Tijon nods.

Walk on, walk on

There is harmony from Caitlin and Scamp. Walk on. The line breathes in the crowd. *Walk on.* It swells in double dumpster beats. *Walk on.* Tijon riffs shamanic exhortations, black gospel. *Walk on. Walk on.* He gathers Teddy's spirit until the courtyard reverberates with it. Then with arms out-flung, Tijon sends him. *Walk on!*

I simply asked, 'Who is Teddy Arnold?'" the woman in the opal earrings complains to Wally. "Didn't I, Frank? That's all I said."

Her husband, a prominent accountant, agrees. "The posters are all over town. Benefit for Teddy Arnold. Maybe he's a child with a brain tumor. Maybe we want to contribute. So when we happen to pass the gate where they're taking tickets, we ask."

"What a piece of work that woman was. Dusky little slut. Do you know what she says to me? 'For twenty bucks I'll let you in *and* tell you who Teddy Arnold was.'"

The husband says, "The signs clearly state five dollar donation. I tell her that and she sasses me. 'It's the free market, man. What can I do?'"

"Oh, the mouth on her. And then we notice this long knife on her belt. Isn't that against the law, a knife like that? At the Peacock Gate?"

A *grande dame* who'd be insulted to be referred to as such drifts into the conversation. "Isn't that gate the most beautiful thing you've ever seen?" She flashes a mouthful of unnaturally white teeth. "That wonderful fan of wrought iron feathers. And there in the center where it opens? The sensual curves of the body? Don't you just love Art Nouveau?"

Wally doesn't feel compelled to demonstrate his ignorance.

Banter is Leilani's element. She's up to the task. "When Wally first showed it to me, I thought, this guy's not so bad. Maybe I'll keep him."

It was thoughtful of Paul and Lois to throw him and Leilani a bon voyage party on the roof of the Halloran, the best address in City Center. He has enjoyed, as always, catching up with old colleagues at the OstarFX R&D Division. But ten days of management conferences, symposia and the like are his limit. He peeks at his watch. Leilani nudges him. He's missed something.

"Shouldn't they?" she asks. "They should renovate that courtyard, bring in quality tenants and send the spongers packing."

Wally says, "I don't know. A little variety keeps things lively."

"With hunting knives?" Mrs. Earrings asks.

"Maybe not the knives."

"Forgive me," Mr. Earrings says. "What did you say you do in Virginia?"

Wally translates this as, Why are you defending spongers?

Leilani answers for him. "He's Director of Program Development at OstarFX."

"OstarFX," the man says, impressed. "That's big. What do you do there?"

Wally issues his standard evasion. "Online pest control. We keep bad guys out of digital networks." Security considerations aside, Mr. Earrings can't begin to appreciate the intricacies of cyber-warfare. Wally flourishes in that arid environment but sometimes he misses the joys of the real world. Sponger disrespect for convention reminds him that his limits are self-imposed. An occasional jolt of sponger attitude is invigorating.

The blond moves on and Paul, Wally's successor at R&D, takes her place at his elbow. "We could use some pest control this afternoon," he says. "Hear the racket down there?"

It's as though a garbage truck has malfunctioned and is banging a dumpster up and down on the pavement. "That's analog," Wally jokes.

Paul laughs but the response of Leilani and Mr. and Mrs. Earrings is bewilderment. Wally has to explain. "Sound information can travel digitally in patterns of 0 and 1 or by analog carrier, such as a sound wave. The information might be the same in both cases but the practicalities of manipulating them are different. Paul and I could write a digital solution for the noise on the street but it's usually simpler to apply an analog fix to an analog problem. For instance, a policeman could tell whoever's down there to stop."

"Today it's noise," Mrs. Earrings says. "Last week water pipes. Not in our building, but all the same. Those people should be in jail."

Leilani seconds the notion. "Our village water system was hit. Wally says the in-home filter strains out the pollution but we ordered tests."

"It's terrorism," Mr. Earrings says. "And Paul, they got you too?"

He pulls a pained face. "Even the Halloran. It isn't the sort of thing we publicize."

Mrs. Earrings stares suspiciously into her cup of punch.

"Don't worry, Naomi," Paul assures her. "Maintenance repaired it last Sunday. The association ordered a surveillance camera and several of us are installing personal filter systems."

The booming sounds increase in volume. Naomi says. "Isn't there a noise ordinance?"

"Only at night."

Leilani fumes, "What *can* they be doing?"

Wally hadn't directed her attention to the benefit fliers. She'd have been upset to read that Caitlin is a headliner. The banging changes to undulating thunder. *Want to bet that's her boyfriend?*

Naomi's husband says, "Why do we put up with it, Paul? We have a right to expect some peace. Let's petition Admin for a real noise ordinance."

The group moves to the boxwood hedge fencing the Halloran's

rooftop plaza, nineteen stories above street level. The source of the disturbance isn't evident but the sound changes again. Tha-thump. Tha-thump. Wally hears chanting, can't make out what's being said.

"You really should call the police," Naomi complains. "There must be a law. That sounds like war drums. What's next, a riot?"

As the music ascends from City Center it's not war drums Wally hears. It's a heartbeat.

The face is weary. Xan's flashlight sweeps across it in the wreckage of the Barboro Hotel. It stares from wood-ribbed cavities under fallen ceilings. It hovers in curtains of dust. It speaks to him. The things it says, he doesn't want to hear. It won't hold still. He swings his sledge at it anyway. Flying shards of concrete sting and stick. His mouth films with grit. He spits, thick, nasty. Takes another futile cut with the hammer. The dying in pursuit of the dead.

The face belongs to Lightning Johnson, Barboro desk manager and old-school bluesman. No card in his deck is a ticket to disagree and he deals them anyhow he wants. The yellowed eyes behind his sleepy lids mean business. "I leaves you be," he tells new tenants. "But if I says a thing, hear me." He jerks a nickel-plated pistol from his pants and thumbs the hammer. "Elsewise, Lightning do my talking."

Xan's first room in Memphis was on the young-buck eighth floor—Mr. Johnson tired of dragging old derelicts down from there, stiff or stroked out. Xan had 861: saggy bed, washstand, armoire with peeling veneer, shared bathroom. He also had the drummer's chair in The Lightning Johnson Band. Mr. Johnson didn't care how it looked, having a white boy play. But for those regular gigs on Beale Street, Xan couldn't have afforded to rent a tiny house the quake didn't knock down.

That first afternoon, he and his neighbors grilled or boiled food that wouldn't keep. Clouds flickered with strange rainbows. Some said from the earthquake. Others thought it the end of the world. He slept in his backyard, fearful of aftershocks. In the morning the couple next door left to stay with relatives in Ohio. Xan walked to the hotel to check on Mr. Johnson.

Few vehicles attempted the obstacle course of the streets. Those that gambled and lost could be unstuck for a price. Several commercial buildings displayed signs of instability or collapse. People congregated where it seemed safest, or kept company with injured folks waiting for medical attention unlikely to arrive.

Mid-morning sun glared on the rubble of the Barboro's east and north wings. Anyone in 861 when the quake struck lay buried under tons of brick. The west side of the horseshoe, including the main entrance, stubbornly refused to fall. No one loitering on the street admitted to seeing Lightning Johnson but those who knew him were sure he survived. Said one, "Devil booted his black ass out of hell three, four times already."

Two days later, with Mr. Johnson still unaccounted for, Xan has returned to the Barboro with a sledgehammer, to lend the devil a hand. The gloom that faded to black in the lobby existed in a reality now lost to him. He has wakened to a darker dream. His body follows a maroon stripe painted on the wall of the service corridor. It delivers him to a dead-end reek of gasoline and corpses where the parking garage should be. Mr. Johnson's face stares from between broken slabs, advises him to reverse course. His fingers bump along the maroon line back toward the lobby.

Walls begin to shake and a thunder fist of dirty air drops him. Somewhere above, a landslide. Rats streak by in the dust, too panicked to concern themselves with another body.

He picks himself up and starts forward again. Beyond the laundry room and kitchen the painted lifeline disappears in the chaos of a fresh cave-in. His route is sealed. The kitchen doors to his right are heavy-gauge steel, pinioned shut top and bottom, warped in their jambs. He takes off his pack, props the flashlight, trains it on the doors. Hammering at them makes his ears ring, but a gap opens. He squeezes through it into a tangle of girders, conduits, tables and scraps of putrid, powdered flesh. The upstairs ballroom is in the kitchen. Mr. Johnson's face is here too.

There's no hope of reaching the dining room, already trashed before this last shock. He hears keening. Not steam. Not rats. Not the face of Lightning Johnson. Not from the dining room. The other direction. He scrambles to investigate. He shouts. It quits.

It begins again, this time accompanied by a voice deeper than Mr. Johnson's. "Praise you, Jesus. We're here."

"Where?" Xan yells.

"The walk-in," the voice replies. Albert Griles says he and his daughters, Shawna and La-trice, are trapped in the kitchen cold room. "Until the food thawed my babies like to froze."

Steel, concrete and close quarters hamper Xan's approach. He almost gets there. The nearness of the voices tells him that. But no gap in the rubble takes him the entire way. At the spot where the crying is loudest he delivers that news and an alternate plan.

Albert tells his daughters everything will be all right, begs Xan to memorize his mama's phone number.

Xan doesn't voice his own doubts. He retreats to the hallway and breaks into the laundry. Empty space engulfs his flashlight beam. Pale rectangles in the distance gel into canvas carts. Linens spill from a dryer. In its glass porthole Mr. Johnson's face bleeds. Xan ignores it. On the left side of the room are washing machines. He climbs on top of one and taps the wall.

Albert's shout comes from farther along, in the sorting area. Xan locates the spot, but not until the dryer doors have been smashed—he'll not have Mr. Johnson staring. The cement-filled block wall separating the laundry from the kitchen area shatters almost as easily as dryer glass, leaving a mesh of reinforcing rods. Across a narrow plumbing gap there's a second block wall. Girls scream as he hammers it.

Albert, however, is elated. "You're almost here, man. I feel you."

Xan exposes a layer of moldy insulation foam he can't reach with his hands. A sledgehammer isn't the ideal tool for spreading rebar mesh but he makes do. The foam covers sheet metal that dents under his sledge. Doesn't want to tear.

Then it does. But it catches the hammer. Albert frees it and a rush of foul air. Outhouse. Rotten meat.

"What did I say?" Albert tells his daughters. "The Lord sent this man. He'll have us out in a jiffy."

Xan attacks the tear, rebar impeding his strokes. "Albert," he says, "if you take the sledge can you widen that hole?"

"If I could see better."

Xan strains to hand him a long flashlight.

La-trice is first into the laundry room, then Shawna. The girls, in grimy jumpers and jeans, hide whimpering under a sorting table. Their father is a while getting through the rebar. When he does, the big man locks Xan in a bear hug, lifts him off the floor.

"Oh, Lordy," Albert says. "Oh, Lordy." Shawna and La-trice scurry to latch onto his legs. He sets Xan down.

"Glad to meet you too," Xan says, catching his breath, trying not to puke from the stench of the man's clothes. "Is there anyone else?"

Albert pats his daughters, apparently twins. "We're the only ones. My wife can't be with us. That's why I bring my babies to my job. How do we go out?"

Xan explains the cave-in, that he's trapped too, that he came for Mr. Johnson.

"That man's not over *me*, praise God. I don't guess you found him."

"He's dead."

"You seen him?"

"He's dead."

"That's hard, man. Not many would come here for Lightning Johnson. What's your name?"

"I was his friend."

Albert arches an eyebrow. "Then we'd best go."

Xan shows them what they're up against. Albert pokes his head into the kitchen. They inspect the rubble at both ends of the passage to the garage. The corridor wall across from the kitchen and laundry room is featureless concrete. The hotel's west wing is on the other side of it. That's their chance.

"Where do we start?" Albert asks.

Xan marks the maroon stripe with his sledge. "Shine a light here." He takes a batter's stance, unleashes a homerun swing at the line separating the lower Mississippi mud color from the pale lemon above. The hammer gets away, helicopters into the opposite wall and caroms toward Albert and his daughters.

"Man, you whipped," Albert says. "My turn." He lays into the concrete like a brawler overdue at his sweet thing's house. A twin cries out, hit by chips. He pauses to check on her, resumes whaling away, breathing hard.

"No telling how thick that is," Xan says. "Let's not both be tired. Take it easy like they used to when the job lasted all day."

Albert pounds on.

Xan claps a slow cadence. "Like this. Like they did laying track for the railroad. Let that hammer ring. Whop. Sing it to the Lord. Let your hammer ring. Whop." Singing along gives the girls something to do besides fret.

Albert listens to his babies. His strokes and breathing calm. He adds his voice to the response lines; "Let this hammer ring."

The concrete is old, hard. Xan's manning the sledge when they encounter a layer of rotten plywood, then brick. Albert sees a white patch at the bottom of the elbow-deep crater. "That's a window ledge," he says, his light tracing an upward diagonal line. "Go this way. Brick is thin where they block up a window."

The excavation inches higher. The hammer song adds verses. They persevere until they have an Albert-sized hole. As predicted, the window brick is only two layers, backed by lath and plaster. Xan's hammer bounces off a 2x4 stud in the opening.

"No, man," Albert says. "I'll show you. Hit between studs." The laths are springier than Albert thought. They crack, but he has to snap them off by hand. Behind the plaster, a wooden obstruction. He shoves at it with the hammer handle, strains until it gives way. They hear a crash.

Xan's light reveals trolleys of folding chairs. An armoire lies face down. He wriggles between the window frame and wall stud. As he pulls La-trice and Shawna into the storage room after him another tremor rocks the hotel.

Still in the corridor, Albert prays at the top of his lungs.

"Give me the hammer," Xan orders. "You girls, sing for your daddy."

Two blows finish the stud barring their father. Xan has no chance to flatten splinters before Albert rolls across the armoire onto the floor, quivering and bloody, wild with fright.

Xan tries and fails to lift him to his feet. "Can't stop now, Albert. Hear that hammer ring? No stopping now. Help us sing."

"La-trice," Xan says, "take my light. See that door over there? Open it for us."

A girl scampers to it. "It's locked," she says.

"Unlock it, if you can." A stripe of gray appears. "Is that daylight you see?" Xan sings. "Let your hammer ring. Stand up now, Albert."

"Let your hammer ring," Albert answers. "Raise me up, Lord Jesus."

Flashlights are unnecessary in the carpeted hall. It's twilight in Memphis. They run through the lobby, out onto the sidewalk.

Electric lights blind them. They drop to their knees, cover their eyes, still singing.

A voice in Xan's ear says, "When you're ready, we've got water." He blinks and squints at the Griles family. They're doing the same. Another voice tells him, "This way."

He gets up, dazzled by the lights, is directed to stand beside a TV personality. "We're live and exclusive at the Barboro Hotel," the woman gushes into a microphone. "Minutes ago this man led three people to safety, more than seventy-two hours after a magnitude 7.9 quake devastated the city."

Lightning's gore-spattered face appears in Xan's mind, shocks him to attention.

The woman says, "What's your name, sir?" She sticks a microphone under his nose.

These people have no right. They didn't lift a finger for this neighborhood. "I'm not here to be exploited," he says. "All is lost; can't you see that?"

The woman begins again. "You saved three lives. How does it feel?"

Her question infuriates him. "Got to go now," he says and walks over to the people with the water.

They urge him to sit but the television crew is on his heels. As he passes their satellite truck a water girl catches up. "Are you okay?" She hands him a bottle.

"What are they doing here?"

"They had microphones in the hotel. We heard singing."

"Vultures." He rinses grit from his mouth, takes a pull of water.

"The camp I volunteer for isn't far."

A pedestrian points at him, says something to her companions. They're about to approach.

"How long was I on the damned TV?" he asks.

"I don't know. A minute or two."

"Long enough for those people over there to ID me?"

She looks, spins ahead to face him, grabs at the sledge. "Keep walking," she instructs, going backwards. "You're my skunk of a boyfriend." She yells, "You like jail, Melvin? Give that to me. Give it to me." They tussle. "Looting? You're lucky they don't shoot you."

The gawkers hustle by, in the direction of the hotel.

Xan smiles, his first of the day. "Melvin?"

She falls into step beside him. "Improv. You take what you get. Here's where we turn for camp."

"I have a place."

"Please, let us help."

"I'll be fine." They detour around a Chevy totaled by a streetlight. "Things are weird tonight, is all."

"There must be something we can do."

Her eyes are innocent, concerned. She believes what she says, but he'll help himself. "They recognized my clothes. Can I borrow your windbreaker? Just until I change? Your camp is in the project, right?"

"The DAN camp, blue and white tents."

"I've been there."

She takes off her jacket, gives it to him. "This is on loan. I'll be around tomorrow morning. Return it then? So I know you're okay? I won't tell anyone. Ask for Caitlin."

"Tomorrow morning," he lies.

Lightning Johnson grins. *Now you learning, white meat.*

Upstairs on The Spouter's mezzanine, in the corner booth under a hanging basket planted with rusty screen door springs, Mari and the money team are counting donations. The benefit raised almost three thousand for Teddy's expenses and another two for legal defense. In the adjacent booth, Caitlin, Tijon and his boyfriend Glenn share a pitcher and enjoy the Mari show. The tough grrrl is giddy with success. Caitlin treats her to a Two-Alarm Ginger Ale. Mari's not much of a drinker.

The joint is jumping. Caitlin wishes Xan could hear people's reaction to the music but he and Denny are still loading out—too fussy with their equipment to let other people help. The praise for her Mary Gauthier song is gratifying but everyone was blown away by Xan and Tijon's performance of "Hammer." They redefined the song, like the Janis Joplin version of "Me and Bobby McGee." Tijon soaks up his accolades.

Glenn, an ad agency videographer, captured the set on his boss's equipment and shows Caitlin the raw footage in playback mode. She's not surprised by the concentration on Tijon. Tijon in tight close-up. Tijon and backup singers. Xan's dervish solo doesn't get enough attention, but it's represented. Glenn's tight shots are rock steady, no small feat in the midst of pandemonium.

"The audio stinks," Glenn tells her. "But Denny recorded off the soundboard. We'll see what we can stitch together."

Downstairs, a commotion. Caitlin looks over the rail; blue shirts are at the door. The bartender hustles upstairs trailed by a friend of Mari's and a few other patrons. They head for the restrooms. Mari's booth companions, Rick and Janice of the International Workers Party, decide they'd rather not be caught holding large sums of cash. Mari stuffs her clothes with envelopes, her fierce disposition restored.

A bullhorn pops to life. "This establishment is closed. Have your driver's license or other official identification ready for inspection. After your ID is scanned, exit the premises. Form a line."

Glenn anxiously switches camcorder memory cards and gives the one containing the performance to Tijon. "Put this in your pocket. Meet me at my place later?"

Tijon thinks it's a plan. "We should separate. No telling who they're after." In his haste for the stairs he doesn't wait for other opinions.

"Mari," Caitlin says. "Can I help with the money?"

Mari nods. "The clowns down there might disbelieve such lumpy tits."

Caitlin slides into Mari's booth as Rick and Janice vacate. "Hold on a sec," she tells them. "Can you give me some privacy?" They block the view as she stuffs her bra and admires the mounding cleavage. "Ooh, a cash bustier, how fun. You can peek now." Rick's gaze lingers. Her hand flutters with Southern delicacy over her chest until he takes the hint: show's over.

Glenn's antsy in the next booth. The longer he's here, the more likely his anxiety is to draw attention. "Rick," she says, "pretend you and Glenn are scouting an ad shoot. Nothing to do with the benefit. Go ahead and leave."

"Without you and Mari?"

"Cash isn't illegal, yet," Mari says.

A hot second later he and the Marxists are on the stairs.

Caitlin asks Mari who skedaddled to the restroom with the bartender.

"Teddy's renter, Steve," Mari says. "You heard him the other night. ISA held him and his wife hostage at Teddy's house. Steve's chipped."

"He's what?"

"Treat yourself to a night in jail sometime. Inmates and people on probation or parole have a Correctional Rehab chip under the skin, like a scannable merchandise tag. Chipped people aren't allowed where alcohol is served. If the blue shirts wand Steve he's busted and The Spouter gets fined. That's why so many consumer bars have door scanners. They're not worried about what sneaks out; it's who they let in."

"The cops are bound to search restrooms."

"Steve won't be there. The bartender unlocks the men's room window."

"This is the second floor. They'll break their legs."

"It opens onto the roof next door. During Prohibition the owners couldn't afford to embarrass town fathers by having them arrested in a speakeasy. No such luck for women, of course."

"But surely the police…"

Mari nods. "A riot wagon might be waiting at the foot of the fire escape."

The crowd below is thinning. "Ready?" Caitlin asks, adjusting envelopes in her bra. Mari's not too lumpy. They watch from the stairs as Glenn, Rick and Janice are carded, scanned and excused without pat-downs.

Caitlin avoids looking at the wall art while waiting her turn at the checkpoint. The nearest canvas is a rendering of Vincent van Gogh's severed ear. The Spouter's taste for the grotesque is a major reason the tavern is low on her list of favorite dives. Ahead of her and Mari in line, the boyfriend of an angry drunk fails to adequately cover up her condition. The blue shirts shift into hassle mode. She's ordered to empty her purse. As they and her boyfriend knew she would, she pops off. The efficiency with which she's tasered, cuffed and dragged away would do a slaughterhouse proud.

Caitlin and Mari have their IDs out, ready for scanning.

"Are you of age?" a buzz-cut cop asks Mari by rote.

"Yes, sir."

"Any legal restrictions on your movements?"

"No, sir."

He scans her license and makes a show of studying the photo before returning the ID. "Free to go."

Caitlin steps forward and receives the same treatment.

She and Mari find Xan and Denny outside in the courtyard. Tijon, Glenn and the others are nowhere to be seen.

"They got Steve," Denny tells Mari.

"Shit. If they activate his sentence, he'll do six months."

"For what?"

"Provoking a Rent-a-Cop at a demo last fall." She and Caitlin detour into a sunken stairway to transfer their envelopes to Mari's shoulder bag.

Danny asks, "Has Steve got family?"

"Wife and baby," Mari answers when they're finished. They walk toward the Burnside Street exit up near the Kava Bar. "Denny, can I catch a ride with you? I'd rather not bike through town holding this cash."

Out on Burnside, they see cop cars and a riot wagon at the Peacock Gate. Denny's pickup and Xan's van are parked close by.

"Let's take the long way around, Mari," Denny says.

When they've gone, Caitlin asks Xan, "Were you hassled?"

"They wouldn't let us inside to meet you, is all."

"Did they say what the bust is for?"

He snickers. "And take a chance on relieving a sponger's guilty conscience? Did they give *you* any trouble?"

"No."

"Then let's stroll on down there like we own the place."

"You do own it," Caitlin says, hugging his arm. "You and Tijon were beyond wonderful today. Take me home and ravish me like you did your song."

Xan frowns. "You don't want that."

rhythms on a flaming drum

dreams

Caitlin's desire for Xan's secrets has come full circle in the months they've been together. At first she was hungry for admission to the experience of an actual hero. What she discovered instead is a painful, fugitive vagueness about Memphis. It's as though he considers himself an imposter. She's ashamed of her early prying. He's vulnerable, ordinary flesh and blood, a guy who incessantly taps out rhythms, dislikes beets and greens. The vicarious thrill she developed in protecting him, or offering to, has faded as well. Guarding him, even from herself, is now automatic. She's surprised at the risk he took in performing "Hammer." He let himself fall into an emotional black hole before hundreds of people. Although he resurfaced with dignity, there will be a next time. *What's he fighting down there?* It's *him* she wants to protect now, not his woundedness; she's afraid of failing.

As they unload the van at Collective Harlequin's theater she says, "People have no idea what it cost you to play like that."

He reaches for an equipment bag above a wheel well. "My ears are still ringing."

"That's *not* what I mean," she frowns, taking the bag from him. "But if you ever do it again without hearing protection, I'll be pissed. Our child shouldn't have to shout for Daddy's attention."

He forgets the amp he was extracting and catches up to her at the back door.

"Audio check." She smiles. "You pass."

"This is the second time you've brought that up. You're not—"

"No. That's *our* decision, not mine. But I think we'd be great parents. Would you still love me if I'm all stretched out of shape?"

"Can I get back to you on that, much later?"

In the darkness of the space where sets are built and stored, she turns to him. "Hold this for me," she says, passing him the bag as though it were a babe in arms. She cups his crotch and maneuvers him against a wall. "Don't drop it," she purrs, unbuckling his belt. "I'll just be a minute."

At the apartment they laze on the couch, grazing like Romans on crusty bread, leftover egg salad, goat cheese and cantaloupe. Melon juice drips down their chins.

"Can I tell you something?" Caitlin hesitantly asks. But having said it, it's too late for never mind. "I was pregnant once."

"Oh?"

That's the best you can do? Oh? "A frat boy I dated at Ruskin told me he had a source for birth control pills. We were aware of counterfeits but he swore he got his from a woman with a legal prescription. I found out too late that he was lying. A girl one of his frat brothers dated made the mistake of going to campus health. Once you're officially pregnant, you're trapped into carrying it. You can be sent to jail for a miscarriage. So I went to Canada. Mom took me to a clinic."

"She was cool about it?"

"Totally. Babies for America is the sort of law that convinced her to leave this country. Dad wouldn't go; so that was that for their marriage. Well, maybe a few other things too. She was into magick. That embarrassed him."

"Did you tell him you were in trouble?"

"He didn't argue. I had the termination and Mom and I devised a system to import genuine birth control. I never told the frat boy he got me pregnant, but I *did* out him and his lying brothers to every girl on campus. And so began my career as an enemy of the state. Do you still love me?"

"Come here."

She luxuriates in the sensation of his fingers combing through her hair. Her mom used to do that.

"Parenthood is the hugest responsibility there is," he says. "Think of it from a kid's point of view. What if things go wrong like they did today for that guy Steve? Unless his wife's got somebody to watch their baby while she works, Social Services will take it. It'll wind up in training school."

"We have resources to prevent that from happening. If you leave us, I'm a big girl."

"I could never do that and wouldn't want to. What I'm saying is: Suppose you're busted and your dad can't get you off? *I'm* the single parent and the authorities decide a professional musician is unfit. Unless I quit, they take our child. If I do quit, we starve."

"Dad's a titan. He'd never leave a grandchild in the lurch."

"Maybe Steve's wife has a pot of gold too."

"I'm not saying it's fair." She settles onto him again and sighs.

He licks melon stickiness from her chin. "I love your titan craziness. And you *would* make a great mom. I couldn't stand it if you were mine."

"What's that supposed to mean?"

"My dad would have to kill me to kick me out of your bed."

The love they make is long and slow. She imagines being off the pill, the future in the balance.

"Find it! Find it!" The frightened moan penetrates Caitlin's dreamlessness. She's being manhandled and wakes confused. Xan's sitting up, breathing hard. This has happened before. She reaches for him, to be sure he's awake. "Xan?"

"Did I hurt you? I'm sorry."

She pulls herself up beside him. "You had a nightmare."

He shakes his head. "I was looking for something. A second ago I could have told you what. Now it's gone."

74

Reba Stein's modernization of the ancient Greek political comedy, *The Birds*, like the Aristophanes original, pokes fun at public figures. Aristophanes' protagonist is Pisthetaerus, a disgruntled Athenian who inspires the birds to build a city in the sky. Because the new city lies between Earth and the Olympian gods, the birds gain power over both. Reba couldn't resist the pun of Pissed Theodorus. She built her play around Teddy Arnold, only to have the ISA Fates so cruelly intervene. *The Birds* was to have been Collective Harlequin's next stage production. Last Friday she emailed the membership announcing her intention to withdraw the work.

The company has much invested in this play. It's a big show: twenty-two speaking roles and a Chorus outfitted as boxy, grade school birds. Opening night was set for Labor Day weekend and people are depending on the payday. While several members of the troupe regret the unfortunate timing, only Mari supports Reba's decision to cancel the show. The collective is in a furor.

Rather than publicly choose sides, Caitlin and Xan debate the merits between themselves. He suggests that Reba might unintentionally be looking out for her own feelings more than Teddy's, a man famous for insults. Caitlin is offended for Reba until Xan reminds her of a fable in the play. Before Earth was made, the birds circled endlessly on the wing. The absence of land didn't become a pressing issue until the Lark's father died. Where could he be buried? She eventually laid him to rest in her mind, and so invented memory. Reba may not want to remember Teddy as a theatrical buffoon. Caitlin hits on an idea that could lay him to honorable rest while permitting the show to go on.

Before what would have been Tuesday night rehearsal—the company has gathered as usual though it isn't clear why—they find Mari and Izzy guarding Reba from the hostility in the house. She's sitting pinched and pale in a corner. Caitlin crouches beside her.

"What if Theodorus and his sidekick are ghosts instead of living men? And the ghost of Theodorus can use his legs? The free market gods murder him but, in death, he takes comic revenge. Can Pissed Theodorus be a clown saint who upsets the economic order?"

"Teddy Arnold a saint? That's rich."

The proposed twist excites Izzy. "Maybe that's the brilliance. His example becomes more potent *because* of his flaws. Why do we airbrush the legends of martyrs? One reason might be that flawless heroes excuse us mere mortals for not really trying. A celebration of Teddy that includes his foibles would counter the temptation to let ourselves off the hook."

Xan hasn't thought it through that far, but he can't fault the logic.

Mari shrugs. She could go with it.

Reba makes them wait. "I like that," she says at last. "It's a minor rewrite. I could have the changes ready for Thursday." She stands and hugs Caitlin with relief. "Bless you. Shall we call the house to order?"

Consensus is swift and rehearsal begins with the company in a slaphappy mood. Xan's testing his acting wings in the Chorus. He'll be attired in a plumed cardboard box and yellow leggings.

Reba, who's directing the show, wants "jive" in the sing-song rhymes the Chorus speaks in unison. They're getting down, having fun, except for Janet, the collective's business manager. She's rhythm-challenged. They try different cues: tapping her shoulder, clapping, dancing together on one leg and shifting to the other at points of emphasis. Reba loves that.

At the conclusion of the rehearsal, Tijon's partner Glenn—the Plover-Page and drag queen parody of local ISA thug-in-chief, Thomas Doak—issues an invitation. "As several of you know, the Teddy Arnold benefit included a stellar performance of 'Let Your Hammer Ring.' Denny and I produced a video of it, premiering tonight. Please stay and check it out."

Xan isn't interested but Caitlin insists. They sit beside the Steins, who weren't at the benefit. Reba leans over and whispers, "We're told your playing was inspired."

Caitlin says, "I won't let him do it again. He'd go deaf."

The upstage projection screen is lowered. The house lights dim. Chair legs scrape the concrete floor as a still shot of the benefit poster appears over the sound of the first dumpster strikes. Glenn follows the poster with a crowd shot and captions.

Tijon P
"Let Your Hammer Ring"
video: Glenn Estevez
sound: Dennis Dempsey

"Tijon P?" Caitlin complains aloud.

"It's okay, babe," Xan whispers. "Couldn't be better."

She steams, arms folded across her chest. From a technical point of view the video is well done. Denny captured the low bass. Glenn got lucky with ambient lighting. As the earthquake solo resolves into the double beat, the Harlequins take it up and spontaneously sing along to the "Walk on" chant. When it's over,

Xan joins in the applause.

Moments later Glenn swaggers by for a pat on the head.

"Great job," Xan says.

Caitlin's less generous. "Glenn, is Xan a random busker Tijon found on a street corner? Did he approve 'Tijon P'? Did Denny?"

Glenn takes a backward step. "Don't misunderstand. The titles are placeholders. I meant to say that and forgot. There's definitely fine-tuning to do on the graphics. But the video itself? Did we nail it or what?"

Izzy isn't ready to let Glenn slide either. "That's some outstanding percussion."

"You're right, of course," Glenn says. "Xan, you were fantastic and so were Caitlin and Scamp. But you're not an established band and I had to call you something. I'm open to suggestions. Please. Tijon and Friends?"

The remnants of a tropical storm forced Xan to reschedule today's landscape clients. He's riding shotgun with Caitlin on a trip to Laurel Ridge, his first visit. Someone's coming to test her dad's water. On the way out of town they stop for dinner groceries and a set of new water filter cartridges—Wally told her the technician will take those in use. They stop at the barred entrance to the titan enclave. Caitlin needs to complete a service vehicle admission form. She parks as close as possible to the candy-striped awning over the gatehouse window. The rain isn't hard but it's steady.

"Can I list your phone as the contact?" she asks. "Dad's landline is disconnected when he's away."

"Of course." She doesn't like it that phones can track their owners. On the few occasions she carries hers, the battery is usually kept separate until she makes a call.

She dashes bareheaded to the protection of the awning. The guard shoves a clipboard at her. She writes and returns it. A discussion ensues.

Caitlin turns and calls out, "She can't see you." Pretends to crank down a car window.

He leans across her seat, lowers the window, smiles, waves.

"That's good," Caitlin says.

The traffic control bar rises.

They pass several drives with ostentatious gates. Caitlin tells him Wally had his taken out soon after buying the place. He's not a snob, she seems to say. Think of him as a regular guy with more money.

A lot more. Some of Xan's clients own McMansions. None has the polish of the Schmidts' mountaintop spread. The grounds are mature and well-maintained. The house, which finally appears behind a landscape planting of decorative conifers, overlooks the Sawligoochee Valley. Two stories of terra-cotta and a slate roof not infested with gables. Although he has no experience of European hunting lodges, he imagines they resemble this place.

Caitlin pulls around back. A pair of double garage doors are tucked under the home's rear deck. She consults a card taped behind her sun visor, asks him for the keypad in the glove box. The numbers she enters raise the door farthest from the house. Another set of numbers copied onto her palm deactivates the building alarm.

There are no hunting trophies on the walls of her father's second home. Otherwise, the lodge impression persists. High ceilings, stone, tile, cherry woodwork. A library with floor-to-ceiling bookcases. Old-school leather chairs in public areas. A kitchen the size of a living room and a sunken dining room that could seat thirty. Upstairs, oak and area rugs. Each bedroom has a private bath.

His phone rings. It's the gatehouse, for Miss Schmidt. Xan switches to speaker. The guard has found a discrepancy on the service vehicle admission form. The technician requesting admission is female, R-i-k-k-i Lyn Buchanan, not Ricky with a "y" as stated on the form. Can Miss Schmidt confirm her spelling?

"No," Miss Schmidt replies, "my father made the appointment and didn't spell the name for me. I'm sure she's fine. Send her on." Caitlin hangs up grumbling, "Life in the gilded cage."

"Do the strip searches here include massage?"

"I certainly hope so."

"Schmidt residence?" a young woman in a neat white uniform asks when Caitlin answers the doorbell. "Oh," the tech gasps, covering her mouth. "I had no idea."

"Excuse me?"

"You're Caitlin Schmidt. You sang that song for Mr. Arnold at the benefit. Wow. I can't believe you live here."

"I don't. It's my dad's house. But come in. You're Rikki?"

"Yes, ma'am."

"Call me Caitlin." She steps aside. "Sorry about the screw-up with the guard."

"No problem. Happens all the time." Rikki is careful to prevent her bulky test kit from hitting the doorframe.

Xan offers to carry the case for her.

"No thank you, sir. It's not heavy unless it's full of samples. Then it rolls on wheels. Which way to the kitchen?"

"You were at Teddy's benefit?" Caitlin asks.

Rikki nods. "It's outrageous what happened to Mr. Arnold. They'd have busted me out there too, if I hadn't been on a job that Saturday."

"No kidding?"

"Water is my living. You wouldn't believe the crap that gets dumped in it. I belong to Sawligoochee Riverwatch."

"Here's the kitchen."

"How long since these faucets were used?" Rikki asks.

"Dad left last Sunday; why?"

"We can estimate the lead contribution from the interior plumbing. I'll collect two samples: initial and one minute. The drop in lead concentration tells us how much leaches into the water from fixtures and solder joints."

Xan's phone rings again. Denny has some sickening information for Caitlin. This isn't the time to deliver it.

Rikki fills specimen bottles from every tap in the house, verifies that the feed lines are plastic throughout. Her final sampling location, as predicted, is the filtration system. They locate it in the basement mechanical room. She expertly switches filter cartridges and seals the used ones in plastic bags.

Samples packed and ready to go, she hands Caitlin a business card. "I'm so honored to meet you. If there's anything else we can do, give us a ring."

The storm has cleared. Xan and Caitlin fix iced tea. She takes him out onto the deck. Steam rises from the flagstones. Fog banks roll on distant mountainsides, shining in the first rays of sun Calhoun has seen in two days.

"Enjoy the scenery," she says. "I'll bring towels and dry us a place to sit."

He pictures parties out here. Tuxedoed men, swanky women, the long serving table loaded with treats. Caitlin breezes out with an armful of fluffy, golden towels. "Nice view," he says, meaning her. She tosses him a towel and executes a grand waltz turn with another.

They dry chairs and a bistro table. He sits. She plops into his lap. He undoes her top shirt button, has a finger playfully bitten in reply.

"So eager," she says, scooting over to the other chair. "Do you like it here?"

"Security might be a tad excessive but we can massage those issues later."

"I meant Laurel Ridge."

"Same thing. Tell me though, all this titan posh and the guard has to phone for instructions? No gatehouse intercom?"

"Dad removed his connection. Intercoms can serve as listening devices. You think *I'm* weird about phones."

"Why so paranoid?"

"OstarFX can't have Dad's projects compromised. Right now there are no hard drives in his computers. It's not much better when he's here. The logon is a bitch. You can't install or run regular software. There's no wireless network. If his computers are operational it's because he plugged them in, logged on and validated system integrity."

"Like your laptop you mean?" He's teasing but it's true.

"Worse."

"Okay, but if you're so worried about surveillance, how come my phone doesn't bother you? *They* could be eavesdropping."

"Never fear. They haven't forgotten you. The information on your computer, your financial records and everything you say on your phone is stored along with the billions of other records generated each month. But sorry to break it to you, baby, the intelligence industry doesn't know Xan Hicks like I do. Maybe the music video will change that. Then you can be paranoid too." She leans over, kisses him. "What was it you said about breaking and entering?"

"Come here and I'll show you."

"Does the television work?" Xan asks. He and Caitlin are puttering toward dinner. He's to chop veggies and cheese while she makes flatbreads for the grill.

"You want to watch TV?"

"Local news."

"The switch is on the wall beside the screen."

He locates a remote on the great room coffee table. The channel selector is already set to News2. He raises the volume until it can be heard in the kitchen. The bizarre case of animal abuse Denny phoned about isn't mentioned until after the weather.

"That call I got when Rikki was here?" he says. "You should see this story."

A flustered mother with a toddler bouncing on her hip tells of finding the Chihuahua she's been caring for dead in the yard. It apparently swallowed a fish hook and bled to death jerking against a line tied to a fencepost. There's a photo of Peaches sitting in Teddy Arnold's lap. The reporter doesn't identify Teddy as the owner, saying only, "Animal control won't speculate on a motive for this senseless act of cruelty."

Caitlin is as upset by the NewsStooge coverage as she is by the viciousness.

Reba's changes to *The Birds* are ready as promised. The most significant alteration, the loss of Pissed Theodorus's wheelchair, has a liberating effect on the actors. Tijon in particular, who plays a king transformed into an exotic bird, has more room to strut his stuff. There's debate about putting Theodorus and the other ghost into white face. Izzy—Theodorus—thinks that's over the top. Reba *does* agree to change the ghosts' costuming from contemporary dress to Greek robes. Caitlin inwardly groans at a suggestion for Pissed Theodorus to carry a small dog, but Mari's impassioned rationale for it achieves swift consensus. The property manager will shop for a stuffed version of Peaches.

When Reba dismisses the company, Xan's sweaty from an hour of practicing the Chorus dance. Caitlin tells him to go on home; she'll be along later. He doesn't have to ask the reason. Digger meetings sometimes occur on short notice.

Denny pumps gypsy music through the sound system, theoretically impairing ISA's ability to listen in on the Street Artists. Izzy circles chairs at the front of the house.

Mari has two agenda items. First, she says, the funeral home received Teddy's body yesterday morning. Soon afterward the funeral director, a mortician with ties to the alternative community, texted a request to discuss arrangements in person. Mari thought nothing of it; Teddy's brother had designated her to act for the family.

The mortician is bothered by a whitewashed death certificate. Several lines, including the location of death, are blank or misleading. Teddy supposedly died of paraplegia, diabetes and obesity. No mention of trauma. But the mortician noticed bruises, broken ribs, taser marks, evidence of recent abdominal surgery and a second, postmortem incision.

"He asked for authorization to contact a doctor qualified to examine the body. If Teddy was beaten to death the World Criminal Court should be informed. They keep a human rights register. I told him, 'Hell yes.'"

Caitlin says, "We didn't raise *that* much money."

"It's *pro bono.* A visiting professor in the Research Triangle works for an NGO that reports to the WCC."

Tijon's not impressed. "The court for senile perps who outlive their protection?"

Mari ignores him. "So anyway, Dr. Sigurdsdottir did the autopsy this morning, there in the funeral home. She said Teddy had water in his lungs and a ruptured spleen. Either could have killed him. We'll know more in a few weeks. She also has an idea about the operation on Teddy's stomach. It could have been to implant a tracking bug. The U.S. has been caught doing that overseas. They install a GPS in a detainee, release him, then drone-strike him when he's with friends."

"I looked it up," Denny says, slouching in a folding chair. "Operation Judas Rat. Implants are probably happening here too. A dude who was previously disappeared had a device show up on a kidney X-ray but the doc who was going to remove it changed his mind. There are other reports of ISA slashing bodies in funeral homes, maybe eliminating evidence."

"Anybody been droned?" Tijon asks.

"No, but it might account for some Digger roundups. These bugs aren't Correctional Rehab chips; those can be cut out. The GPS is sewn into your guts and you don't know it."

Izzy asks whether the X-ray Denny mentioned is available online.

"It disappeared."

"So, no proof it wasn't a standard medical device?"

The gypsy music careens and wails. "Not until a domestic unit is available for study," Denny says. "But true or not, the rumors play into ISA's hand. If you're afraid somebody's a Judas Rat, you avoid him."

"If the plan was to track Teddy, why kill him?" Reba wants to know.

"Evil *and* incompetent," Tijon replies. "Par for the course."

Reba's looking queasy. "Anything else? No? Mari, you have another agenda item?"

"I need an understudy for *The Birds*. The company I work for has contracts with places where filtration systems were bypassed. ISA questioned my boss."

"Can they prove anything?" Caitlin, who also was grossed out by the previous discussion, is fully engaged now.

"Who knows? I wouldn't care except for what happened to Teddy. I'd rather disappear myself than be a security risk."

Izzy doesn't like the sound of that. "Won't that be taken as a sign of guilt?"

"There's no record of me servicing those water systems."

Izzy shakes his head. "ISA could squeeze anyone they pull in with an offer of leniency for being the first to talk."

"We're doing a daily check-in. If somebody misses a contact, we scatter. I'd try to let you know."

"Should we start that too?" Caitlin wonders. "At the darknet chatroom, like we did before?"

Reba asks, "Is that a proposal? Any discussion?"

There is none.

"Consensus?"

Fingers twinkle around the circle.

"We'll begin tomorrow morning," Reba says. "I'll understudy your part, Mari. The troupe needn't be informed."

"Thanks. The other thing is, remember the redneck in the woods?"

Denny says, "Oh, shit. The fisherman. Teddy's dog."

"That creep was too seedy for an undercover. More of a hate group type."

"Or a loyal Palomar employee who lynched a dog," Tijon adds.

"Huskins has a reputation to uphold," Denny says. "I doubt the fisherman was sent by Palomar or the Southern Mountain Alliance. Could be a nut case, or the Brotherhood of the Fiery Sword. Mari's in danger if he IDs her."

Izzy breaks an extended moment of concerned silence with a proposal. "Reba and I are involved with the Humane Society. I think we can talk them into sponsoring a reward. Law enforcement won't object to a mainstream group mobilizing against a community menace. We'd innocently publicize the fact that Peaches was Teddy's dog, and if I put up the reward money the Society will share any tips it receives with me. It would be a Street Artist action by proxy."

Xan's boating lessons commenced this morning with learning to tie a borrowed canoe on top of the van. Although he's dubious of the straps and foam blocks, the boat's still up there when he and Caitlin arrive at the Lake Hollister public landing off Highway 7. To him, lakes are mysterious novelties. The farm ponds he occasionally fished in high school were muddy, full of snapping turtles. He prefers the reliable smell of pool chlorine to seaweed funk, and blue concrete to haphazard shorelines. Admission to the landing is twenty bucks a car. Plus ten a day for vehicles locked in overnight. Payable by cash or credit card at the automated kiosk. He presses the button. The machine issues him a ticket, raises the crossbar.

Across the parking lot from the group shelters, potbellied adults stake beach territories with lawn chairs and umbrellas. Girls on towels sun like oily seals while mothers and sisters at water's edge tend little kids squealing in colorful armbands. Teenaged boogie board captains harass each other out as far as a line of red buoys. In the distance a speedboat plies the open water with a thumpety, mosquito whine. He'd scoffed at Caitlin's decision to borrow lifejackets. Now he's glad she did.

Her summer camp system for sliding the canoe off the van and flipping it upright reminds him of a drill team exercise but it does the job. She has him lash the cooler and dry bag into the center section of the boat. They march it to the launch area. He's knee deep in the pleasantly warm lake before she tells him to let the bow float. She thinks he ought to get out and board from the stern, crawling over their gear to the front seat. That sounds unnecessarily complicated; he tries to board where he is. The canoe doesn't quite tip over. He doesn't quite sit in the lake. Caitlin doesn't quite laugh herself silly. His second attempt succeeds but not without further excitement. The canoe shifts under him, then surges when she climbs in. He grips the gunwales as the red buoys swing drunkenly out of his line of sight.

The strokes she demonstrates are relatively simple. He digs the blade of his paddle through the water, careful not to lean too far off-center. The boat moves. Within minutes they're paddling like islanders, bound for the far shore. The water glints clear and deep. There's no sensation of forward motion. Only a white bow wave and ripples slapping the hull.

A pontoon boat crosses ahead, raising a mini-tsunami. Caitlin steers to take the wake head on. The canoe bucks and settles. *I could get the hang of this*, he decides. She schools him on turns and spins. He accidentally splashes her. She rains retaliation on his back. Too soon, the wooded shore. They glide along, over crowns of deadfall trees where minnows hide. At a small clearing he draws the bow onto the mud, disembarks, drags the boat ashore with Caitlin in the stern.

After a swim they drip dry on a shady outcrop. Lunch is pasta salad and fresh plums. He arcs a pit into the water. Fish converge, fighting each other for the prize. "Check it out," he says. "Fish rugby."

"Don't," Caitlin scolds. "They might choke."

She brings up the "Hammer" video again. Why won't he allow his name to be included in the titles? It's a golden opportunity to promote himself. They've had this discussion so often her lines are as familiar as his. She's relentless, wearing him down, knowing he'll eventually realize his objections are nonsensical to anyone other than himself. They don't even make sense to him. The performance is out there. He can't take it back any more than he can undo his dread of Memphis.

"Okay," he concedes, "You win. I'll call Glenn. Who taught you to nag?"

"My mom."

"Who left your father for Canada?"

"When I was fourteen. She was born and raised there. We're on good terms now, though."

"You haven't told me much of what she's about."

"Lots of stuff; take your pick. Socialite, Pagan priestess, life coach. Her partner serves on the Toronto City Council."

"Toronto?" *Try not to laugh.* "He's not that guy—"

"Geoff's thoroughly respectable. So is Mom," she says. "Take me exploring. Was that a trail where we landed the canoe?"

He toys with her swimsuit, to no avail. She's on the move, shimmies into a sundress from the dry bag.

There are frequent stops for breath and flailing at spider webs on the steep footpath. The summit seems just out of reach until they emerge from the trees onto the broiling, lichen-painted dome overlooking the dam and both arms of the reservoir. The cove to their right is busy with boats. Pinpricks of sunlight glare off car windows at the public landing. Although the left cove is longer, nothing's happening there except jet skis near the confluence. Caitlin says the land on that arm is mainly private. She draws his attention to industrial buildings and a red, white and blue smokestack at the head of the cove: Palomar.

Someone thought this ridgetop was so right for romance he went to the massive trouble of hauling up a mattress. Once upon a time that alternative to the blistering hot rock may have been worth it. Today the mattress is a filthy mess. They leave it to the ghosts of past glories and beat their retreat down the gnarly track.

Xan could learn to love lake water, seaweed smell and all. His dive off the lunch rock raises an almighty splash. Sweat and cobwebs immediately dissolve in the cool. Caitlin wades in behind him, floats on her back, hands sculling like dainty fins. She's Ophelia from the painting, hair and translucent dress billowing. *Hamlet was a complete idiot to send her away to die.* In fun, Xan swims under her reincarnation and surfaces, gathering her into his arms. The water is too deep for the scene he has in mind. He can't touch bottom, is forced to let her go.

She laughs at the ineptitude. "You're better in a boat," she says. "Let's take the canoe around the Palomar side, see what's over there."

Once again he's stationed in front. They follow the shoreline to the rocky point where the left arm of the lake joins the right, staying as far from the choppy wakes of watercraft as possible. The Palomar side is calmer but, except where Caitlin swings wide of private docks, they hug the bank anyway, taking in the scroll of forest and mossy stone formations. Sycamore limbs lean low over the water, the white bark alive with reflections. Toward the head of the cove the tranquil rhythm of paddle strokes is ruined by a smell of paint fumes and picket line of floating notices.

PALOMAR COATINGS, LLC.
PRIVATE PROPERTY
KEEP OUT
NO TRESPASSING

The smokestack isn't visible behind the bend where the lake narrows. They parallel the signs across the water and encounter a large catfish, belly-up and bloated in a rainbow slick. The stench overpowers the industrial chemicals blackening a stretch of shoreline in the restricted area.

"What's that gunk?" she says, steering them between warning signs to investigate. They sidle close enough to the bank for her to collect some goo with her paddle. "It's a gummy film, like old grease," she tells him. "Ick!" An inky blob has dripped onto her dress. She scoops up a handful of water for an attempt to rinse it off.

He hears a motorboat rounding the Palomar bend, heading directly for them. "Clean that later," he says. "Get us to the other side of those signs."

They're clearly legal before the boat arrives but it bears down anyway, at speed, almost sideswiping the canoe, the driver yelling about private property as he roars by. Caitlin strokes hard to take the wave on their stern. The canoe lurches badly but doesn't swamp. The maniac swings about for another pass. If he's a security guard Xan can't tell it from the street clothes or unmarked boat.

"He's trying to dump us," Caitlin shouts.

"Face him." Xan pretends to reach for something, raises his hand as if it's a pistol. He levels it at the approaching boat, braces the imaginary weapon with his other hand. The driver veers away, soon disappearing toward Palomar.

Xan grabs his paddle. "Seen enough here? I have. Time to go. Stay close to shore in case that fucker makes a second run with a real gun and we have to hightail it through the woods." They put their heads down and stroke, not slacking until they reach the protection of other watercraft. "I've got to ease up," he says. "I'm gassed."

She's also puffing. "You did great. Who knew a canoe could go so fast. And that gun trick? I never dreamt I'd be saved by pantomime."

"By dumb luck, more like. If that guy was armed we'd be dead.

Thanks for keeping us right side up back there. I thought he had
us rolled."

*P*romise me you'll stop."

"*Hmm?*"

"*Promise you'll stop.*"

"*Stop what?*"

"*Taking risks.*"

"*After what you just did to me, you want to fight? I can't focus.*"

"*Not fight. Have an understanding.*"

"*The Palomar crazy? We weren't doing anything.*"

"*Enough for him to try to drown us.*"

"*We didn't deserve that. Or their pollution. It ruined my dress. Did you see the sores on that poor fish?*"

"*Don't change the subject.*"

"*Baby, I'm no Teddy Arnold. My most heinous crime was aiding and abetting graffiti.*"

"*Details don't matter, do they? To them, you're an enemy of the state.*"

"*I am an enemy of the state. You too.*"

"*I'm not a Digger. That's a mandatory ten, picking peaches for Correctional Rehab.*"

"*I should drink the water and pretend to be happy?*"

"*Just be less in their face.*"

"*Drop out like you?*"

"Isn't learning to live without free market paychecks valid? I don't want to lose you, and if you want to be a mom someday—"

"Children need parents who aren't afraid to do what's right."

"I had parents like that. It didn't work out so well."

"But they gave their students a better chance and you inherited their courage. Where'd you learn the gun trick?"

"A man in Memphis. He told me he shot the fool who tried it on him. Lightning sometimes exaggerated. What will it take to make you stop? Would motherhood convince you?"

"Now you want me barefoot and pregnant?"

"We'd have to get married or something. Parental rights."

"You're not serious."

"I'll do whatever it takes. But promise me."

"Oh, I do. I do."

"I'm not joking."

"Me either. But like you say, parenthood is huge. Maybe we should sleep on it."

"Okay, but not quite yet."

In this, Wally's fourth year of teaching the Electronic Battlefield seminar at the University of the Potomac, the required orientation session for adjunct faculty is an exercise in boredom. The code of ethics has again been tweaked to discourage grade inflation. Appearances will change, little else. Professors beholden to sponsoring industries for their jobs—a majority of the graduate school faculty—are rewarded for pandering to their benefactors' potential employees. Academic transcripts are as unreliable as weight-loss testimonials for the BBQ Diet. Observed classroom performance better indicates who might cut it at OstarFX.

As he's leaving the hall his eye is drawn to a blast from the psychedelic past advertising a lecture honoring Alan Watts in the centenary year of his birth. When Wally was an undergrad at Columbia, the pop philosopher's paperbacks were a soothing counterpoint to the coke-fueled alienation of the punk scene. Life is a game, the trickster guru agreed; why not play it with understanding and compassion? Wally's still sympathetic to those ideas and thinks Leilani would benefit from the broader perspective on spirituality.

She'd rather model lingerie for him than be subjected to the teachings of a false prophet. The offer of frilly fun might have been more tempting if the Laurel Ridge water report hadn't arrived in the mail and she hadn't already diagnosed herself with lead poisoning. The main thing she'd model for him tonight is a new snit.

She's overreacting. As he's said all along, the in-home water filter does an excellent job. Contaminants possibly related to tampering at the village waterworks weren't detected at the faucet. Some samples *do* contain lead slightly in excess of European Union guidelines and are higher than the lead level in municipal water. A note describes this as a common finding. Faucet fixtures gradually leach lead. When water stands inside them for a length of time, the increase can be significant. Surprisingly, the corrosion in older fixtures has a protective effect; corroded brass gives off less lead.

"The report says faucet filters are effective. I'll have Caitlin look into it for us. We might need them here too. The fixtures are newer."

"Those filters are so ugly."

"Would you rather run the water for a minute before drinking or cooking with it? That's another solution."

"I shouldn't have to do that. We don't live in a trailer."

"True. We could go to a strict regimen of bottled water and wine. No dining out, though. Restaurants cook with water. The hot and sour soup could be laced with lead."

"Don't say that."

"That's an even better idea. We could stop worrying and forget it. Lead poisoning hasn't killed us yet."

He twists her arm another notch on Watts, reminding her that he attends church when asked.

Reluctantly, she acquiesces. "But if you think I'll doubt my faith, you're sadly mistaken."

WarpCom Auditorium has an aura of regimented austerity Wally finds intriguing. *Would the Buddhist half of Watts approve this minimalist interpretation of colonial style?* The plain white walls, pine stage, brick-red carpet and matching theater seats are nonstick surfaces for attention. He'd like that. But they also represent the industrial illusion he encouraged people to wake from. Then there's the corporate wallpaper of WarpCom logos behind the podium.

Baby boomers dominate the meager audience. What a shame. *Hasn't the younger generation heard of Alan Watts?* Wally wishes Caitlin were here. Her negative outlook is too common these days. Boycotting the system doesn't correct social ills; it's petulant. She could do with a dose of *The Joyous Cosmology.* Perhaps he'll buy her a copy for her birthday. *No, isn't that the one about LSD?*

The speaker is a fellow at a think tank known for training government officials. He invokes Watts as inspiration for a dry inquiry into contextual constraints on value systems. While yes/no is typically understood as an either-or proposition, he says, in quantum contexts they may co-exist in superposition. Similarly, depending on context, true/false may properly be treated as a polar dyad, superposition, or irrelevant—he brilliantly observes that the Potomac River is neither true nor false. And since all contexts are themselves contextually defined, none has a legitimate claim on ultimate primacy. That being said, decisions must be made. The choice of *controlling* context is a critical administrative function. In the Department of Justice, "projected economic impact" proved superior to "criminal code violation" as the optimal controlling context for initiating enforcement actions. Appropriate sauce for the consumer goose may be disastrous for the national security gander.

Wally recalls the fiasco of imposing the regime of rationality on Caitlin. First graders can't go around speaking to trees and working "magick" without being thought strange, he'd told her. Maeve accused him of small-mindedness. They settled the question with a jointly designed experiment. At the dark of the moon they bought a flat of petunias and set them out in the flower garden. Caitlin's job was encouraging half to grow by magick. The others would serve as controls. Six weeks later, on the full moon, both groups looked the same. Magick had no demonstrable effect. "This is why people don't believe in it," he explained to Caitlin. "Your mother has different beliefs but she doesn't make a spectacle of herself. You shouldn't either. No more public displays of nonsense."

That evening, long past her bedtime, he and Maeve heard singing in the backyard. From Caitlin's bedroom window they watched as she twirled and sang in her nightie.

"Wait here," Maeve said. "I'll handle it."

Instead of bringing Caitlin directly in, the backyard conversation became a mother-daughter song and dance. They spun themselves dizzy and fell in the grass.

Before he got to them, Maeve had Caitlin in the house and on her way to bed, silent and teary. Maeve told him Caitlin had been casting a spell, aligning her will to his. "You should know she confessed to violating the rules of your experiment. She thought it was mean to ignore half the plants. So she encouraged them all."

Caitlin forgot magick after that but not the reserve she adopted in his presence. For him and Maeve the incident was a marital step downhill. He wishes he had it to do again. *Who cares if a kid talks to trees?*

The lecturer drones on. "Individuals may function as societal brain tissue, muscle, skin, hair or dandruff."—someone in the audience is audibly amused—"Each must be carefully monitored for the optimization of systemic stress in the controlling context of market performance. Stressors may need to be increased by external threat or internal scarcity. Excessive stress must be vented. The sports industry is a win-win in this regard, channeling aggressive tendencies and stimulating economic activity. Acute perturbations in systemic stress may necessitate ad hoc methods…"

This isn't Alan Watts. It's Orwell. Big Brother would love it.

Wally's applause at the end of the lecture occurs in a context of relief.

Leilani has detected no heresy but asks, "Why do they make things so complicated?"

"It's their job. Sorry I dragged you along. This wasn't what I expected."

"You owe me."

"Remind me to call Caitlin when we get home. She uses faucet filters. We'll find out how she likes them."

"Hey, Dad," Caitlin says.

"Did I ever tell you how sorry I was about the petunias?"

"Petunias?" She sounds distant, impatient.

"When you were a kid. But never mind that; are you okay?"

"We're kind of exhausted."

"What happened?"

"We were attacked in an alley this afternoon. Xan hurt his hand fighting them off."

rhythms on a flaming drum

memorial

Across the street from the Living Spirit Fellowship Hall where Teddy Arnold's memorial service is being held, Palomar supporters denounce him as a communist Nazi. The harassment began before the service with drive-by abuse from men in pickup trucks, some flying Confederate flags. A plywood sign in the bed of another displayed the flaming-sword-in-the-stone emblem of the local redneck underground: the Holy Brotherhood of the Fiery Sword. Blue shirts trained their cameras on arriving mourners, not hecklers. Xan loaned Caitlin his phone to remedy that disparity. Denny had his own citizen journalism thing going in front of the hall. While Caitlin went in to find seats, Xan stayed with him to watch a shuttle bus drop placards and red-white-and-blue-vested organizers at the chain restaurant opposite Living Spirit. When the bus pulled away, cops closed the street to vehicles but allowed a protest march to reach the eatery. Marchers were offered a choice of signs: JOBS PATRIOT. *ONE LESS ECO-NAZI.* DRINK THE WATER, NOT THE KOOL-AID. News2 interviewed protesters. Denny videoed a blue shirt lieutenant joking with an organizer. The demonstration was steadily increasing in numbers, volume and venom as organ music drew Xan into the sanctuary.

He spies Caitlin near the front with Mari and Brent McWhorter, both of whom are scheduled to speak. They've saved him a space. Mother Prentiss, the senior minister here, assures the congregation that police have the situation under control. Noise from the protest is tolerable with the front door closed but the temperature in the sanctuary climbs. Shirts and dresses are damp after the first song. Service programs rustle in the pews, stirring the air for what little that's worth. Brent keeps it together during his eulogy. Other speakers, including Mari, digress from prepared remarks to address the situation in the street.

An hour stretches to two but the interminable does eventually terminate. People clog the aisles, eager for air but hesitant to venture into the belligerence.

"Is there another way out?" Xan asks Brent—the Sawligoochee Riverkeeper is a Living Spirit parishioner.

"There's a fire exit onto the alley. I'm sure Mother won't mind."

"We should confront those assholes, not sneak away," Mari says.

Xan disagrees. "Haitians taught me how shit like this goes down. Avoidance is survival. The Man's henchmen are free to shoot you. You shoot *them*, you hang."

Brent mounts the stage. "Follow me."

A sign at the exit warns that an alarm will sound. If it does, it's silent. Alcoves and garbage cans line the narrow alleyway. They hear a diesel engine rumble to life. The white pickup with the Fiery Sword sign rolls toward them from the near end of the alley. The church door has relocked.

"He's herding us," Xan says. "Expect an ambush." He dumps a trashcan, chooses a stinking bag for himself, hands another to Brent. "You and I go first. If anybody jumps you, hit him with this."

Mari draws her knife.

"Put it away," Xan orders her. "You and Caitlin run while the garbage is flying. We'll meet at the parking deck." The driver behind them guns his engine, creeps closer. "Here we go."

Fifty feet ahead two good old boys waving ax handles step from an alcove. The one on Brent's side is a sunburned Bubba. His camo-wearing companion is smaller.

Brent halts. The truck behind them doesn't.

"Walk," Xan whispers, "or get your ass kicked. When I say to, charge Camo Man. Whale him with the sack. Then run. I'll take Big Boy. Mari, I'm counting on you."

At forty feet Camo Man calls out, "What you'ns up to?"

"Taking out the trash," Xan says, continuing forward, the truck keeping pace.

"That's funny. Us too," Camo Man says.

He's a twitchy weasel.

At twenty feet Xan hisses, "Now." He dashes in front of Brent to catch Big Boy's club at half cock. The man takes a rotten food explosion in the face. Camo Man goes down. Brent's past him; Caitlin on his heels. But Mari isn't with them. She stomps Camo Man, whips out her phone. Big Boy takes a swing at Xan. Misses. The truck is almost on them.

"Go, Mari."

Finally, she does. Xan sprints after her. Big Boy isn't quick but he's coming too and Xan would rather not be chased around the corner. He slows, sidesteps, pivots. Big Boy runs into a short, straight left that lands with a tooth-spitting crack and pitches him onto his garbagy face. Xan hurdles him, beats feet for the street. The truck honks. Honks again. Kills its engine.

Mari, Brent and Caitlin are waiting at the sidewalk. "Let's go," he urges. "That guy could be on us any second." They walk fast, away from the barricades and mayhem near the fellowship hall.

"Xan," Caitlin says, "your hand."

He's leaving a blood trail from a gash between his knuckles. He can look into an empty space between the meat of two fingers. His wrist feels like he punched a wall. "Got a handkerchief?"

Caitlin gives him a pack of tissues. He tears off the plastic, clutches half the tissues—as best he's able—in the injured hand, applies the remainder as a compress to the back of it.

"I'm taking him to Urgent Care," she tells Mari and Brent. "We'll talk later."

Big Boy and Camo Man aren't at Urgent Care West but the waiting room is slammed with their pals. Xan can't smell the garbage on his clothes for the pepper spray on theirs. He has to have Caitlin fill out his forms. She writes that he had an accident with a dumpster at the apartment.

Clinic TV is tuned to PGA golf. Palomar supporters gather around when News2 breaks in with a live report of mass violence near City Center. The reporter stands before a backdrop of cop cruisers with flashing lights.

"Police say a peaceful jobs rally was disrupted this afternoon by irate mourners attending the funeral of well-known radical, Theodore Arnold. A number of rally participants were injured in the melee."

"By pepper spray," a man shouts.

"Well done, NewsStooge," Caitlin gripes.

"A Calhoun PD spokesman tells News2 that dozens of activists were detained. Charges of incitement also pending against officials of the nontraditional house of worship."

Caitlin isn't allowed to accompany Xan to the treatment room—immediate family only. The nurse who cleans his wound questions the cover story.

"I threw something away by mistake and had to go in for it. There was a sharp edge."

"If you say so," she replies. "Right now I'll take the smell of garbage over pepper spray."

X-rays don't show any obvious fracture. He's sent home with stitches, a splint, tetanus shot, and prescriptions for antibiotics and a painkiller.

He and Caitlin are listening to music, chilling. Mari calls. The gist of Caitlin's conversation with her is that blue shirts corralled mourners with plastic fencing, brutalized them with batons and pepper spray, then detained them in droves. Denny escaped because cops mistook him for a NewsStooge staffer.

Caitlin passes Xan the phone. Mari is sorry for slowing him down in the alley.

His painkillers are kicking in when the phone rings again. Caitlin checks the screen and mouths, "Dad." She goes into the kitchen to talk, leaving him in peace.

Fifteen minutes later she brings a glass of wine. "Dad wants faucet filters installed at Laurel Ridge," she says. "I've been telling him for years…"

rhythms on a flaming drum

Pain pills and a wine chaser sent Xan early to bed. His wrist was bothering him. Caitlin hopes he won't have nightmares. Flailing around tonight could hurt them both. She doesn't want to contemplate how hard he must have hit that man to do the damage he did. He'll be lucky if the cut doesn't get infected and his wrist isn't broken. The doctor said he'll need another x-ray in a few days. Until then, Xan is supposed to avoid manual labor. That won't happen. His customers depend on him.

She has work to do as well. No better time than now to upload her photos of the redneck trucks. She goes to the bedroom for his phone. He's out, on his back, the splinted hand propped against the headboard. To prevent it from going to sleep she lowers it to his chest and kisses his forehead. Despite her nonviolent principles she was thrilled to see the big oaf fall.

Her pictures aren't the best but fiddling with the images renders two license plates legible. One belongs to the Fiery Sword truck. She hadn't noticed the Southern Mountain Alliance sticker on the back window of the cab. Any link between those organizations could be a news bombshell. SMA poses as mainstream. The smiling face of its philanthropist founder, Bobo Huskins, is everywhere. It would be too perfect for him to be the truck driver. Sadly, he's not. This dude has dark curly hair. She didn't get the face of the man driving the other vehicle with a readable plate but instantly recognizes the driver of a truck amateurishly painted in camouflage colors: the mugger Xan named Camo Man. She's sick she didn't get his tag number. Mari really, really dislikes that guy. He has short hair, a bony face and a gun on the rack behind his head. The mugger Xan hit isn't shown in her photos.

She saves them to a temporary file and goes online. Denny has her computer strongly encrypted and running freeware instead of corporate products. If she follows his procedures, her online activities are untraceable—he's almost as finicky as her dad. But usability suffers. It's a slow system even without the darknet complications. She's nostalgic for direct access to Google.

A roundabout search for pictures of Bobo Huskins eventually yields pages of image results. Bobo at charity events. Bobo testifying before Congress. A former president with his arm around Bobo, wanting to be seen as a friend of industry. Bobo with the chairman of the World Bank, various foreign heads of state, an action movie star, Mrs. Bobo. None shows the men in the alley.

She moves on to the chat room Diggers in the Southeast favor for secure communications. Denny, aka Wraith, has already opened a Palomar subtopic on the day's events. He reports that text and video from the fellowship hall are up on PeoplesWiki, the Digger darknet cousin of Wikipedia.

BasqueGoddess, otherwise known as Mari, writes that Camo Man was the fisherman who accosted her in the woods—she didn't get his picture in the alley. She doesn't post the other thing she told Caitlin by phone, that Tijon is among the riot detainees. That's bad but could have been worse. He and any other Digger caught in the sweep will blend into the mass of detained mourners. ISA is unlikely to devote much energy to sifting through that haystack. Calhoun Admin will probably be satisfied with the thousands of hours of community service it expects to receive from plea deals.

Caitlin, screen name ShakenIt, informs the chat room that her photos, including the fisherman BasqueGoddess recognized, will shortly be linked to the PeoplesWiki page on Palomar. She types the license plate numbers and asks if anyone has access to the North Carolina Department of Motor Vehicles database. She thinks the possibility of a direct connection between the Fiery Sword and Bobo Huskins is also worth pursuing.

The Palomar Coatings page at PeoplesWiki has been active lately. The former paint manufacturer is now rumored to have a classified contract for an unknown product. Solvents associated with the paint industry are among the list of municipal water contaminants. Other sections of the article summarize the Sawligoochee Riverwatch lawsuit and demonstration at Lake Hollister. Caitlin adds information to a new paragraph on the events at Living Spirit and uploads her images of trucks and drivers. These she annotates and links to PeoplesWiki pages on Bobo Huskins, The Southern Mountain Alliance and the Holy Brotherhood of the Fiery Sword.

It's after midnight before the computer hygiene program finishes erasing all record of tonight's activity from her laptop. "If you don't have it," Denny says, "they can't find it."

rhythms on a flaming drum

"Put your foot down, Wally." Leilani's in the bathroom scrubbing residue of the dreary Watts lecture from her pores. "Next thing you know, she'll be in jail."

"What do you suggest? Caitlin's a grown woman, twenty-eight next month." *Here we go*, he thinks, studying the Laurel Ridge water report in bed, trying to understand the presence of carbon in the first stage cartridge of the in-home filter system. To the best of his recollection there's not supposed to be backflow from the activated charcoal second stage.

"Take away her money."

"I can't. The trust fund belongs to her and it's probably doing better today than when she took over. For a person down on capitalism she has quite a head for finance."

"So you approve of her hoodlums and riots?"

"Of course not."

"Then do something."

Leilani doesn't comprehend idealism or that experience is the cure for it. He was idealistic himself once and, thanks to Maeve, Caitlin inherited a double dose of starry eye. *So romantic, thinking you can save the world.* What worries him is that she may not wise up before Leilani's prediction becomes fact. *Riots? Beatings? Xan cuts grass for a living? Wasn't he supposed to be a drummer?*

When Caitlin introduced him after the Collective Harlequin performance he'd seemed a decent sort. Leilani didn't like him; she didn't like anything that night. *Do female realists still have women's intuition?*

"Caitlin says the faucet filters are no problem. She can install them herself."

"We'll test the water again afterwards, to be sure?"

"If you want."

Leilani comes to bed in pajamas. Hadn't she promised him fancy undies?

"Explain this to me?" she coos, snuggling against his shoulder. "I wasn't good at science."

Are we playing professor and fawning student? I'll give it a shot. He shows her the municipal water sheet. The reason for the carbon in his particulate filter is now apparent: city water has carbon in it.

"What we have here, little darling, is a long list of chemicals and compounds, and the amounts in city water. These other pages are results from our filters and faucets. See? Much cleaner."

"Except for lead."

"Strictly from taps that haven't been in use."

"Water should only have water in it."

"That's why they make filters."

Leilani's not fawning. She peruses the list of municipal water contaminants. "Benzene? Gobbledygook letters with stars beside them?"

"Stars are bad. They indicate concentrations in excess of European guidelines. One star per order of outlier magnitude. Trichloroethylene gets three stars because it's present in concentrations greater than a hundred times the EU limit. Benzene and vinyl chloride have two stars. They're elevated between ten and a hundred fold."

"But why?"

"Have you ever poured paint thinner down the drain or

owned a car that leaked oil? If you did, you added chemicals to somebody's water. Industries are the same. The failed lawsuit against Palomar was an attempt to discover which of these might be from the plant."

"Bobo Huskins wouldn't poison us."

"No, but dumping is cost-effective. Water quality downstream isn't Palomar's concern."

"It should be."

Wally nuzzles her cheek. "Turning idealistic on me?"

"It shouldn't be allowed."

His prospects for sex are zilch after she enters one of these tail-chasing mental feedback loops. "Ironic, isn't it?" he says. "If not for that court case, we'd never have known any of this."

"There are right ways and wrong ways to make things known."

"What's on television?"

She cues up a documentary on the construction of Hoover Dam and Lake Mead. What a feat of engineering and determination. Workers desperate for jobs during the Great Depression endured abysmal living conditions, low wages and average temperatures in excess of a hundred degrees. Scores died in accidents. Others succumbed to heat or foul air in the river diversion tunnels they blasted through the canyon walls. Labor strikes were ruthlessly suppressed. Superintendent Frank Crowe's no-nonsense approach brought the dam to completion two years ahead of schedule. Companies that partnered in the project went on to become multinational giants and Lake Mead remains a major supplier of water and electricity to the Southwest.

"Inspiring, isn't it?" Leilani says when it's over. "The American spirit in action."

"Tell that to the poor bastards who slaved there."

"They sacrificed for their country."

"Or couldn't let their families starve to death. Their welfare wasn't among Crowe's bottom lines. Same with the Palomar dumping. Business goals drive business behavior."

"It's not the same at all. Hoover Dam is a wonder of the world."

The sonic masking Denny chose for tonight's Street Artist meeting at the Harlequin Theater is a jagged concerto by a pioneer of experimental rock. "He had a following," Reba Stein says, sympathetic to Mari's complaint, "including Izzy. This piece always reminded me of an extended car wreck. What's it called, love?"

"'Cacaphonia LA'; not his most accessible piece for the uninitiated."

If Denny's miffed at being second-guessed he hides it and shuffles to the soundboard. The driving rhythms of Brazilian Carnival fill the room with high energy dance music.

Much better, Caitlin thinks. Xan's irritation at hearing she wouldn't be straight home after rehearsal hasn't left her in the mood for dischords, if that's a word. She hates to rub activism in his face so soon after the alley fight—his hand is better, thank goodness—but there's really no choice. In this climate of violence, ignorance is dangerous.

The agenda begins with a recap of the memorial service. Per the Steins' usual practice, they hadn't attended. Their artsy but mainstream reputation protects Reba at the university and the couple's extensive social connections, both important Digger assets. Had Izzy not overheard a conversation at a community board meeting, Denny wouldn't have been alerted in advance to the likelihood of harassment from Palomar supporters. The evidence he anonymously passed to Gil Punshon of Hotwired Free Media refutes the manufactured outrage of NewsStooge and other corporate outlets—not that the average consumer is aware of Hotwired FM's existence as an internet radio station.

Six Harlequins, including Tijon, were among the 137 mourners corralled by police kettle nets. His account of the ordeal sobers the Street Artists: pepper spray, bruises, zip tie handcuffs that cut off the circulation in his hands. During the hours of confinement on transport buses awaiting Detention Center processing, detainees secretly cooperated to phone relatives—Caitlin can't imagine how hard that must be with hands cuffed behind. Then the mug shots, strip search, fingerprints, DNA swabs and assignment to segregated bullpens. No explanations. Diabetics and heart patients went without medications in fetid, overcrowded cells. One man cut his head during a seizure. Another began vomiting the first night and lay on the floor until guards dragged him out for his bond hearing.

Outrages against decency didn't end with the detainees' release on Monday. That night, last night, Teddy's house burned to the ground. Witnesses interviewed by Hotwired FM say the fire department made no attempt to douse the flames, only prevent them from spreading to adjacent structures. Teddy's renters weren't home when it happened; Steve's wife and baby had skipped town. Fear of the sicko who fed Peaches the fishhook probably saved their lives. Izzy worries that the arson could intimidate tipsters to the Humane Society.

"It had the opposite effect on Teddy's brother," Mari says. "That and getting busted—"

Tijon interrupts, "Did I see him? What's he look like again?"

"A thinner Teddy with slicked-back hair. Was there an older man on your bus who kept his distance from brothers of a darker persuasion?"

"Several like that. Couldn't tell them apart."

"Anyway," Mari continues, "Levon's pissed. He couldn't shut up about getting even when we talked this morning. Dr. Sigurdsdottir had questions."

Denny's curious. "She couldn't think he knew Teddy's medical history?"

"Just general stuff: where Teddy worked, whether he'd been exposed to asbestos or coal dust. His lungs were black and he had spots on the inner lining of his chest and stomach."

"What sort of spots?"

"Some condition. I'll write it down next time. My point is, Levon's ready to kick ass."

"I hope you talked him out of it," Caitlin says. "Things are too crazy as it is."

Denny has identified the owners of the license plate numbers she posted—more unsettling news. "The yahoo with the white pickup and Fiery Sword sign is Joshua Rice. He works for Bobo Huskins, who, as we know, owns Palomar and runs SMA. If Huskins doesn't own Admin too, he's the loudest noise in Hufnagel's ear."

"Superb!" Izzy exclaims, "and incredibly stupid of this Rice character. It's the link between SMA and the Flaming Sword."

Denny says, "Yeah. But maybe we've reached the place where Huskins can do whatever he wants with impunity."

"Massa never went away. Didn't hardly change clothes," Tijon says.

Caitlin is oppressed by a level of foreboding she hasn't experienced since the ISA interrogations at college. Mari's update on her personal situation only worsens it.

"Blue shirts were at my house a few hours ago. A guy who lives downstairs talked to them."

"And?" Caitlin imagines the worst.

"And they left."

Izzy drops into counselor mode. "How are you doing with this, Mari?"

"I can handle myself."

Caitlin has another Ruskin flashback. "Don't underestimate them and don't say peep without an attorney."

"Do you have one?" Reba asks.

"I did a kitchen remodel for a cool lawyer. She'll be there if I need her. Meanwhile I'll be less predictable. My computer won't be at the house when they break in to steal it."

Denny volunteers to delete any incriminating files.

"Better safe than sorry," Mari says. "Which reminds me, what's with the 'Death to Pigs' email?"

It had been in Xan and Caitlin's in-boxes this morning as well. The message from the suspected ISA informant proposes a gathering of "comrades" to organize a punishment action against the City of Calhoun. While the form this might take is unspecified, the intent is clear. "Hufnagel and his tools at the Chamber of Commerce must be made to understand that violence against the masses will be met with force."

The wannabe comrade-in-arms hid her distribution list. Cautious inquiries lead Denny to doubt that a Digger network was penetrated. The common thread between known recipients seems to be a public role in Teddy's benefit or memorial service.

"That woman is a snake," Caitlin says.

Tijon replies, "Sister Obvious isn't the only viper in town, Sugarpie, just the one you see."

"I know," Caitlin frets, "and if it isn't her, it's arson and rednecks and blue shirts and ISA in Black Mariahs." A vision comes to her. She's sitting at home, humming a lullaby to a baby drowsing at her breast, eyelids aflutter with dreams. The image is irresistibly appealing. "I may need to step back from actions for the time being."

The Street Artists stare, open-mouthed. Samba drums and whistles strut with an audacity nobody in the room shares. But as Caitlin hears her half-lie of an excuse, it rings true to her. Naïveté—and her dad's intervention—saved her at Ruskin. She's not innocent anymore. Catastrophe can lurk around any corner. *The Steins don't take chances, why should I?*

Xan is tensed for a fight. "Before you start," she says, "I told them I'm done with doing actions."

"You're out?" The look on his face is pure joy.

"Not entirely. They're letting me stay in the information loop, at least until things settle. I'll do meetings. Those people are like family. I can't abandon them."

"My family is you."

She holds him tight. "You're more than that to me. You're the one I never thought I'd meet again. There are a zillion other ways to work for a better future."

He kisses her. "Someday when we're old and rocking on the porch with grandkids in our laps I want to remember this moment."

Her orphan boy can offer her no greater gift.

rhythms on a flaming drum

Hello?" Xan can't fathom what possesses him to answer telephones at inconvenient moments. He's grimy from mowing and trimming. He's thirsty. His wrist aches. The gauze pad over his stitches is soggy with sweat. When the landline rang he'd scarcely had time to step out of his work clothes and read Caitlin's note: she'll be home late. It's not as if telephones are living things. Yet he answers, in his underwear, and proceeds into the kitchen for a cold drink.

"Oh, hi. Is this Xan?" The caller pronounces it correctly and doesn't include his last name as a telemarketer would.

"Who's this?" The tea jar in the fridge is full. He shoulders the phone against his ear and considers how best to maneuver the jar to the cutting board by the sink without dropping tea or telephone.

"Caitlin's mom, Maeve Duggan. It's so good to finally hear your voice."

Success. He clamps the phone, hugs the jar with his bad arm and begins unscrewing the lid. "You too, Mrs. Duggan. Caitlin's—"

If the scrape of metal threads on glass carries to Toronto, she lets it pass. "I'm not Mrs. Anyone. Maeve is fine."

"Caitlin's not home. She had a shoebox of receipts waiting at the credit counseling center."

"A shoebox?"

A glass. "The filing system of the self-employed. Mine was a boot box."

"You wouldn't do such a thing."

"Of course I did. Can't get away with it anymore though." *Pour quietly.*

"I'm so proud of Caitlin's volunteer work. You two must be busy, busy."

Ice. "Busy enough. I'm trying to get her to cut back."

"On the political front, I hope?"

He opens the freezer door, takes cubes from the bin. "Excuse me?" *How much does Caitlin tell her?* The ice slips into his glass silent as a shadow.

"I spoke with her father last evening. What he told me was more frightening than he realizes, but I left his ignorance intact. He said you hurt your hand?"

"They sewed it back together. The wrist is sore but nothing broke." The tea isn't organic but the peach flavor can't be beat. His first swallow shoots delicious arrows of cold through his chest on the way down.

"What happened?"

He summarizes the escape from Living Spirit, hears sharp intakes of breath on the other end of the line. There'd have been another if she'd seen him almost drop the jar returning it to the fridge.

"Will your country never grow up? But I shouldn't say that. Forgive the commentary and accept a mother's gratitude for protecting her daughter. Heal your hand, well and strong."

"We were lucky."

"Your skill and resourcefulness are a comfort to me. By the way, Caitlin sent the link to your YouTube performance. Orpheus himself would have been chilled by the escape from the underworld you conjured. This witch is jealous."

"It just sort of happened."

"Magick is a curious brew of preparation and circumstance. Fifty thousand views already. Gaia is vibrating with you."

"Thanks." *Gaia is vibrating?* "I'll tell Caitlin you called."

"Yes, please. Another thing: my partner Geoff and I might fly down for her birthday. Would she like that? Be honest."

"Her dad will be here."

"He told me."

"I'm sure she'd love to see you. We're throwing a birthday bash at the theater. It'll be fun."

"A surprise?"

"No. The play opens the previous week. The collective is taking a night off to party. Live music, the works."

"Oh, goody. You'll perform?"

"The wrist should be fine by then." *In fact, now I think of it, the sprain feels better already.* "You should catch a performance of *The Birds* while you're in town."

"We plan to. And I so look forward to meeting you. Caitlin's not good at hiding her feelings."

"She's the world to me."

"So, for all of our sakes, keep her safe. Will you?"

"I'll do my best, Mrs. … Maeve."

"Of course you will. You'll be a wonderful father."

"Excuse me?" he says again.

"The heavens are full of gossip. It's been wonderful speaking with you, Xan. Welcome to our family. Ring me anytime."

rhythms on a flaming drum

We rise naked, from a cascade pool. Stand on a wide, flat stone. Behind us the roar of falling water. Below us thick moss. Air traces invisible designs on wet skin. We shiver with living fire. Before us a forest, dark, uncertain.

A flowery vine binds my wrists. The other end binds him, close in body, far by vine. I twirl, dancing steps I've always known but don't recall.

The flowers burn bright, yellow, now white
His body ripples in their light
We turn and dip, spooling garlands
This is the pull of inevitability. A child's sing-song.

I have no will but this. Consent radiates from me in silver beams and tendrils of green. He answers with ribbons of blue, red and gold. Twining colors draw down the moon and sun, to an ending in the middle.

What was before, leads to this
What will come, springs from this
With this clasp of hands, right to right, left to left,
the knot is tied, the figure complete.

rhythms on a flaming drum

> *Bedded by Earth*
> *Blanketed by Sky*
> *Water sings to us*
> *Fire glows within*
>
> *At one with necessity*
> *This is happiness*
> *So simple.*

dancin' in the rain

Caitlin's decision not to participate in future Street Artist actions has opened a deeper dimension for her and Xan. Where once her urge to be of service radiated outward, it's now reflected into the space they share, concentrated there, aching to take form. The motherhood remarks she thought of as mere conversation were actually messages from her body, addressed to her consciousness as much as his. She can't pretend any longer that they carry no weight. She's ready, and equally sure he is as well. He worries he's bribing her out of selfishness. Partly true, but given his feelings on parental commitment, that willingness alone is tribute beyond measure. It's easier for him to speak of bribery than the larger hollow inside. After Haiti, it's a leap of faith to dare having a family. He admits it, admits wanting one anyway. Not to overcome. To be whole in a manner they both understand, but laughably beyond the fumbling words they use to point at it. Late at night, hearing themselves, so earnest, it all dissolves in jibber-jabber. *Who are we fooling with these pep talks? We're no different than millions of other clueless couples standing at the edge of this cliff. That's life. No sport for weenies.*

They celebrate the end of birth control with a candlelight dinner at home. She floats from room to room, immune to the early gloom blowing in with a line of storms. Rain pulses against the windowpanes. Down on the street, cars splash pothole solos. The occasion demands her sunniest yellow sundress.

Along with blueberry pie and yogurt for dessert she serves him her waterfall dream. "It was so beautiful, a skyclad handfasting," she says. "We should totally do that. Someday."

He has attended a few of these antique Celtic ceremonies. They're a popular alternative to consumerist weddings. No tuxedo or wedding dress required, but people do wear clothes. "I'll save my bare ass for you," he says.

"Just an idea."

They bring candles to the living room, where dusk in the city makes Rothko paintings of the drawn window shades. Xan dances her to the beat of rain on glass. Slinking and slithery, dirty blues. He reaches for the bow of her dress. "If you get naked, you could show me the moves in your dream."

"I thought you liked clothes?" she says, resisting. "We haven't disposed of the pills yet."

She leads him to the bathroom, hands him her unopened pack from the medicine cabinet. "Let's do it outside," she says, eyes flashing mischief.

Instantly drenched they stroll arm in arm, the sidewalk theirs alone. At the corner, in a streetlamp's golden cone she stops, her dress a clinging violation of decency standards. Rivulets stream from her chin. "Where to?" she asks.

"Any cop sees what I'm seeing, babe, the answer is jail. The river park won't be doing much business tonight. Plenty of dark corners there."

"And the pills?"

"A trashcan?"

"Disposing is different than throwing away." She brushes draggled ropes of hair from her face. "Disposing is meaningful."

"Then I don't know." They walk. At a construction site where a dozen artists and studios are being displaced by another mixed-use development for up-scale consumers, new walls sprout behind a chain link fence. "Nothing suck-cedes like gentrification," he says.

"Perfect. That's where we'll leave the pills. Birth control for the free market." They climb the fence, slog across bulldozed mud and gravel and conduct a brief ceremony of disposal in a watery trench.

Guided by pavilion lighting visible through the trees, they negotiate the river park entrance gate and splash along an asphalt path flowing teal in the distant glow of mercury vapor lamps. They circle around in the shadows, to a dim picnic shelter remote from park surveillance cameras. He unties her dress.

"Now show me your dream," he says, "over in the grass."

"It needs you too, minus clothes."

Arms outstretched, they whirl like fallen leaves. Apart, closer, spiraling, elemental as the storm. She'll recall aligning herself with the design of the future. He'll say they danced until the force of attraction became irresistible.

They're aware of sharing their lovemaking with an unseen other. *What must you think of us rolling around in the fringes of your dream? Can you relate to the slippery heat of lovers' skin on cold ground or what it is to be pelted by rain, pricked by blades of grass? To consciously dissolve? To wonder whether you'll thank us?*

rhythms on a flaming drum

Mushrooms interest Xan. He finds them on the job and wishes he knew which are edible. Mari, a local expert, has identified several types for him. None safe to eat. She says he'll do better in the woods and has offered to lead him and Caitlin on a hunt. He's amused at Caitlin's idea of bushwhacking attire. The spaghetti strap blouse, peasant skirt, straw hat and hiking boots are theatrical, not practical. Expecting briars, he chooses jeans.

Mari lives in the back of an old two-story house but they find her on the front steps—canvas pants, denim shirt. She loads peach baskets and other gear into the trunk of Caitlin's car, creates space in the backseat wardrobe department, climbs in.

The mushroom lecture he anticipates on the drive out of town doesn't materialize. Instead, Mari tells them she's anxious about *The Birds*. She's normally offstage crew but the large cast requirements forced her into a speaking part as well. She fears blanking on her lines. The play opens in two weeks. Panic city.

"Nerves? You?" Caitlin teases. "Talking in character is like talking to us. You'll be fine."

Xan's comfortable doubling as sound effects guy and Chorus bird. The chicken dance has gelled. Janet's sense of rhythm is improving. But he does question the durability of his costume. He can't do sound effects inside a cardboard box covered with faux feathers. Will it survive quick costume changes? Tuesday's the first dress rehearsal. *Fingers crossed.*

Past the Lake Hollister public landing they round a curve with a flashing caution sign. A flagman signals Caitlin to brake. Ahead, a tractor trailer escorted by state troopers pulls from a side road onto the highway.

Mari says it's a Palomar shipment. "Down there is where they disappeared Teddy. Wouldn't we love to know what that trailer is hauling?"

With the procession on its way, the flagman reverses his sign and stands aside. Caitlin steps on the gas. "Yes, but this close to Mordor is too close."

"Damn straight," Mari says. "Huskins wasn't satisfied to murder Teddy. He had to send his orcs after Teddy's dog, and torch his house, and desecrate his memorial service."

"Cops don't like firebugs," Xan says. "They'll get that clown."

Caitlin has doubts. "Not unless Huskins says so. A pickup with a camo paint job was seen the day Peaches died and on the night of the arson. Teddy's neighbors told the fire investigator. I photographed it before the memorial service. How many trucks like that can there be around Calhoun? The arson squad knows who the perp is."

"That truck you and I saw?" Xan reaches for his phone. "The one that looked like it was painted with a brush?"

Caitlin nods. "I erased the pictures. But they're online. The driver was the short thug at Fellowship Hall."

"Camo Man? Did you tell me that?" If she did, he has forgotten. He was loopy on pain pills that first night. The stitches in his hand have been out a week. He makes a fist too limp to flatten a dollop of mashed potatoes. His wrist is still tender. "Does our friend have a name?"

"Not so far."

"But he has a face," Mari says, "If I see it again, he'll regret it."

Too macho for her own good. "Do the blue shirts have your pictures?" Xan asks Caitlin.

"If they do, it's not from me. There'd be questions we don't want to answer."

We? So … Digger business and Mari is involved. No surprise. She's a good lady but he's relieved that Caitlin's activist days are over.

The forest service road to the remnant of public land on the upper Sawligoochee is paved as far as the Painter Falls Recreation Area where the user fee is only ten dollars a vehicle.

"Not here," Mari says. "There's no charge where we're headed. Keep your wheels on top of the ruts." The road changes to washed-out gravel. They wind uphill paralleling Painter Branch, cross it on a wooden bridge. The water is rocky and fast. Another half mile brings them to a trailhead lot. The only car in it is topped by an empty bike rack.

While Mari excuses herself to cast a spell for an abundant harvest he and Caitlin dawdle near the cars. Sunlight hasn't touched this piney woods in decades. The needles underfoot are sparsely littered with mossy branches and logs, the air scented with turpentine. The chanting they hear lends reality to the term enchanted; he'd not be surprised if a fairy popped from behind a tree. But Mari is the presence that manifests. She declares the hunt underway.

Equipped with baskets, paper bags and scissors they prowl the pines. Almost immediately Mari stoops before a mushroom he and Caitlin in their meandering might obliviously have stomped. The scruffy maroon and yellow cap blends in with the pine needles.

"Toxic Tony likes these for meat sauces," Mari says. "He'll buy all I bring him. Fan out. Take the young, firm ones. Brush them off; remove the stems and bag the caps."

"Toxic Tony the chef?" Caitlin asks.

"Yep. The pharmaceutical phenom himself. His pores exude altered states. The titans aren't worthy but only they can afford his food."

Xan spies a reddish mushroom at his feet. And another. The things are materializing before his eyes. They're everywhere.

"No sense in carting these around," Mari says moments later. They've harvested dozens of the sharp-smelling caps. "We'll stash them under the car to stay cool."

Baskets emptied, they search along the road beyond the parking lot. Progress slows to a crawl as she calls their attention to mushrooms he would have missed. Some bleed milk. There are yellow corals, pink parasols with wiry stems, and rubbery fungi resembling Reese's cups. She has them smell the root of an enormous dirty-white toadstool. The odor reminds him of a ham bone.

"Is it good?" Caitlin's voice doubts it.

"No."

"Too bad," Xan says. Others of its kind are visible under stands of mountain laurel. "A few of those could feed a lot of folks."

"You can eat any type of mushroom once," Mari says. "The question is whether you live to try it a second time. Ah, a chanterelle." In the roadside leaves she uncovers a squash flower of a mushroom, snips it off at ground level.

He spots more below the embankment. The trees here are hardwoods. Undergrowth abounds, including poison ivy. He isn't allergic, hopes Caitlin is careful.

"Everybody likes chanterelles," Mari says, sniffing it. "They have a peachy aroma. Let's see how many we can find, but leave the young for the woodland folk."

Chanterelles *do* smell peachy. Above him on the other side of the road Caitlin's peering at the ground, skirt gathered around her legs. "These are in poison ivy," she shouts to Mari, who's crouched twenty yards away, reaping.

Like a dutiful husband Mari rises and obeys, leaving her basket as a marker. "Nice," she tells Caitlin.

Her basket is lying in the road. Xan's about to take it to her when she forms one with the front of her skirt. "Use this. What fun. Thanks for inviting us." Chanterelles are even more numerous than the red mushrooms in the pines. A search of the mountainside yields full baskets.

With afternoon heat and humidity bearing down, Mari shows them a trail cutting down to Painter Branch. At the bottom of the washed-out goat track an informal camping area has been created alongside a swimming hole fed by a ten-foot falls.

"It's like my dream," Caitlin exclaims, scampering to a section of exposed bedrock at waterside. She takes off her boots, hikes up her skirt, wades in. "So cold! Want to skinny dip?"

"I will if you will," Mari tells Xan. The mannish clothes do no justice to her curves. The tattoo he's familiar with on her arm continues around her shoulder and under her breast, like a viny piece of armor. Rather than be caught staring, he studies the overhang of the falls. "I've always wanted to go behind a waterfall," he says.

The girls slosh out to a submerged sandbar and lie in the shallows, feet downstream, wavelets Vee-ing around them. He cautiously maneuvers among algae covered rocks and waist-deep holes to the base of the falls, and scrambles through the torrent into the undercut. He can stand. The space is a feast of rumbles and shifty ribbons of light.

"Caitlin," he yells into the shimmering curtain. It reflects his voice. *Can she hear me?* He speaks more slowly, enunciating. "When we're rich and famous, let's have one of these at home."

A squealing commotion brings her to him. She ignores the watery spectacle and presses herself against him.

"You should at least look," he says.

She pouts, obediently surveys the scene. "Pretty. Do we have room for Mari?"

"Not with you misbehaving."

"Mari," Caitlin shouts. "Over here."

"I'll get her for you." He escapes as Mari gets to her feet, sleek and glistening in the sun. *These women. Out of the fire and into the frying pan.* "Your turn," he tells her.

He assumes her former position on the shoal. Before the swirling water erases that last image of her entering the falls he has cooled, from pleasantly chilled to cold. He climbs onto the flat rock to dry.

The girls pop into view, laughing. The olive and the pink. *Which do you prefer, sir? Amazon or Faerie Queene? As if the question need be asked.* They splash and stumble in his direction.

At the edge of the pool Caitlin extends her right hand to be helped onto the rock. He crosses her up by taking it with his right.

"I'm sorry," she says, hesitating. "Does the other one still hurt?"

"That's not it." He extends his left over the top of their clasped hands. "Will you take this one too?"

Her dawning realization that she's being offered the figure-eight connection from her dream will stay with him. "Yes, yes, oh, yes. I do. I will," she sputters, taking his left as if it's a sacred object. He draws her up slowly onto the rock.

"Look, Mari. Xan's proposing and I'm going to cry."

Mari, who didn't need assistance getting out, is wringing water from her hair. "Well, blessed be. Congratulations, man. She never let *me* past second base."

abomination

Wally earned his seat at the OstarFX directors' table by coaxing agile development teams to industry-leading heights of software innovation. He's an enthusiastic whiz-kid whose single-mindedness assumes everyone else shares it. Because his coattails have furthered many a career, that expectation is generally well-founded. His staff regards him as a mildly autistic uncle and he pretends to be unaware of the condescension.

But lately the women in his life have been testing the limits of his emotional detachment. How could Caitlin assume he'd be pleased to learn that she wants to start a family without benefit of marriage? To Maeve this nonsense actually makes sense. "Marriage is an institution," she'd told him on the phone. "Many free spirits today reject that authoritarian symbolism. Handfasting affirms their love and commitment without the baggage. And don't worry, Wally; Xan is definitely her guy." How she can be so positive, never having met the man, is beyond comprehension.

Naturally, Leilani is revolted. "Your daughter *plans* to get herself knocked up by a sponger who punched out a man's teeth, and you go along with it? No law in heaven or earth recognizes the abomination of witchcraft weddings."

Hell no, he doesn't agree with Caitlin on this. But it's *her* life. She has as much right to it as Leilani does to hide behind

God Almighty when issuing her selectively applied moral pronouncements. As always, her interpretation of His rulings is absolute. Her god doesn't trade in fractions, probability clouds or temporary working solutions. Tonight, while she's occupied with a singing contest on TV, he's holed up in his home office when Caitlin calls to say they've set a date for the handfasting.

Again he asks whether she's certain.

"I think you're telling me you aren't."

"How could I be, sweetie? Consider my perspective. If your daughter's fiancé cut grass for a living, what would *you* think? Let's be frank. You were brought up with uncommon privilege. Nothing against Xan but how can he be expected to adapt? And with what? Does he have an influential family? A professional degree?"

"No and no."

"It's much easier to fall out of society than to claw your way in. What are his ambitions?"

"To play music? To live as honestly as possible?"

Wally washes that down with the last of a bourbon and soda. His leather chair audibly winces. *Are you kidding me?* "What else?"

"You'll never see a more devoted dad. He believes parenthood is the supreme responsibility on the planet."

The leather groans again. "Have you met his family?"

"His parents were murdered when he was a kid. An aunt and uncle took him in but he ran away a few years later."

The Schmidt family is no paragon of Prussian virtue but it grounds Wally in centuries of tradition. Heritage informs his decisions, and Caitlin's. She's talking like a Duggan. That grates, but still, it's a standard to test her impulses against. *Xan's only standard is childhood tragedy?* "Sweetie, it's commendable that he wants to be an involved father. But what else can he offer a child? Shouldn't we factor that?"

"He's resourceful, ahead of the curve in knowing how to live outside the market machine. He teaches me more than I teach him."

She's flirting with sedition here. "Are you on your landline?"

"Of course."

"Even so, watch your language. I'm a member of that machine and so are you. It pays your bills. Your trust fund is invested in it."

"Less than you may think," she says. "But can you check your calendar for me? October fourteenth. The leaves here should be gorgeous."

Leilani will kill him if he says yes and Caitlin will forever blame him if he doesn't.

"If you can't spare the time for a second trip so soon after my birthday, we'll understand."

"Your mother says this is like a formal engagement for a year? Then what?"

"A year and a day. Then we make it permanent by tying the knot. It's an old custom from the British Isles."

Time enough to change her mind. Is there an anti-fertility god to pray to? "Why doesn't he give you a ring? Can't he afford one?"

"I wouldn't wear it if he did. Our love isn't monetized by the carat. We just want to share a special day with special people. October fourteenth, Dad."

If this phone were cordless he'd mix another drink. "You say people have to hike into the location? How does that accommodate your grandparents?"

"It doesn't. The guest list is limited to a few friends and immediate family. We'll tie the knot some other place."

"If you're into waterfalls I know of one with a nifty gazebo. It's accessible by service vehicle. You might have to be flexible with your date though. Let me talk to Bobo. I'll take care of everything."

"Bobo?"

"Huskins. You've met him. Big guy, blond going gray, quite the talker."

Caitlin's voice turns icy. "Involving that man would disrespect everything I believe in. His goons … never mind. I appreciate your offer, but no. We have things under control. Mom's conducting the ceremony, nothing too freaky for Christians. In case of rain we'll move it to the theater. Think engagement party in the woods. October fourteenth."

He consults his calendar. *A Wednesday?* "That's the middle of the week."

"Mom says we should do it on the first day of a new moon. It'll be late in the afternoon so more people are off work."

"You'll still be cutting it close with daylight. Why not wait until summer?"

"We looked at other dates. September's out because of the play. By next spring I may be pregnant. There shouldn't be any hint of a shotgun wedding."

Oh, lord, the very thought.

"So can you make it?"

If you don't, you'll die regretting it. "I'll be there, sweetie. I can't promise for Leilani."

"Now it's an 'engagement party'?" Leilani scoffs, lying stiff in bed beside him. "Makes no difference what they call a sanctification of Godless lust."

"You mean sex?"

"And to think her father—"

"Now hold on. You and I didn't wait until we got married."

"But we were *going* to be married."

"You knew that in the beginning? I didn't."

"You'd never have touched me if we weren't."

Wally's chest swells with pride at Caitlin's birthday bash. Xan, who's scarcely found time to say hello, rearranged the warehouse theater to clear a dance floor. The party boasts a well-stocked bar, a live band on stage—complete with lightshow—and a mostly edible selection of health-conscious finger foods. Everyone sang "Happy Birthday" and blew out candles on organic cupcakes—organic cupcakes? It was a wonder the smoke alarm didn't go off. But what really gets to Wally is that his daughter has become *somebody* in Calhoun. He and Leilani have been introduced to heads of non-profits and a courtly veterinarian. Caitlin's on two boards she hadn't got around to mentioning. Business people are here—startups he's never heard of but so was OstarFX once upon a time—and artsy types, including the creator of a music video featuring Xan and a local singer. It has 100,000 views according to Maeve and her partner, Geoff, who flew down for the occasion. She's a bit thicker around the middle, not hiding her gray, a Canadian sweetheart aging with elegance. Leilani's on the dance floor, a popular partner this evening. The occasional rigidity of her ideas doesn't impede those Hawaiian hips. They coped admirably with a slow swing through a bluegrass rendition of the rock classic "Forever Young." They even carried her and the veterinarian through a weird number about a little girl who keeps spiders in her pocket, paints huge books and lies in the bathtub on her birthday smoking cigars. That image takes him and Maeve back, big time. Caitlin's bathtub obsession had been a bubble pipe. Maeve recalls it for Geoff and Caitlin's professor friend Reba, who's kind enough to coo at the cuteness before asking Maeve and Geoff their reaction to *The Birds*. Does the satire translate for those unfamiliar with the civic leaders being lampooned?

Geoff says, "We have our share of blowhards and imbeciles in leadership positions. They're much more entertaining at a distance."

Caitlin and a balding man with a ponytail insert themselves into the mix. She's excited. "Reba, Ed's giving us a rave. A full-page write-up."

"Fantastic job, all around," Ed says. "Four stars. The writing is superb, Reba, your best in years. If you have a moment I'd like to add a sidebar on the challenge of adapting an existing work."

"You don't mean *now*?"

"Layout deadline is day after tomorrow."

"Only for you, Ed." Reba rolls her eyes and sighs. "Excuse me, please," she says to Wally and Maeve. "So wonderful to meet you at last. Your daughter makes me wish I were thirty years younger, starting again myself." She hands her wine glass to Caitlin. "Can't have *InCalhoun* putting me down for a lush."

As Reba and Ed leave in search of quiet, Wally asks Caitlin where Xan's hiding.

She tips Reba's glass and says, "Slowly he turned…"

Xan has materialized at his elbow. "Sorry, Mr. Schmidt. Our regular sound guy just now arrived. Enjoying the band? Friends of ours."

Wally nods. "Leilani's having a fine time."

"Tell us, Xan," Maeve says, "what was that one they played? The birthday in the bathtub? I can't quite remember."

"'Birthday' is from the *Sugarcubes*," Xan says. "Björk sang it. Caitlin was afraid it might be too in-your-face." Wally could swear, even in the low light, that his daughter blushes.

"Björk. That's right," Maeve replies. "Geoff's eldest son worshipped her. The innocence is the charm. After all, what are friends for?"

Wally searches his memory in vain for risqué lines.

"Blownglass has the chops to try anything," Xan says, giving a thumbs-up to a server passing with another tray of cupcakes.

Caitlin adds, "They promise to end the show by backing Xan on a hot R. Kelly cover."

Whatever that may be.

Leilani, shiny with exertion, walks up with her latest partner.

"Wally," she says, "meet Brent … McWhorter, isn't it?" Brent has the emaciated features Wally associates with excessive fruit and vegetables. "He was with Caitlin when they were attacked in the alley."

Caitlin nudges Xan. "My turn to dance. Let's go."

"Thanks for keeping Leilani busy, Brent," Wally says, shaking the man's hand. "Have you been introduced to Caitlin's mother, Maeve, and Geoff Atherton? Geoff is a member of the Toronto City Council."

"Brent, tell Wally how helpful Caitlin's been," Leilani urges, leading the innocent witness.

"She and Collective Harlequin are a godsend to our water quality campaign. The benefit they staged for Teddy Arnold raised as much awareness as it did money. *The Birds* will reach so many more."

"Brent says he and Caitlin and another woman might have been killed if not for Xan."

"I'm no fighter," Brent admits. "Those rednecks would have beaten us to a pulp."

Leilani prods again. "They belong to the Brotherhood of the Fiery Sword? Who did you tell me they are?"

"White supremacists relitigating the Civil War, similar to the KKK."

"Wally, buy me a drink," Maeve says. Out of earshot of Leilani and Brent she asks him, "Has it really come to that in the States?"

He hadn't thought so. "Still drinking daiquiris?" He orders for them both. Caitlin and Xan are dancing, carrying on like they're alone in the room. Wally directs Maeve's attention to it. "She's known him for what, six months?"

"Can't you see they're perfect together?" The drinks slide across the bar. Wally stuffs a five into the tip jar.

"What can he offer her?"

"Other than being a talented percussionist, an old soul and the man of her dreams?"

"Come off it. She's your daughter too."

"He has twice saved her life, and that's not the half of it."

"Twice?"

"Ask her about the canoe."

"What canoe? Maeve, he cuts grass for cripes sake."

"And drums like Evelyn Glennie." Wally has no idea who that is. He could swear Maeve suppresses a smile as she looks down her nose at him. "We in the Commonwealth consider Dame Evelyn a musical treasure."

Well, la-di-da. "It's too damned soon. Caitlin hardly knows this guy."

"The timing *does* concern me and I've told her so. We're due for a lunar eclipse. Next month is Blood Moon, a better season for communicating with the dead than conducting a handfasting. But she won't wait. Other factors must be involved."

"She's not already…"

"Not to the best of my knowledge."

The band follows a jazzy tune by inviting Xan and Tijon Porter to the stage. They kick off a Caribbean number with Tijon doing a fair impersonation of Harry Belafonte. Xan's on steel drums.

Wally has visions of beaches and planter's punch. Geoff, on the dance floor with Leilani, is tentative with the calypso rhythm; she cuts him no slack. Caitlin jiggles with her odd-duck friend, the knife lady. After a second rum-soaked tune someone shouts, "'Let Your Hammer Ring.'"

Xan takes the vocalist's microphone. "Not tonight," he murmurs in a come-hither baritone. "This is a birthday party. Baby, where are you?" The crowd hoots as Caitlin waves her arms. "This is for you."

Wally's no stranger to setting moods with R & B records. He frowns at the smoky, romantic number Xan croons. *Damn him. He can also sing.*

The party is bookended by Xan's real introduction to her family. On the day prior, he and Caitlin had taken Maeve and Geoff to the falls on Painter Branch. Geoff marveled at the size of the trees, gamely negotiated the trails in city attire. Maeve declared the falls an ideal spot—something to do with tarot cards. On a sandbar exposed by the drier weather she drew a symbol invoking love in its natural element, had Xan and Caitlin stare at it while holding hands, then wash it away with creek water.

Tonight he and Caitlin are due in Laurel Ridge for dinner. The current Mrs. Schmidt requested menu preferences a week in advance. She's having the meal catered by Calhoun's hottest chef, Anthony Kochinowski, aka Toxic Tony. Caitlin ordered organic vegetarian, including wild local mushrooms if possible. Cake? Chocolate, of course. Xan was up for the mushrooms but also meat; he doesn't get it often. Caitlin took the precaution of having a personal chat with the chef. No special seasoning please. She says Tony didn't categorically deny the rumors of spicing an occasional dish with a pinch of Ecstasy.

Caitlin has Xan buttoned-down for the event, as preppy as she can make him. She goes for the same. The rationale for this decision isn't fully apparent until he lays eyes on Leilani's baubles and bangles. Her father's casual trousers are sharply creased, his canvas shoes spotless, tied with meticulously even bows. *We're laughable*, Xan thinks. *Mismatched mannequins in a foyer.* Wally breaks the women's wear tension by inviting Caitlin to accompany him and Xan on a guided tour of the estate while Leilani supervises dinner preparations.

Wally is especially proud of a rock garden with a monster view of the Sawligoochee Valley. Fruiting prickly pears decorate mossy humps. Cracks and basins in the bedrock hold ferns, thyme, wild oregano and a frosty-leaved mint.

"Sweet garden and a view to match," Xan says. The ridge above Lake Hollister might have looked like this if it was maintained.

Wally, leaning on a walking stick like the titan squire he is, acknowledges the praise then cuts to the chase. "What's the rush, kids?"

Caitlin hugs Xan's arm. "No rush," she tells her dad. "We've been around enough to know what we're doing."

"Then what's your plan for the day after? And children, good lord. If your mother and I had done whatever felt good to us you'd be flipping burgers for a living."

Xan tries a different tack. "Sir, maybe the question is what future to plan for."

Wally jabs his stick into the dirt, dislodging a weed. "Same as always. A man provides for his family and strives to achieve." He flips the offending plant toward the woods. It falls short, lands on a rock. His phone rings.

"Yes, dear.... I'll send her." He pockets the phone. "Caitlin, Leilani would appreciate your assistance. It's a nice evening. We thought we'd eat on the deck."

Caitlin slips Xan a questioning glance.

I can handle this.

She says, "Moving the table won't take a minute. When I come back we'll pick prickly pears. The juice is loaded with goodness. Tony'll find a use for it."

"Bring gloves," Xan tells her. "The fruit doesn't look prickly but it is." When she's gone, he adds, "She's everything to me, Mr. Schmidt. I'll do my best for her. You have my word."

Wally won't meet his eye. "I'm indebted to you for protecting her in that alley. Send me your medical bills. It's the least I can do. But, son,"—there's nothing familial in his voice—"providing for a wife and child requires more than good intentions. How do you expect to finance a college education by cutting grass?"

"Music is my profession. Lawn care pays bills on a temporary basis." He pauses, decides Wally deserves a better explanation. "No disrespect, but why condemn a kid to college? Student loans have to be repaid, job or no job, and hey, look around. Jobs come and go. When a bank sinks its hooks into a kid, the only financial security it buys is for the bank."

"Debt isn't an issue for those with adequate means."

"True."

"It's the way of the world, son. I don't say one man is better than the next but people have different skills, different roles. When Americans recognize that fact and work together, we build a great nation."

"It built *me*," Xan says. "The system is happy to accept my labor and money and otherwise couldn't care less." He picks up the weed Wally left lying on the rock, tosses it into the trees. "I respect the market's power and stay clear of it as best I can."

"You're forthright; I give you that. What else are you, an anarchist? Communist? Digger?"

Xan shakes his head. "Not a joiner. Money owns the system, lock, stock and barrel. Corporations don't go to jail and wouldn't fall if John Wayne himself shot them. But I get it why some people fight anyway; don't you? If your water's polluted, it's self-defense."

"So you vandalize filter systems?" Wally's brows furrow. "A groundskeeper might have access."

"My only connection to Teddy Arnold was an outdoor market

when I was new in town. He told me a wackadoodle story and I bought a sea charm from him." He pulls it from his shirt. "That was the afternoon I met Caitlin."

Wally forces a smile. She's approaching with a plastic bucket.

"Are you two behaving?" she asks.

Wally sucks in a long breath. "I'm getting quite an education."

She distributes gloves. "Twist the pears off the pads. Tony also wants a few sprigs of mint."

They see little of Chef Tony at dinner. His assistant presents the courses. Sundown on the deck is pleasantly cool. Scattered puffs of pink and orange cloud fade to gunmetal in the twilight. The food is better than the conversation. Xan hopes Tony ignored Caitlin's prohibition on a dusting of Ecstasy.

Leilani's pursuit of Xan's résumé isn't as off-handed as she'd probably like him to think. Prior marriages? None. Children? No. Early childhood in Madison, Wisconsin, then Cleveland. The Haitian coup. Not fitting with the farm boys or military mindset in Leavenworth but staying in contact with a high school music teacher there. Running away to Kansas City. Lying about his age for session work. Touring with the roots group Tarkeo—Leilani hasn't heard of them. A stint with a Beale Street blues band. On to Nashville and well-paid years as a studio musician—adult alternative, mainly. A Calhoun stopover to catch up with Scamp Wallace before trying his luck in New York. Meeting Caitlin revises the plan.

Leilani rattles off the names of pop musicians she's met and the venues involved. He strokes her consumerist ego, remarks on her dance moves at the party. She credits gymnastics—her Olympic aspirations were thwarted by an adolescent growth spurt—and years of training in Chinese and Hawaiian martial arts. The mind-body control she gained made dance styles a snap to learn and served her well during a national security stint that she declines to discuss. Xan's mildly intrigued. Caitlin looks bored.

Chef Tony personally serves a fancy chocolate cake and prickly pear daiquiris. He says the watermelon tang of the cactus juice perfectly complements the richness of the chocolate. His pandering is as accomplished as his cooking.

rhythms on a flaming drum

the fiery sword

Janet, the Collective Harlequin business manager, is on the phone, talking fast, informing Caitlin that the theater has been vandalized. "I called 911 and left messages for Reba and Mari. Denny's at work. Can you meet me here?"

"Of course," Caitlin says. She scans her morning appointments at the credit counseling center. They'll have to be rescheduled. "I'll call Xan."

The crude hammer and sickle graffiti on the front façade is the attention grabber. Had Janet not said her office smells of gasoline, Caitlin might have missed the broken window. She parks in back of the building, beside a police cruiser. Janet and two cops are talking near the fire-blackened rear entrance. She's gesticulating—she does that when nervous. Caitlin's grateful for the brick construction and steel door. *Where's the fire department? This might have been Teddy's house all over again.*

Rotund Sergeant Mackey asks for ID when she introduces herself. She can't help imagining him as a gun-belted blueberry. His partner, Officer Hoover, scans her license and returns it.

"You the owner?" Mackey asks.

"We're a worker-owned collective. Every Harlequin is an owner."

"And how many would that be?"

"Thirty, thirty-five. It varies."

Hoover, a coltish kid, blurts, "We'll need the complete list."

"It's in my office," Janet says. She unlocks the door and wraps a tissue around the sooty handle. The hinges screech drily when she pulls.

Caitlin hears tires on gravel. *Xan, and Mari's with him.* "I'll be there in a minute," she tells Janet as the blue shirts follow her inside.

Mari hops from the van, clothes streaked with sawdust. "How bad?"

"We may be looking at the worst of it," Caitlin replies, opening Xan's door. He steps down. She needed his hug more than she'd realized.

"Then if Janet's okay," Mari says, "I'm leaving. I'll board up the window after the blue shirts go."

Oh, come on. "They're being nice. We're victims."

"Right," Mari snorts. "I had my fill of face time with those pricks when they caught up to me about Teddy's benefit."

Xan says he'll take her back to work.

"Four blocks? I'll walk. Call me if we need kitty litter to soak up the gas."

Caitlin says, "I'll peek inside and let you know. Only be a minute."

"And have the next cop to drive by catch me loitering at a crime scene? I'll rent a pressure washer for the paint and soot." She stalks away, not waiting for a response.

"In that mood, we're better off without her," he says. "Let's walk around. See if the firebug left us any other presents."

The sides of the building are undamaged. Along with the broken window and graffiti in front—the communist symbol is captioned DIE COMMIE FAGS—they discover a police utility vehicle and a tan, federal sedan.

Hoover's in the lobby. He demands Xan's ID.

"Yes, *sir.*"

"Remove it from the billfold. You an owner here?"

"A probationary member of the collective." Xan hands his license over, reclaims it and hurriedly pockets his wallet.

Caitlin smells gasoline fumes. Next to the business office, in the ticket booth, Mackey and a man in a dark suit sit on the counter, backs to the glass. Hoover speaks into a radio clipped to his epaulet. A pair of jumpsuited technicians emerge from the house, one carrying a video camera.

"You have keys?" the cameraman asks.

"Why?" Caitlin replies.

"Come with us." It's an order, not a request.

"I'll go," Xan tells her. "Find Janet. See what's happening."

"We'll start in the backstage areas," the second investigator tells him. "This way."

Hoover instructs Caitlin to have a seat on a lobby bench. "Are we expecting anyone else?"

"I have no idea. Where's Janet?"

He nods toward the ticket booth. "Stand by." He speaks again into his radio as Caitlin finds an angle that lets her see Janet in a chair, Mackey and the other man towering over her. She doesn't return a wave. Mackey brushes off Hoover's message with a shooing, over-the-shoulder gesture.

Caitlin sits and rereads Ed's review of *The Birds* in the latest edition of *InCalhoun*. He judges the play a campy reminder of theater's feisty heritage, a daring assertion of artistic relevance to a routinized culture. The interview with Reba adds nothing of substance. Her answers are too cautious.

"Miss Schmidt," Hoover says. "They're ready for you now."

She and Janet cross paths in the business office. Janet whispers, "They're impounding our laptop." Shards of window glass are strewn across the desk and floor. Caitlin spots the neck of a broken wine bottle and a large stain on the concrete, evidently the source of the gasoline smell.

Hoover looks in to interrupt.

"Call our lawyer," Caitlin mutters, hoping Janet hears.

Mackey fills the doorway to the ticket booth. "Come join us, Ma'am," he says. "Watch your step."

The man in civilian clothes has a gold badge hanging from the breast pocket of his jacket. No nametag. "And you are?" he says.

Caitlin tells him.

"Seems like somebody takes exception to what you folks do here," the man observes. He's older, has a military bearing, gray hair, wire-rimmed glasses. "Sit down, Miss Schmidt. Have you received threats?"

Caitlin remains on her feet. "Vicious comments were posted to the *InCalhoun* website after our play was reviewed. I'm sure you have methods of identifying those people. You might also talk to the arsonist who torched Teddy Arnold's house. That was a firebomb too, I believe. Then there's the Brotherhood of the Fiery Sword. None of those leads has anything to do with our computer. You don't need it. And while we're introducing ourselves, who are you?"

"Your basis for suspecting the Fiery Sword, assuming such a group actually exists, is what?" the man asks.

"Calhoun PD must have video of the white pickup with the Fiery Sword sign cruising around before Teddy's memorial service. I asked who you are."

"No evidence then?"

The radio on Mackey's shoulder pops to life. Hoover again. "Attorney incoming. Requests we cease and desist until she arrives."

The man in the suit nods, "Noted."

Mackey leans close to his mic and repeats, "Noted."

"My name," the suit tells Caitlin, "is Special Agent Thomas Doak. I'm attached to the Calhoun detail of Integrated Security."

"This is vandalism and attempted arson, not an ISA matter."

The man stares at her as if she'd questioned the right of a janitor to sweep a floor. "Palomar Coatings is of interest to us, Miss Schmidt. We investigate any and all threats to the operation there. You people, some of you anyway," he consults notes on his tablet, "participated in a fundraiser for an enemy of the state. And the handbill for this new propaganda show of yours dedicates it to the late Mr. Arnold. These highly suspect activities are most certainly of interest to ISA. I assume you wish to cooperate."

"Our lawyer said to wait."

"I'm a busy man, Miss Schmidt. Your attorney will tell you that in matters of national security a special agent acts at discretion. We're almost finished. Your computer and files will be returned."

Mackey tries to give her his clipboard. "Sign here," he says.

Caitlin crosses her arms. "And if I refuse?"

"Sergeant Mackey will detain the lot of you." Doak smiles again. "Obstructing a national security investigation is a serious offense, Miss Schmidt. Your father's an important man, a loyal American. He'd be heartbroken to learn of his daughter's seditious tendencies."

Shaken, Caitlin accepts the clipboard and adds her signature under Janet's, acknowledging the voluntary nature of the seizure.

"Not so hard, was it?" Doak grins. "Cooperation is much less stressful. Mackey, slap evidence tags on those file drawers and get them out of here. Then we'll leave these folks in peace. They have options to consider."

Caitlin allows him and Mackey to pass. Glass crunches under their shoes.

"Mackey," Doak says, "be careful. Glass everywhere." At the door to the lobby he turns to Caitlin. "And, miss, a friendly word of advice. The auteur of this theatrical trash, what's her name, Dr. Stein? In future she may want to avoid controversial issues. You were lucky last night. Next time the wick might not fall out of the bottle."

smokin'

News2 and other free market outlets don't cover the vandalism at the Harlequin Theater, let alone the sham police investigation of it. The fix is in for Palomar. If not for alt media crusaders such as Gil Punshon, people might never have heard of the attack. Caitlin suspects the talk show wild man is an associate of Denny's in the NetBat affinity group, though it's not a question Diggers ask. Homebase for Hotwired Free Media, "Internet Radio for Calhoun and the World," is Gil's basement.

The former television producer has been a tireless advocate for citizen journalism since being fired from News2. He'd unearthed evidence of sweetheart deals between the general contractor for administrative services in Calhoun/Lumet County and unacknowledged subsidiary providers. After his bosses spiked the story he gifted it to a colleague from a competitor outlet. The exposé based on his information is rumored to have yielded a goldmine of contributions to the governor and members of legislative oversight committees, but cost Gil and the regional director of Municipal Administrative Service Group their jobs.

Gil's request for Caitlin to appear on the Hot Live News Hour to discuss the arson should, in her opinion, have been a no-brainer decision for the collective. It wasn't. There wasn't even consensus on future performances of *The Birds* until Tijon channeled Jim

Crow fighter Jesse Jackson to convince the Harlequins that they too must keep hope alive. Some members, including Xan, expressed concern that rednecks could twist a Hotwired interview to foment additional violence—in private he confessed that his actual concern was her serving as spokesperson. That hesitation to respect and support her investment in Collective Harlequin caused their first real argument.

She rings Gil's doorbell conscious that the city air she's breathing is the cleanest she'll get for a while. He's a chain smoker with nicotine-stained fingers and a face frozen in a smoke-deflecting squint. The bib pockets of his trademark overalls contain two tins: one of loose tobacco, the other a travel ashtray. When he opens the door his house exhales a malodorous fog.

"Enter!" he exclaims, a hand-rolled cigarette waggling in the corner of his mouth. "We'll rock this town tonight." She trails him downstairs to the studio guests refer to as the Hotwired Gas Chamber.

Sweet Sue Andrews, his on-air sidekick and acid-tongued life partner, is waiting for them. Would Caitlin like a cup of coffee? "Fresh two hours ago, or we have water or iced tea."

EuroPop music plays softly in the background. A young man in the studio kitchenette says, "Caffeine alleviates bronchospasm."

Caitlin prefers tea.

"A little late in the day for coffee," Sue concedes, "but burnt joe lends an Alcoholics Anonymous ambience. Gil's guests can't wait to confess." She hacks up a phlegmy chuckle. "Have you met Egghead, boy scientist?"

Caitlin recognizes the name from countless Hotwired broadcasts. "You're Egg? You've taught me so much. I thought you'd be older."

"Bill Ramseur," he says, rising to introduce himself. "It's truly a pleasure, Ms. Schmidt. My girlfriend and I loved *on 2nd thot*. And *The Birds* is a hoot, pardon the pun. I hope the vandalism won't intimidate you."

Gil says, "Caitlin, after you and I finish, we'll go to Dr. Sigurdsdottir in Brussels for a report on Teddy's autopsy findings. Egg will explain what she says. Ready for a sound check?"

The Gas Chamber is carpeted, furnished with a round dining table and swivel chairs bolted to the floor. There are table-mounted microphones on swing arms, remotely operable videocams in strategic locations, and a cluttered bulletin board. A window looks into the closet where Sue engineers the broadcast from a rat's nest of electronics and wiring. She dons a headset, signals Caitlin to do the same.

Sue's voice comes through the earphones, "Caitlin, look at Gil and count to ten as though he doesn't speak English. And remember, we're live with video as well as audio. Don't pick your nose."

Gil moistens the tip of a hand-rolled cigarette and spits a flake of tobacco toward the corner of the room. "Go ahead," he says. Streams of smoke issue from his nose.

"One," Caitlin begins, "two…"

He's a skilled interviewer, eliciting details without baiting her into direct accusations. Xan needn't have worried. That's all it was, she'd decided after their fight: worry. Ironic coming from a guy who only trusts Denny to schlep his equipment.

At the conclusion of the interview Sue cuts to a public service announcement on low-income daycare. Gil rolls smokes and arranges them in a neat row. Talking over the last of the PSA, Sue alerts Gil, "Doctor's online."

"Welcome back to Hot Live News on Hotwired FM," he growls. "Our recent spate of violence follows allegations of water pollution by the Palomar Coatings plant on Lake Hollister. An early victim was former Palomar employee and gadfly Teddy Arnold. This summer Arnold died in federal custody after disappearing from a protest demonstration outside the plant. The cause of his death was listed as quote unquote Natural Causes but his family arranged for a private autopsy."

Gil selects his next cigarette. "Joining us now by telephone is the pathologist who examined his body, Dr. Astrid Sigurdsdottir. Welcome, Dr. Sigurdsdottir. Sorry you can't be here in person. Your re-entry visa into the United States was canceled? You're speaking to us from Europe?"

"Thank you, yes," a female voice says with a British-inflected Scandinavian lilt. "It is a problem."

"You were a visiting pathologist at the University hospital in Chapel Hill; is that correct?" Gil licks his new smoke and gets a light off the roach of its predecessor. A curl of smoke rises.

"Teaching, yes. It is true since last year. For the future, I do not know."

"How did you come to be involved with the Arnold case, Doctor?"

"It is a service we provide—not the hospital you understand—but an international organization to which I belong. We document allegations of human rights abuse. If it is appropriate we refer the matter to the World Criminal Court."

"Can you tell us what you found when you examined Teddy's body?"

"Mr. Arnold could not have survived the rupture of the spleen. There were signs of trauma."

"He was beaten?"

"It appears so."

"To death?"

"The rupture occurred many hours before the death."

"Did you report the case to the WCC?"

"It was received there, yes."

"What happens next?"

"This is for them to say. As you may know, your country does not recognize the jurisdiction of international courts."

"Hmm," Gil says, underlining her statement. "Do you have other findings?"

"Mr. Arnold had a most uncommon medical condition. Lesions in the chest and abdomen."

"Lesions?"

"Very rare. There are reports from industrial zones of other advanced countries. We believe it is a condition similar to the diseases of asbestos exposure, difficult to diagnose. Electron microscopy is required for confirmation. The lesions are usually discovered at surgery for other causes, so the prevalence may be higher than it appears in the literature. Patients complain only of nonspecific symptoms. We fear that the lesions may become malignant over time as they can following exposure to fibers of asbestos."

Caitlin rummages a pen and paper from her purse.

"Do we know the cause of the lesions?" Gil asks.

"Tiny fibers are inhaled or swallowed. The body attempts to sequester them, producing the lesions."

"What sort of fibers, Doctor?"

"Nanotubes of carbon."

"Nanotubes?"

"A few atoms in diameter. Certain manufacturing processes may be responsible but there is confirmation of this only in Germany."

"So you're telling us nanotubes didn't kill Teddy Arnold but they might have eventually?"

"It is possible."

"This is the first we've heard of nanotubes. Are they found in water?"

"Or air. In this instance the source is unknown. I should not speculate. Your medical doctors should be aware. That is all I can tell you."

"We appreciate your willingness to stay up late and alert us,

Doctor. You've given local residents a real wakeup call. Best of luck with your visa problem."

"Thank you. Goodbye."

"When we return," Gil croaks, "our neighbor Egghead will explain what you just heard. The boy scientist doesn't know everything but give him a minute and you'll think he does."

What Egg says, Caitlin's notes will read, is that nanotubes are a new technology. The hollow fibers may be inches long yet 100,000 times thinner than a human hair. They can be woven into bulletproof fabric, act as superconductors, improve solar panels or find uses in nano-scale machines. The final application Egg mentions boggles her mind. Nanotube films can also create invisibility cloaks. *Is the world ready for Star Trek?*

"Films, you say?" Gil asks him.

"Thin films, fabrics, paints."

"Call me crazy, Egg, but try this on for size. Our little old paint factory has the clout to get an environmental lawsuit dismissed. A Black Mariah squad, never before seen in these parts, rolls into town and disappears Teddy Arnold. ISA kicks in his spleen, ransacks his house. Over what? Poisoning people with industrial solvents?"

"Seems excessive."

"Could they have been afraid he'd spill the beans on nanotube research?"

"We have to assume war machine interest in that technology," Egg says. "The fibers must be produced somewhere. Why not in the backwoods privacy of Appalachia? There'd be some percentage of waste product, maybe bad batches and failed experiments to get rid of. Who cares about slow-developing health risks when there's profits to be deposited today?"

"In whose bank, Egg?"

"Palomar's a privately held corporation."

"Right. The majority of voting stock is controlled by Bobo

Huskins, that prince of good old boy virtue and defender of the Southern Mountain heritage."

Caitlin doesn't need to write that down.

"Sweet Sue's sending me the cutthroat sign," Gil says. "Join us next week for more Hot Live News on Hotwired FM. My guess is we'll be discussing water filters. Don't forget the lunar eclipse this evening. And if you're the praying kind, say one tonight for Teddy Arnold and Dr. Astrid Sigurdsdottir. Despite the goons, it seems like Teddy spilled a whole mess of beans."

rhythms on a flaming drum

Seldom since childhood has Wally's grip on reality felt so tenuous as this afternoon. The sensation isn't unpleasant exactly, closer to wonderment. He's helpless to wake from what must obviously be a dream. The Steins have guided him and Leilani deep into the Lumet County boondocks to the secluded glade where Caitlin will be formally engaged to a working-class oddball/musician in a Pagan ceremony officiated by the mother who abandoned her and the United States only to return as a witch. Cue opera singers in horned helmets.

Thus far, Leilani is managing surprisingly well. She and Reba Stein can't get enough of the golden carpet of autumn leaves, the vibrant shades of red and copper still clinging to the trees, the festive greens of holly, evergreen ferns and laurel thickets. Reba declares the harlequin colors of the maple leaves especially appropriate for a handfasting of Harlequins. Leilani agrees that the maples steal the show. Wally's amazed at the turnabout in her attitude. It's as disorienting as the occasion itself.

Rhododendrons frame a waterfall at the ceremonial site. Off to the side of a large circle marked out on the ground with white rope, musicians play Celtic tunes on recorder, fiddle and hand drum. The fifteen or so other guests—he recognizes several from the birthday party—also wait outside the circle. Inside it Maeve,

Caitlin, Xan, and Caitlin's knife-wielding friend wave a dagger around, sprinkle powders and perfume the air with burning sage, all the while chanting doggerel rhymes. Maeve's a white-robed figure from fairyland, crowned with holly and oak leaves. Mari's robe is black. *Waggling her blade like that she'd pass for the Grim Reaper's delinquent daughter.* Normal dress suffices for Xan and Caitlin. If not for her green garland and bouquet of roses, she could be attending a civic function.

The other witnesses seem oblivious to these peculiar goings on and chat amongst themselves. Izzy fills him in on the afternoon of cleanup that went into preparing the area for the ceremony. Leilani, Reba and another woman discuss water pollution and the attempted firebombing of the theater. The woman isn't happy with Bobo Huskins. Someone's been detained for something. Leilani is bursting with questions. She'll fill him in on the details later.

The music ends. At the edge of the circle nearest the water, Maeve, Xan and Caitlin take positions reminiscent of a wedding. Mari steps slowly to the perimeter opposite, chanting about a "circle cast thrice nine." When she reaches the rope, she pretends to cut a man-sized hole in the air with her dagger. Then she explains the rules. Guests are to enter through the doorway she's created. It will be sealed behind them. None may step outside the rope until she reopens the door. Leilani obediently leads him in but her cooperation isn't complete. She maneuvers him to a spot where Maeve and the musicians won't notice her standing on the rope.

The service begins innocuously. Maeve's not proselytizing, which Wally appreciates. Her invocation of the four directions, sun, moon, et cetera is the sort of babble he and his friends concocted while playing Indian as kids. The part that chills him occurs toward the end.

Maeve has the couple join right hands and asks Xan, "Will you cause Caitlin pain?"

He answers, "I may."

It's like a punch in the gut.

"Is this your intent?" Maeve asks.

"No."

Is that supposed to make it okay?

"Caitlin, will you cause Xan pain?"

"I may."

"Is this your intent?"

She gazes into Xan's eyes then tells him, "No."

"Will you share each other's pain and strive to minimize it?"

When they promise they will, Maeve lays a long multicolored ribbon over their hands. She asks them to join left hands and lay them on the ribbon, holding it in place.

"Xan, will you love Caitlin with the wholeness of your being?"

"I will."

Good intentions don't cut it, son.

"Caitlin, will you love Xan with the wholeness of your being?"

"I will."

The ribbon takes a second wrap around their hands. Wally recalls his trepidation the day a childhood pal thought he could ski jump a bicycle off the roof of his house. Today is worse.

"Xan, will you be faithful to Caitlin for a year and a day?"

"I will."

"Caitlin will you be faithful to Xan for a year and a day?"

"I will."

The ribbon is wrapped a third time. The ends flutter loose in the slight breeze. Caitlin and Xan share a blissed-out moment while Maeve and Mari look on. Phones appear. Photos are taken. *This is temporary*, Wally reminds himself.

Maeve's concluding remarks invoke various protective powers. The audience is asked to respond to each of them with "Blessed be." Leilani glowers at him for doing so. Then it's over. Mari leads Caitlin and Xan around the circle, cuts a new doorway with her dagger. The couple walks through, followed by the guests and musicians, who strike up a lively tune. Maeve and Mari lag behind. There's evidently more chanting to do.

Caitlin's eyes sparkle as she pulls Wally along with her and Xan to the head of a receiving line. Her excitement reminds him of moments past when he believed his little girl could never be lovelier. Bittersweet though it is for him, this is another of those moments. For her sake he does his best to get into the spirit. By the time a photographer calls for family pictures beside the waterfall, he's faking it pretty well.

Leilani's remedy for the ungodly handfasting is a quick dose of church. Wally considers that a reasonable price for her tolerance. He's still amazed that the day unfolded without friction. They excuse themselves from the after-party as soon as the photographer finishes with him, missing out on a vegetarian potluck and the risk of religious sparring between Leilani and Maeve. Caitlin, perhaps sharing that concern, doesn't object. But there's no opportunity for a bite to eat elsewhere before the prayer meeting.

Salvation testimonials from church youth are blessèd distractions from the hunger pangs that beset him during intervals of prayerful contemplation. Tonight's program also features the installation of church deacons, among them Bobo Huskins' groundskeeper, Josh Rice. Bobo, who bankrolled the elevation of James Street Baptist to megachurch status, solemnly occupies a gilded elder's chair behind the pulpit. Leilani's rumor mill accuses him and Palomar not only of polluting the water with industrial solvents but also carcinogenic fibers used by the military. A lady Leilani spoke with this afternoon lays responsibility for the up-tick in social unrest at his feet. Reba Stein believes Bobo's influence hinders arson investigations at a torched house and the Harlequin Theater. The senior pastor closes the witnessing portion of the service with an extended prayer on behalf of several dozen parishioners—disrupted for Wally by rumbles of regret at his decision to forego Caitlin's tofu and beans.

Elder Huskins rises to invite the new deacons forward. Rice's curly hair is slicked back and his suit is a half-size too large. The coats of the men filing onstage behind him are similarly ill-fitting. Wally wonders whether this is an intentional declaration of spiritual values. The gaudiness of the sanctuary suggests otherwise. After the final amen Bobo sheds the grave elder's face to congratulate his newly minted deacons.

"I'll have a word with him about the water allegations," Wally tells Leilani as they reach the end of the pew.

"Not without me," she says.

Bobo's delighted to see them. "Wally! Leilani, what a pleasant surprise. We don't often see you folks out on Wednesday night. I want to personally express my gratitude for that generous contribution to the Rise Up fund. It'll help a lot of kids. When did you fly in?"

"We're down for a family visit," Wally replies. "Back to Arlington in the morning. If you have a minute, Leilani and I are interested in your perspective on some rumors around town."

Bobo raises an eyebrow. "That so?"

Wally ticks off the charges. "What the devil's going on down here?"

"No need to linger around for this, fellas," Bobo tells his deacons. "Welcome to the James Street team. Josh, tell Lucy I'll be along directly."

Leilani asks, "Does Palomar produce or use nanotubes?"

"Where'd you hear *that* nonsense?" Noticing Leilani's offense, he withdraws the question. "There's a loony tune in town who fancies himself a journalist. Several years ago they drummed him out of News2. Punshon set himself up with an online 'radio station' to spew whack-a-doodle stuff to other malcontents. A couple of weeks ago he interviewed some broad, supposedly a doctor in Europe, who claims that a dead Calhoun jailbird had secret fibers in him. This woman's so nuts the United States won't allow her into the country. But Punshon believes her and takes a flying leap to blame Palomar. The spongers and malcontents ate it up. But Punshon has peddled his last baloney salad. Calhoun PD busted him and his lady friend on dope charges. If and when he gets out of prison he won't have a pot to piss in."

Leilani can be dogged in pursuit of a point. "Does Palomar make nanotubes, or use them?"

"I don't know what a nanotube is and I own most of the company. Relax, your water's fine."

Wally says, "Some idiot tried to burn down my daughter's theater building."

Bobo seems caught off guard by this. "She's mixed up with that bunch? Sorry to hear it. No defense for arson, of course, but take it from a friend. That load of propaganda they call a play gives aid and comfort to water crazies. If they set out to rile the working man when the economy's in the tank, boy howdy, they succeeded. Folks are steamed. Get your girl away from those seditionists, and quick."

Leilani asks Wally if he believes Bobo.

"The unrest part? Yes. Caitlin and I need to have a serious talk."

"Palomar *does* have an SDI designation."

How could she know such a thing? "Bobo could sell fog in Foggy Bottom but a Secure Defense Industry designation for a paint factory? Who says?"

"I read it somewhere. They don't issue those for no reason."

"I'll check into it."

"Pray that Caitlin repents. Before it's too late."

rhythms on a flaming drum

you've changed

Xan sees lights on the third floor when he rolls the van to a stop in the residents' lot after midnight. Caitlin's awake. He kills the engine. The cooling motor ticks in the stillness, unwinding. He's on the glide path to a mellow touchdown after band practice. Collaboration with the Blownglass Trio revives memories of Nashville session days with Scamp. Tijon's the joker in the mix. His Trinidadian rhythms take the band to new places but if he wants to pursue singing he has a lot to learn. If not, the island flavor is fun while it lasts.

Caitlin's usually in bed by now. While fumbling on the landing for his door key he hears Mari inside. He walks in to find her scowling at one end of the sofa. Caitlin's coiled at the other, legs tucked under, hunched with tension. The women stare at him like he interrupted a spat. There's an empty wine glass and bottle on the table beside Mari. She seldom drinks.

"What's happening?" he asks, braced for turbulence.

Caitlin uncoils and crosses the room to welcome him home. "*The Birds*," she says under her breath.

"Can I help?"

She shakes her head. "Go on to sleep."

"You're in this too, Xan," Mari objects, tongue thick with wine.

"Mind if I take off my coat first?" He hangs his jacket in the closet, goes to the kitchen for water. When he returns to the living room Caitlin has reclaimed her corner of the couch.

"Mari still thinks we should reinstate the performance schedule."

He's not fool enough to sit between them, chooses the chair across the room. Emotions concerning the play's future have been intense. He'd been among the majority faction in the collective to favor pulling the plug on *The Birds*. Better to live and fight another day. Mari disdained surrender. Teddy can't be allowed to die in vain, etc. Denny volunteered to beef up building security. Those precautions and completion of the local performance schedule eventually achieved consensus. With members on both sides threatening to quit over an unfavorable decision on road performances, that question was tabled.

Caitlin had been negotiable on the issue until a call from her father moved her to the fight-another-day camp. According to Wally, Bobo Huskins hinted that the risk of violence against the collective is ongoing. She was advised to consider his warning the informed opinion of a man with an ear in the police department. The collective heard Huskins' expression of concern as a veiled threat delivered through Caitlin's unsuspecting father. *The Birds* is now on complete and indefinite hold. Mari didn't block consensus on that but apparently isn't ready to let it go either.

"Palomar can't be allowed to continue poisoning people, Xan. Or silence those with the guts to speak the truth. Thank Goddess Dr. Sigurdsdottir's interview was uploaded to mirror sites before the Hotwired FM raid."

"It sucks about Gil," Xan agrees. "But between his work and the controversy over the play, the word's out on Palomar. That's what you wanted, isn't it? Mission accomplished, I'd say."

"Not hardly," Mari sneers. "NewsStooge explained everything away. Gil and Sue are dope fiends. A 'reliable source' doctor at Lumet Regional discredits the nanotube allegation, and a mouthpiece for the Business Council accuses Europeans and malcontents of endangering American jobs."

Here we go again, Xan thinks. "But the pollution isn't a secret anymore. Caitlin's dad may be an out-of-touch capitalist but he's not stupid. He had us install water filters in his house. You know his friends are doing the same. Titans don't believe the media whitewash. Palomar's catching heat."

"So a few titans install filters and read their leftie kids the riot act about the dangers of political activism. Does that stop Huskins from slapping down people who call bullshit on Palomar? It does not. That asshole's attrition tactics aren't stupid. Memories are short. Barring a massive popular revolt, Palomar keeps on keeping on."

"That's not fair," Caitlin says, wounded. "How would *you* feel if we lose the theater or somebody else is hurt? There's less up-side to the play than before. It doesn't justify the risk."

Mari snaps, "What happened to you? These past few months, you've changed."

"You're right, I have." Caitlin's tone is conciliatory. "Things *are* different. We thought you understood. That was the importance of the handfasting. It draws a line. New commitments change priorities."

Xan's heard enough. "Mari—"

She doesn't let him finish. "Caitlin thinks you're the second coming. For a minute at Teddy's benefit I thought she might be right. You played 'Let Your Hammer Ring' like your life depended on it. But that was a load of show biz."

Caitlin's aghast.

Mari's on him like a junkyard dog. "It's not just another tune, music man. 'Walk on' doesn't mean shit should be ignored. 'Let Your Hammer Ring' is sacred to us. I don't care how wizard a musician you are. Posers should leave that song alone."

The absurdity of the indictment convulses him with laughter.

Caitlin says, "Shut up, Mari. The person with no clue is you."

Xan composes himself, hopes he didn't strain a muscle. Mari is pig-eyed angry. *Maybe this is why she shouldn't drink.* He tells her, "You'll be glad to hear I felt the same about 'Hammer' when we rehearsed it tonight."

As he suspected she would be, Caitlin's shocked out of her annoyance. "You played 'Hammer'?"

"Sang it too. Tijon was late."

"How?"

"Like Mari said, it's just another song. The band can't do a public performance and leave the only song we're known for off the set list."

"Unbelievable." Mari pops to her feet, wobbly. "Fucking unbelievable."

"I'll drive you home," Caitlin says. "You're in no condition to ride your bike or deal with blue shirts."

"Screw them."

"Caitlin's right," Xan says. "No sense chancing the potholes on a wine buzz. I'll take you."

"Fuck you too."

Caitlin puts on her shoes. "I only had one glass of wine." She grabs her coat from the closet. "Here," she says, thrusting Mari's backpack at her. "I'm driving."

Feverish clouds blanket the mountains, sweating November drizzle. A fine day for a landscape installation, from a plant's point of view. Xan's breath smokes the heavy air. Heavy soil clings to his spade and boots. Heavy balled and burlapped saplings belie the bouncy tunes in his earbuds. The steaming mulch he distributes is heavy with woody fragrances that sustain him until the new residents are tucked into their sodden bed. He's due for a hot shower.

Caitlin's parking space is empty. *Was she scheduled at the credit counseling center? Maybe the food co-op, we're low on groceries.* Though his boots had a rough scrape at the jobsite, they're too mucky for indoors. He leans against the wall in the bushes flanking the building entrance, sets to work on them with a twig, hears the door. Sounds of panting and skittering claws tell him that Bitsy the bug-eyed Yorkie is taking his owner, Mrs. Letourneau, for a walk. Bitsy squeaks, alarmed that Xan might pee on his bush. Mrs. Letourneau freezes, startled in the process of raising her pink umbrella.

"Mud," Xan tells her. "Didn't want to track it in."

Though he's lived with Caitlin since May, Mrs. Letourneau and her disabled husband remain standoffish—Caitlin says they're staunch Catholics. "Very thoughtful of you," the old woman replies with a heavy stare. "Shush, Bitsy. Come along." The two of them continue on toward the street.

The note on the kitchen counter says, "Back late. I love you."

"Bummer," he says to his damp sock tracks on the linoleum. Caitlin sometimes volunteers as a support person for women with unwanted pregnancies and is secretive about the details. Pickings in the fridge haven't improved since morning. He peels off his socks, his shirt, drapes them on the rack above the washer. Shower first. Groceries after.

She's still out when he returns from the co-op. He dials her mobile number. It rings in the bedroom. *Should have known.* He empties a bag of split peas into a pot, adds water and vegetables, sets the pot on to cook, listens to a recording of band practice.

Soup's ready and no Caitlin. That's irritating. He wishes he'd bought a ham hock for flavoring, placates his inner carnivore with a stiff dose of pepper and onion powder instead. Two bowls into the soup, he decides it tastes okay.

His fingers are experimenting with a Caribbean rhythm when the red light on the landline answering machine catches his attention. It isn't blinking. She listened to the message. Rikki at Turtle Valley Water Services says, "We have the sample bottles you requested. You can pick them up or I'll deliver them. Have a great day."

At ten o'clock he transfers the congealed soup to the refrigerator. Could she have been in an accident? *Don't be a ninny.* He calls the Steins. Izzy says they haven't heard from her. To the best of their knowledge nothing's happening tonight at the theater. Xan tries the business office anyway, gets the recording. Tries Mari, gets the same. He rings Laurel Ridge on the chance she might be on an errand for her dad. No answer. He reluctantly hits the sack, tries to think sunny thoughts.

He lies balanced on a razor's edge. Boundless blackness to either side. If he moves he'll fall in.

The clock radio explodes with chatter, jerking him to consciousness. Alone in the dark. He reaches for the volume knob, fearing to hear why that's so. Louder.

"Speaking at a summit of *Alianza Bolivariana* leaders, Brazilian President Chagas vows a socialist cure for the cancer of capitalism. In Washington State, authorities foil a Digger plot to impede weapons shipments…"

Xan's feet find the pants on the floor.

"Gasoline prices ticked up again yesterday as Hurricane Reuben churns in the unseasonably warm Gulf. Meanwhile, tourism officials across the Southeast grapple with the negative effect of traffic stops and aggressive civil forfeiture policies on their industry. What many motorists call highway robbery, law enforcement agencies deem a critical source of revenue."

He shuffles to the kitchen, brews an extra-strong pot of coffee, organizes his thoughts. Who to call first? Who's awake?

The voice in the bedroom informs him that another popular contestant has been voted off another reality show. "Your Povogram.biz celebrity hook-up of the day…"

Come on. Come on.

"Calhoun/Lumet Administrator Bryce Hufnagel hikes property tax rates to cover the cost of courting new business."

That'll be popular. Xan takes his mug of coffee to the bedroom, sits on the bed.

"A Lumet County man remains in serious condition following an altercation outside the Lucky Seven Lounge on Highway 7. The assailant is described as a Negro male. Anyone with information is urged to contact the crime hotline. The Calhoun Thanksgiving Parade steps off this Saturday afternoon at two. Come early. Shop late. Motorists can expect dense fog for their morning commute. Clearing skies later, with highs expected in the mid-sixties. Your Morning Read on 99.6 is brought—" Xan clicks the radio off.

Online versions of News2 and *The Calhoun Journal* are equally uninformative. *That's good.* But the coffee is oily and acid. He sets the mug aside, rings Mari. She's hardly spoken to him since the argument over *The Birds*. No answer. He leaves a message. The thought of calling Caitlin's parents embarrasses him—it implies failure or incompetence or both—but it can't be helped. Their numbers aren't in his phone. He uses hers, is shunted to voice mail when he tries her mom. He asks her please to call.

As he's scrolling for Wally's number, the phone rings. Maeve.

"Xan?" She's groggy with sleep. "What's wrong?"

It's a relief to have someone to tell.

"Was there a fight?" she asks, fully awake now.

"No."

"Have you called the police, the hospital?"

He hasn't and hesitates to explain. What if Caitlin's on a Digger mission? The wrong question could get her busted. "I just wondered if maybe you'd have an idea."

"Why ever would I?"

"If there's anything she isn't comfortable talking to me about? I don't know."

"Is there?"

"I don't think so. But I thought I should ask."

"This isn't like her, Xan. Notify the authorities and get back to me right away. I'll tell her father."

"Please let me do that."

"Asking a mother to wait quietly by the phone in these circumstances is asking a lot. But you may have a point. Promise to call the minute you ring off with Wally?"

He does. Law enforcement agencies haven't received an accident report involving a Honda Civic. Is there a missing person? Probably a misunderstanding, he says. He's officiously reminded that alerts for missing adults can't be processed for unexplained absences of less than seventy-two hours. The automated attendant at Lumet Regional has nothing on patient name Schmidt. The human operator tells him no information is available on emergency or urgent care patients.

"Good morning, sweetie," Wally says, assuming Caitlin's on the line. The ensuing conversation rapidly shifts to problem solving. Wally approves of Xan's intention to visit the hospital and walk-in clinics. "Cast the widest possible net."

The lack of progress Xan reports to Maeve has the expected effect on her anxiety.

Caitlin isn't being treated at the hospital emergency room or Eastside Urgent Care. Southside is next on his list. His phone rings: Chip Hagadorn, the photographer for the handfasting. Pictures must be ready. Xan toys with letting it go to voicemail, decides to take it. "Chip," he says, "what's up?"

"Have you heard from Caitlin?"

"She didn't come home last night. I'm out looking for her."

"Oh, shit. Dude, she borrowed my boat yesterday and promised to have it back first thing this morning. I *told* her it was a rotten day to be on the water. Shit."

"Just a second. Let me pull over." It was Hagadorn who'd lent his canoe for the day on the lake. Xan noses into the nearest space at a fast food. "Did she say where she was going?"

"No, only that the weather was perfect. Your lady's good in a boat and everything, but the river's up from the rain. What if she dumped?"

Fucking Mari. "I don't think she went to the river, Chip. I'll be in touch."

Xan leaves the van idling at the gate for the Lake Hollister public landing. On such a wet, cold morning, nobody's likely to complain. A white Civic is the lone vehicle in the lot. He ducks under the barrier for a look. Her car has been here all night. He wipes at the dew on the side window. Chip's ratchet straps and car-top carrier blocks are on the front seats. He unlocks the door. Along with the clothes in back he finds a box of plastic bottles— four are missing—and a sales receipt from Turtle Valley Water Services.

He reaches for his phone, but it's his, not hers. He pockets it again, cursing himself for not copying down Wally's number, or Maeve's. *Can't call 911, at least not yet, or trust Chip not to. If Caitlin's here I need to find her, not the sheriff.* It's a long hike to the head of the cove where she'd collect samples. He can drive there in minutes.

The Palomar access road terminates at a checkpoint, gates and a security fence. All marked NO TRESSPASSING. He waves at the guard in the kiosk, wheels the van around, begins to retrace his route. Out of the guard's sight, he parks on a wide shoulder. Before he can get into the woods a Palomar four by four rolls to a stop behind him, bubble-top lights flashing. The passenger door opens and a uniformed officer crouches behind it, gun drawn. He orders Xan to place both hands on his vehicle and step back, legs spread.

Xan does as he's told.

The Palomar cop holsters his weapon and swaggers over. "Private property, sir," he says. "Don't you read signs?"

"I assumed the fence was the property line. Sorry, I don't mean any trouble."

"Left hand. Show me some ID."

The next minutes are a royal hassle but the private cops have nothing on him, not even trespassing. He's told to leave and not return without an invitation.

In the rearview he watches the four by four execute a U-turn. He starts for the highway and the long hike he should already have begun. It's past eleven. *Caitlin must be hypothermic. At least the clouds are breaking.*

A chainsaw whine cuts through his self-recriminations. He eases off the gas, creeps by a mailbox at the mouth of a gravel drive. A camo-painted pickup sits near the place in the woods where a smallish man, also sporting camo, works on a fallen tree. *If that isn't the weasel from the alley, it's his brother.* Xan tucks his hair up under his hat. Puts on sunglasses. Maybe Camo Man won't recognize him.

The stickers on the pickup tout bass lures and the Southern Mountain Alliance. A fishing rod is racked with the shotgun behind the seat. Xan flashes on Teddy's gut-hooked dog. "Hey, partner."

Camo Man shuts off his saw. "Who are you? What you want?"

"I need a way down to the lake."

"All private land along here."

"I wouldn't ask but a friend went canoeing yesterday and didn't make it back."

"Call 911."

"They said they'd send a boat," Xan lies, "but you know how it is. A guy's got to do what he can."

"Like I said, most of this is Palomar land. Nobody don't go nowhere on this side without their say so."

"I know it. Just had a run-in with the guards. Is this *your* land? Maybe I could—"

"Said this was yesterday?"

"That's right."

"Rainy day, yesterday. Tell you what, friend. I got an idea you might be on the wrong side of the cove. They's state land on the other side. Fish camp along the water. I seen a bonfire last night. Try that."

Camo Man's directions take him to a county road that crosses the Upper Sawligoochee, then another mile and a bridge over a creek. The fire road to the lake is supposed to drop off to the right, right … here. A flattened twelve-pack marks the spot. Puddles shine along the rock-studded track. On the lurching descent he thinks that if Caitlin was here, she'd have found this road. She could be at her car by now. He should have left a note. *She'll call me when she gets home.* He skirts a deep rut, checks his phone. No service.

The fish camp doesn't swing into view until the last minute. He wonders why he and Caitlin didn't notice it last summer. *Might have had something to do with a Palomar speedboat.* Recalling the rotten fish and black glop he asks himself who'd eat anything caught here.

The van spooks some crows. They give him a raucous fit from the trees. Camo Man had the location of the bonfire pegged. There was a whopper here last night. A green fringe of pine boughs surrounds a huge, overflowing fire pit. The air's still thick with a dank, smokehouse reek. *If Caitlin did this in the rain she's a heck of a woodswoman.*

No canoe. The drag marks in the mud appear to be from firewood. A few girl-sized boot tracks. Most are larger. He investigates a disturbed area at the edge of the campsite. Blood, a lot of it. *What did they catch, Moby Dick?* He turns to the bonfire again, spots a white twig in it. Not wood. It connects to a contorted cinder. *Bone*, he realizes, *and a body, a human body.* The crows jeer.

So little remains. Empty eye sockets. Ruined face, no hair, no clothing. It could be a shriveled store dummy, crusted and cracked. The twiggy claws are flecked with ash. *Can't be her*, he tells himself. *There's no canoe.*

A silver glint the size of a bottle cap drops him to his knees. He gathers up the familiar sea charm, undoes a shirt button to feel for his. She'd taken it into her mouth when it dangled near her lips that afternoon in the other cove. Hers was salty with sweat. Now it's muddy, cold.

Caitlin is dead.

He'll never stitch together the events that follow. He's at the top of the trail speaking to 911. Down at the lake when deputies arrive. Passing into deep shadow at the jailhouse mouth. Assisted from the back seat of a squad car, in handcuffs.

rhythms on a flaming drum

*T*he crow plucks its gobbet and flaps away, a blue-black horror beating like a heart through trees endlessly done for the season. Wing and branch, weft and warp. Now you see it; now you don't. Illusions are eternity's stock in trade. Jump forward, back, up, down or sideways. Call the search for other possibilities free will. But the pattern is indifferent to justifications, deaf to begging, already complete. It is present. Only the eye is moving.

rhythms on a flaming drum

fragments

"New customer in F," a muffled voice says through the cell door. Faces appear in the narrow window. "Suicide watch. Standard precautions."

"Bad case of the shakes. Detoxing?"

"Intake doesn't mention it, but maybe. Lover boy offed his girlfriend at the lake. Torched her for good measure."

"The actress chick? What's he got against pretty things?"

"Felt so bad in the morning he returned to pay his respects. Called 911 himself. Claims not to know how it happened."

"Fricking head cases. Anything else?"

"D transferred to general population. C's still trying to start the revolution. Must get off on being tased. Faster than he looks though. Made Lockwood miss."

"No surprise there. Only time I've seen Lock cut a ten ring at the range was on the next man's target."

Paper clothes and flip-flops, shackles, chains, the works. "Try to run; you'll be on your face." He clanks when he walks. The room they take him to is painted sick green. Steel chair. Steel table. Two men: the ISA agent from the arson investigation and a blue shirt who identifies himself as Lieutenant Dillingham. Dillingham recites fill-in-the-blank statements.

The prisoner in the wall mirror is unmoved. "Don't I get a phone call?" it asks. That much it knows to do.

The cop sighs. "First, why not square with me? Your story's a load of crap. The boys at Palomar never heard of you. Same with the landowner who supposedly gave you directions. How'd you know where she was, Xan?"

"I want a lawyer."

"Out of my hands. If we could convince Special Agent Doak this was a crime of passion, ISA might back off. You were high. You fought. You didn't mean her to die."

He can't think. He hasn't slept. He's freezing. When he tries to settle in the chair the computer chip they jabbed into his back pokes him. "Inventory control," the booking clerk had said. "You'll get used to it."

Sleep is something he remembers but that's over now. The plastic mattress is a joke. He'd rather lie beside Caitlin, on cold steel. What they did to her, the detective won't say. If there's a reason not to kill himself, it's to keep her parents from believing she fell for the sort of man who … But he *would* kill Mari. She played on Caitlin's feelings right before his eyes and he never suspected. What a fool. What else was said when he wasn't around to hear?

A familiar voice rasps through the ventilation grates. "My name is Gilbert Punshon. I'm a journalist, a political prisoner of a corrupt system. I'm here because I told the truth. Palomar Coatings is poisoning us. Power tries to crush people like you and me. But we shall prevail." He sings,

Gonna break this old jail
Let your hammer ring
Breathe some fresh air
Let your hammer swing

Rhythmic thumping in the cellblock. A jailer shouts over it. "I got five says Lock can't hit shit. Jump Digger, jump!"

Is this daylight I see?
Let your hammer ring
Make a joyful—

"Ahhhh!" Gil screams through the vent. "Ahhhh." The singing ends. The thumping from the other prisoners fades.

No daylight for Gil. That's the ironic line, Mari, not "all is lost." No daylight for any of us, you reckless bitch, just another tease.

"That headshrinker friend of yours, Stein, says you spoke to him on the night of the murder, and the girl's parents heard from you like you said. Not that it matters. You could have called from anywhere." Dillingham taps his pencil on the table. "I'm curious, though. This Chip what's his name, Hagadorn? Can't seem to locate him. Some other folks around town have gone missing too. Strange coincidence, don't you think? Why do you suppose that is?"

"I want a lawyer."

"We've gone over that." The lieutenant leans on his elbows, exasperated. "Xan, I'll be straight with you. Segregated Housing is worried. You took the mattress off your bunk. You don't sleep. Don't talk. Don't leave your cell for exercise. Don't eat—not that I blame you; the smell turns my stomach. Thing is, though, SHU-pod doesn't like suicides. Too much paperwork. Unless I can convince them otherwise they're moving you to Enhanced Suicide Watch. I don't guess you'll miss the mattress, for a while anyway, but paper clothes are *clothes*. Hear what I'm saying?"

"My name is Gilbert Punshon…"

There's a rapping on the door of his cell. The tray slot opens. An orange jump suit—cloth—is pushed through. "Moving day," a new voice announces. Xan doesn't recognize the face in the window, a crewcut cracker with a neck wider than his head. The lips move. "Put this on."

Xan complies.

"Step to the back wall. Face it and straddle the pot."

He hears the door buzz open. The shackling procedure is becoming routine. He offers no resistance as the cuffs are locked.

A second voice says, "Open your mouth. Open it wide." Hands grab the belly chain and fabric between his shoulder blades.

He opens his mouth. A black-gloved hand reaches in front of him. Suddenly he's gagged. He bucks, tries to yell as a strap is cinched behind his neck. His head bounces off the wall, and again.

"Hold still," the first voice orders, "or I'll crush your Digger skull."

He's jerked away from the wall. A bag slips over his head and he's shoved into the wall once more, with a pressure that squeezes the air out of him.

The voice in his ear murmurs, "Give my baton an excuse to play taps on your punk ass."

Hot wetness drips along the side of his nose. His forehead tingles.

"Walk backwards. Straight back. That's a good boy."

buried alive

He's in a file cabinet at a cold, noisy factory. With arms outstretched he can touch both sides of the drawer. No observation window or bookshelf. There's a bean slot, combination plumbing fixture and a raised steel bench, bereft of bedding. The metal screen overhead blasts nonstop light. It bleaches gray walls white, sucks the pink from skin. A pitiless sky. Fugitive colors hide in the few suggestions of shade his body throws. Behind the curtain of his eyelids he's assaulted by blood-red reminders of animal endurance. He shields himself from them until his hands drop aching with fatigue. Bowing his head is better than nothing.

He's naked except for a corset with a heavy-duty loop in back. If he tries to take the thing off, it zaps him senseless. The cell and shock belt are in cahoots. At the least sign of misbehavior the sky strobes angrily and a warning tone throbs. Has he been caught shoplifting? Electricity bites his midsection with muscle dissolving ferocity.

No sleeping allowed. No lying down or sitting in a corner where he might doze. He must stand or move or sit in such a way that the cell believes him awake. If guards are on patrol he neither hears nor sees them. It occurs to him to count the number of times the bean slot presents a tasteless cake on a napkin of folded toilet paper. The appearances are seemingly random but his senses could be playing him tricks. Flutterings in the illumination warn him to eat. If he doesn't, he's shocked. If he throws the sticky lump of food, current rips through him like the bullets that slammed his father against the blackboard. The slumping body painted a crimson smear in the shape of an apostrophe. Haitian contraction from the possessive case. The sanitary light in Xan's cell erases the smears of his repetitious demise.

Coup images blur his parents' features; he begs them for relief. Caitlin hovers eyeless, charred. Her words fall as silent ash. In the distance a light pulses, a buzzer sounds. Expecting to be cut in half again, he screams. The jolt doesn't happen. He must have been asleep.

At first he ignores the presence that plagued him in Memphis. In the subterranean darkness of the Barboro Hotel, Lightning Johnson stared from the wreckage of fallen ceilings and portholes of laundry dryers. Now Xan feels him as a companion on the bench.

The tray slot clicks open. Xan blindly reaches for the food cake, scoots along the bench to the rear of the cell for water. Lightning avoids him, content to hum an antique blues the cell doesn't hear.

"Go away," Xan tells him.

Lightning condenses to visible form in a black tuxedo, skinny tie, silver-trimmed belt, the satin-striped pants mended by a ladyfriend.

"Go away."

"They does it to break you," Lightning whispers. "In jail, a nekkid man got no pride."

"Go away."

"Ain't nothing lower than the hole. In here you find out what you got."

"I got nothing."

> *"Now she gone, but I don't worry*
> *I'm sittin' on top of the world."*

Xan launches a fist to smash the vile mouth. Hits concrete instead. The shock belt snaps open his eyes, lifts him off the bench, deposits him on the floor. Sometime after it turns him loose he catches his breath and throws an elbow onto the platform, levers himself to his knees. His knuckles are bleeding, the wrist already swelling.

Lightning shimmers faintly in the foul air. "It all about invisible, boy. Can't have 'em expectin' what you bringin.'"

"Why'd you make me do it?"

"You took your damned time, but you did for me. I appreciate that."

"I didn't want to."

"Them kids and they daddy was happy to see you too. Could have been famous, bringing them out. But you too good for it."

"That's not what I meant and you know it."

"A man pay his debt."

"Yeah? Then where's your pistol? Give it to me."

"Done lost it. Like I told you before."

"I want it. Give it to me."

"You don't want it no more than I did, white meat. Wantin' ain't havin.'"

rhythms on a flaming drum

the great memphis quake 3

For two days Xan has prowled the streets, talked with displaced Barboro tenants, visited hospitals and relief camps springing up in the neighborhoods free enterprise ignores. Nobody's seen Lightning Johnson. He must be in the hotel, might still be alive.

Memphis continues to tremble, a landscape of urban fruits with damaged rinds. Rubblefields stretch the fifteen-minute walk to the Barboro to twice that. More rats and pigeons out this morning than people. *What a shame,* he thinks, *to sleep away the cool hours.* He's as prepared as scavenging permits him to be: sledgehammer, flashlights, backpack stocked with batteries, rope, water, folding knife, stout wire cutters. He'd hoped for a hardhat. Tells himself it wouldn't make much difference.

The hotel's north and east wings collapsed in the quake but the west side and main entrance still stand. Though he recognizes the irrationality of feeling safer inside the building, he does. The lobby smells no more than usually of vomit. Deeper in the gloom, he sees Lightning's long, mahogany counter. Behind it the hotel safe lies on its side, intact. Looters had better luck in the resident property room; the lockers have been jimmied one and all.

His inspection of the west corridor roils the dust hanging in bars of light cast by open doors to street-side rooms. Shards of glass litter the stairwell at the far end but the steps are serviceable. The second floor door is off its hinges. He walks that hall, shouting for Mr. Johnson, irritating men unhappy to be disturbed. Beyond the north wing elevators and stairwell he's stopped by a fallen ceiling. Ditto on 3. North corridors on higher floors gape in open air. The commons area and parking garage infilling the hotel horseshoe lie buried under debris.

He returns to the ground floor. The north wing is navigable past the elevators, service corridor and west entrance to the dining room. The stench in there turns his stomach. Dozens of residents would have been at lunch when the quake hit shortly after noon. His flashlight plays across tables and overturned chairs, dangling fixtures, remnants of suspended ceiling and exposed sections of fallen girders. The first bodies don't appear until he's inside, hugging the wall shared with the service corridor.

"Mr. Johnson," he shouts. "You in here? Anybody?"

He waits, thinks he hears a living groan in the sounds of subsidence.

"Somebody there?"

"Yeah," comes a weak reply.

"Keep talking."

"That you, white meat?"

"Yes, sir. Where are you?"

"I see your light. Now it gone. Over this way."

Xan kicks aside chairs, plows through a litter of tableware and acoustic tiles. In a space where the ceiling slants abruptly from five feet to nothing, his light finds the grime-powdered dome of a bald black head. Beside it, a hand slowly rises. "Over here."

"Man, am I glad to find you." Xan drags a table out of the way, crouches at Lightning's side.

"It got me by my legs. Lord a'mercy; take that light from out my eyes. Bring me a drink of water." The voice is parched, exhausted.

Xan stands the flashlight on end, redirecting the beam. "Can you sit up?"

"Not hardly. Can't hardly breathe neither, for the grinding bones in my side." Lightning's thighs are mousetrapped by a mangled girder, high, near the waist. Xan takes a bottle from his pack, unscrews the cap. Lightning struggles for a sip, spills most of it, sets the bottle down with a sigh of pleasure. "I been waiting these long days for that."

The gap between girder and floor where his legs are caught can't be more than an inch. The sledge is useless here. Xan reimagines his route through the hotel, looking for a lever to slip under the girder.

"Are you in much pain?"

Lightning coughs and gags. His shoulders buck convulsively. A moan and pink foam drool from the side of his mouth. "I know what you thinkin'," he says, his yellowed eyes rolling to meet Xan's. "Ain't nothing can lift this. Tell you what you can do for me. Lightning ain't in the back of my pants." *He means his pistol.* "Not nowheres around. Did find my shoe, though. Here it is." He taps the sole of a shoe resting against his side at the edge of the girder's clamped jaw.

The foot's still in it.

"Find Lightning for me." The implication is plain.

Xan sweeps the area with his light, avoids a bloated corpse. No sign of the nickel-plated .38. He says, "The devil doesn't want you. You said it yourself."

"Well, he done got me now. Don't listen to none of them old preachers. This right here? Worse than all they rumbling. Ain't no hell to touch this. I been prayin' for it."

Nothing I can do here alone but watch him die. "I'm going for help. Back as soon as I can."

"Best thing you can do, white meat: fetch me a pistol."

"I'll bring help. We'll have you out of here."

Lightning Johnson isn't a popular man. The tenants Xan

approaches laugh at his pleas. On Linden Avenue he flags down an NGO relief vehicle. The driver, a nervous volunteer with a Jersey accent, says he'll forward the request for assistance but this isn't a critical infrastructure district. "Does the hotel have an emergency services contract? If you have the provider's number—"

"Can't you round up some men and crowbars?"

"We're under strict orders to avoid unstable structures. The risk is too great."

A TV satellite truck pulls up behind the NGO wagon, taps its horn. Xan presents his case again. "A man's alive in there. Your network must have resources."

"Buddy, we're here to cover the story not be part of it."

The prick deserves a sledgehammer retort but Xan promised Lightning to return. He runs into the hotel again, appropriates a water-pipe closet rod and a set of bedrails from a room in the west wing. Longshot levers. If all he can do is sit with the poor man, that's what he'll do.

Hours later, the gap kept open by the bluesman's crushed thighs is stuffed with bent angle iron, pipe and chair legs splintered by hammer blows awkwardly struck in tight quarters. Where Xan had more room to work, he pried with broken floor joists. The girder hasn't budged. In desperation he floats the idea of amputating Lightning's legs.

"Hell no," Lightning sighs. "Sooner stick myself. But your blade dull and I'm too weak for it now anyways. Told you to find me a pistol. That what I need. You fixin' to leave me lay like a dog in the road?"

"I'll stay with you." Xan's not the weepy sort but he does, quietly.

"You goin' to have to do for me."

"What?"

"Ain't you never killed nothing?"

"Of course not."

"Ain't had no sick dog or cat?"

"My uncle in Leavenworth took me quail hunting once. I missed."

"Nobody say you got to like killing. Sometime it have to be done."

The idea is too abhorrent for words.

"Shit fire, boy. If I had Lightning… You goin' to *have* to do for me. I'd yelp and holler for you if I could. It strangles me too much to do it now."

Xan stammers, "I should what? Cut your throat?"

"What I look like, some kind of hog? Don't be sawing at me with that paper cutter of yours. Do it like I was something you cared for. I don't want to know nothing about it. Whop me upside the head with that hammer you brung."

"I couldn't do that. I'll go out again. Somebody will help."

"Help do what you ain't got the grit for? This how it is in the world, white meat. Ain't nobody gets out these blues alive."

"I can't." But Lightning will certainly die. They're arguing over how much to prolong his suffering. "The pistol must be here," Xan says. "Are you lying on it?" He reaches under the urine-soaked old man, provoking another round of coughs, retches and whimpers. He searches the surrounding area again in minute detail. Nothing. It's a horrid thing Lightning asks, more horrid to condemn him to the slow agony of additional hours or days. Xan admits defeat. "I can't find it."

Lightning fixes him with a weary stare. "Ready now, white meat?"

Xan goes cold. "How do you want it? I can't just hit you in the face."

"Ever play golf, boy?"

"No."

"Too bad for me. Do it like that, though. I'll just have me another taste of that sweet water first. When it done, you tell Mr.

Morrison and Mr. Hooker I gone. Have 'em make out my last check in your name. It the least I can do."

Xan assists him with the water bottle.

Lighning drinks, moans appreciation. "What I'm goin' do," he says, "is close my eyes and hum me a little 'Stagger Lee.' Get up on your feet, good and strong. Let that hammer swing like my head a golf ball and you a mile from the hole. Not no love tap, hear me? Rear back."

"Are you sure?" Xan blubbers.

"Boy, if it wasn't for the Klan and the sheriff, I'd think you white meat was *all* pussies."

Xan's first blow sends Lightning rigid, back arched, arms jerking. The second relaxes him. He stops gasping for breath.

Xan's body follows a maroon stripe painted on the wall of the service corridor. It delivers him to a dead-end reek of gasoline and corpses where the parking garage should be. Mr. Johnson's face stares from between broken slabs, advises him to reverse course. His fingers bump along the maroon line back toward the lobby. Walls begin to shake and a thunder fist of dirty air drops him. Somewhere above, a landslide. Rats streak by in the dust, too panicked to concern themselves with another body.

The ceiling doesn't fall. He wishes it would.

one less digger

Inmate. On your feet."

Xan sits on the shelf where he'd sleep if it were allowed. He's not propped against anything, but the cell flickers at him, throbs the warning tone. If he doesn't discover why, he'll be zapped. He opens bleary eyes. Nothing swims by. Closes them again.

"On your feet." This isn't Lightning's voice, or his own. It's the cell, speaking from on high. He hadn't realized it could speak.

The light steadies, satisfied. "Slide your hands through the bean slot."

The cold steel soothes his swollen wrist. He lingers, absorbing the chill.

"Farther."

He pushes his arms through to the elbows. Yelps as a handcuff bites his injury. He tries to jerk the hand free.

"Hold still."

The other cuff is applied, ratchets to a tight lock. On command he retracts his arms, retreats from the door, turns around. Hears motors and moving metal. A breeze flutters against his butt. Blackout goggles are placed over his eyes before his head is bagged. *Why bother?* The cell knows his eyes are closed. Breath stink. He imagines spitting rotten teeth.

Guided backwards by the loop on the shock belt he stumbles,

is grabbed by the hair. He's being evicted? *Lightning too?* Hands control his arms and shoulders. "Sidestep, to your left," he's told. Shoved against a wall. Belly chain. Handcuffs hooked to it. His ankles swiftly shackled. A squeak rolls up behind, stops at his heels, trips him when they pull his shoulders. Mid-fall, a hard surface catches him. Straps across his chest, legs, waist. He's tipped to a horizontal position and covered with a crackling sheet. Pressure on the sides of his head. His ears ring with subtle music on the conveyor ride through the robot factory.

Electricity shrieks through his bones. He's trapped at a precarious angle, can't escape. *Was there a warning?* The head bag is gone but he still can't see. The goggles.

"What's your name, inmate?" This voice, like the cell, is male. "Speak up." The words are calm, distinct, have a Texas accent.

"Xan Hicks."

"Good. Mind if I call you Xan?"

Another machine? He hates when cars talk to him. "No."

"Then we'll get along fine. Do you believe in God, Xan?"

"Uh-uh."

"Speak up."

"No."

"Didn't think so. That's okay. But do yourself a favor. Believe in me. Will you do that?"

The warning sound pulses. Xan screams, anticipating a jolt.

"Stop," the voice commands. There's no shock. "Do I make myself clear?"

"Please, don't."

"We're going to talk, just the two of us."

"I didn't do it."

"Didn't do what?"

"Kill her. I loved her. I…" He forgets what he was going to say next.

The voice is bored. "First you did; now you didn't. I wasn't going to bring it up today but since it's on your mind: What were you jabbering about in the cell? After you punched the wall you said, 'Why'd you make me do it? Where's your pistol? Give it to me.'" The voice pauses. Pages are audibly turned. "So on and so forth, duh-ta-duh-ta-duh. Ah, here. 'I didn't want to kill you.' You say that a lot."

"I was talking to Lightning."

"Lightning made you do it?"

"Yes."

"Do what?"

"Kill him."

"Interesting. You didn't kill *her* but you *did* kill him. Was there lightning that night?"

"What?"

"Report says it was raining. But forget it; I don't actually care. Who you killed or think you killed is between you and the State of North Carolina. Far as I'm concerned you did the country a favor. I have one less Digger to catch. You're here to help me round up the others."

The threads of Xan's thoughts have unraveled. All he can say is, "That's not right."

"You must be tired. Lord knows you reek to high heaven. Your cooperation has earned you a shower and jumpsuit. Get some sleep. We'll talk later."

rhythms on a flaming drum

"Who is Marie Errandonea? Am I pronouncing it correctly?"

As always in the Texan's presence, Xan is strapped to the transport cart, fitted with blinder goggles. But since he was issued the orange coveralls, no swaddling sheet.

Lightning smells a setup. "Watch yourself, white meat. He tryin' to hang you."

"She pronounces it Mary."

"How did you meet Errandonea?"

"She was Caitlin's friend."

"What was your relationship with her?"

"I knew her from Caitlin and the theater we belong to."

The Texan presses. "Mari Errandonea is a Digger, a member of the Monkeywrench cell. You can confirm that without giving away any secrets. I've been talking with her associates. Care to guess who?"

Lightning doesn't have to advise him on this answer. "Monkeywrenchers?" The claim of ignorance is a lie but not by much. Caitlin rarely used the term. Mari never did in his presence. He's glad he doesn't know more. If anyone ever deserved to be snitched out, it's Mari Errandonea.

The warning tone sounds.

"Please," he cries. "I don't know."

A shock rips him in two.

"Caitlin Schmidt is a Monkeywrencher. Acting with others, she sabotaged the water supplies of the people of Calhoun. Then she attempted to steal discharge samples from the Palomar Coatings campus. That's espionage, Xan. A capital offense. You were involved." The punishment paralyzes his muscles until he passes out.

"Tell me about Wallace Schmidt. You've met him, I believe."

"He doesn't like me."

"Sensible man. Computer bigwig, isn't he? What are his political leanings?"

"Republican maybe. I don't know. We never talked politics. His wife's a Dominionist."

"This would be Leilani?"

"She drove Caitlin nuts."

"Got a nose for Diggers, does she? And the former wife is Canadian? What's her name again?"

"Maeve."

"What sort of political discussions did you and Caitlin have with her?"

"None really. She officiated at the handfasting."

"She has Digger sympathies?"

"It didn't come up in conversation."

Lightning butts in. "You bein' played. Watch your fool mouth."

Although the shock belt was removed the day he transferred to his new cell, he still cowers at the warning signals. The food here is no better but the lighting isn't as harsh. He has a shower head and a back door that sometimes allows him into a narrow exercise run. Other doors and fences line the walls of the enclosed space.

He never sees anyone there. Beside the bean slot, where he has to put his hands for cuffing, an inscription reads:

> Servants, be obedient to them that are your masters according to the flesh, with fear and trembling, in singleness of your heart, as unto Christ.
>
> Ephesians 6:5

The Texan is unaware that Xan has discovered a bodily escape from Prison World. There's a shifting, invisible boundary where it adjoins the Free Territories. When he slips across he never knows where he'll land or how long he can stay. He likes most places he's visited but a few are terrible. The rules of that reality are different than those in Prison World. He's learning by trial and error. Prison World is coming into better focus as well. He has glimpsed purple latex gloves. Been cursed in Spanish. The cell doesn't speak; the Texan only wants him to think it does. His captors aren't robots; they're human.

For the first time in the Texan's room he's unstrapped from the cart, told to stand. The squeaky wheels roll away.

"You've been holding out on me," the Texan says evenly. "Allowed us to believe you're just another Digger. Couldn't be further from the truth, could it? Gentlemen, this secret squirrel is actually a people's hero. He's freaking famous. Goes to show you should never judge a book by its scrawny-ass cover. You want to introduce yourself, Xan, or should I?"

A Free Territory nightmare? What's the Texan doing here? "Go away. You're on the wrong side." Xan wills himself to float through the ceiling. Nothing happens.

"Cut the crap. I'm not buying it anymore. Since you won't tell them, I will. Gentlemen, behold the great John Henry."

Lightning offers urgent counsel. "Here it come. Keep your

mouth shut and ball up if you have to, best you can."

The Texan continues, "I've met you more than halfway, Xan, or John, or whatever you call yourself. Took away the stun trainer. Allowed you to sleep, exercise. Gave you clothing. How am I repaid for my Christian charity? You string me along. Didn't the inevitability of DNA testing cross your feeble mind?"

"I'd tell if I could. Anything. What do you want me to say?"

"We've known for weeks, of course, but too late. Caitlin Schmidt crossed the Canadian border. I tip my hat to your ingenious line of BS."

I'm in the Free Territories after all. Take me to her! From Prison World, the warning tone throbs. Guards prevent him from collapsing in a quaking heap. "No, please," he whines.

"Drop the games. Hear me? It's over. Get that through your rancid pudding of a brain. The body in the fire pit was Errandonea's. You and your girlfriend killed her because she was talking to ISA."

"What?"

"Then you covered Schmidt's escape. Maybe in some diseased, sponger fashion you *do* love her. But, like it or not, you'll help me catch her and the rest of the Monkeywrench outfit. Xan, I've done all I can for you. This is end of the line, your last chance at voluntary cooperation. What do you say?"

"It another trick, white meat," Lightning whispers through the hallucinatory confusion.

A gut punch launches Xan across the border into Prison World. He's dragged backwards, retching. Thrown against a wall. At the crack of his head, cameras flash behind his face.

She's alive in the Territories. He won't forget that.

The guards kick him, roll him onto his stomach. A knee digs into his spine, forces the wind out of him. He chokes on vomit, breathless. Something stings his leg.

They haul him up gasping, apply the head bag and earphones, strap him to the cart. *She's alive. She's alive.*

"Only in your mind, white meat," Lightning says. "You saw what they done to her. These crackers fuckin' with your fool ass."

Consciousness stretches, smears, thins to transparency. *Find her.*

Her voice is low, terrified. "Xan, is that you? I need help. Where are you?"

At the moment, he can't say. He's too groggy to move. Has a fierce pain in the belly.

rhythms on a flaming drum

Your former wife wishes to speak with you." Leilani's making an effort to tread lightly. Since their arrival in North Carolina she has answered the phone that won't quit ringing. Everybody's got an angle. Everybody wants a piece. "I told her you weren't accepting calls but she says it's an emergency and insisted I put you on."

These hours, since the police notification, have visited impotence and harassment upon Wally he'd never imagined possible, although he also can't imagine why not. He is as guilty as anyone of ogling tragedy cheapened to titillation for the viewing audience. It's standard news-ghoul fare dished up between pitches for cars and precious metals, safely quarantined behind a monitor screen. No one wants actually to see with the unseeing eyes of the traumatized or comprehend that those wails are not prayers. They are the sounds of evisceration.

An OstarFX jet landed him and Leilani at the Calhoun Sky Park before dawn. Pragmatically the rush was useless, but how else to contend with the hellish eternities before and between and after the hastily arranged arrangements? He's jigging like a soul on fire, pacing, engaging in meaningless motion. He could no more have delayed the flight to a reasonable hour than prevented the sun from rising on this desolation of a day.

The Victim Assistance counselor they'd met with at ten, a volunteer named Treva, delivered the first gratuitous torment. Caitlin's body is too disfigured for visual identification. No viewing is possible at this time and it might be best, she'd said, if they spare themselves the ordeal later. "Grisly images tend to stick in people's minds. The medical examiner requested dental records, although I'm told there was severe damage to the facial area." In cases like this the request is a formality. Caitlin's car was found near the crime scene. They have statements from Xan and a piece of jewelry he identified as hers. Wally didn't recognize the photograph of an ancient coin. Leilani thought she might have seen Caitlin wearing it but couldn't be sure. "No problem," Treva said. "DNA testing eliminates any doubt. We obtained reference material during a search of your daughter's apartment. By the way, that premises is off limits to unauthorized personnel, including family, until further notice."

Next came the insult of a loyalty grilling administered by ISA Special Agent Doak and Lt. Dillingham of the Calhoun PD Major Crime Unit. They told him Caitlin may have gone to the lake for purposes of espionage. Were Wally and Leilani unaware of her radical activities? The subversive theater? The benefit concert for an enemy of the state? Associations with Digger elements? Leilani, bless her, held her tongue.

"What about that episode of feminist agitation in college?" Doak asked.

Wally didn't deny his role in quashing the sedition inquiry.

Dillingham rubbed in the salt. "We have the utmost respect for your service to our country, sir. Your patriotism is unquestioned"— *Not much it isn't*—"but might your judgment have been clouded by sharing some of your daughter's concerns?"

That was too much. Wally terminated the interview by blistering Tweedle Doak and Tweedle Dum's officious ears.

And now he's supposed to deal with Maeve's emergency.

"What?" he barks into the phone.

"My old love," she says in the soothing tone she used during Caitlin's childhood illnesses. "Parents should never be subjected to what we're going through."

"What is it, Maeve?" Leilani's hanging around, listening in. *Can't the woman rest from gathering ammunition for a cat fight she's long since won?* "Hold on."

He turns to Leilani, "It's okay, dear. I can handle this."

"Is she gone?" Maeve asks.

"Yeah. What's on your mind?"

"I need you to trust me. Our futures depend on it though I can't tell you how just yet. Do you understand?"

"Don't play games. I'm in no mood."

"Nor am I, I assure you. You never thought I paid attention when you tried to explain your work, but I did listen. What I have to say is to the father of my child, not the man from OstarFX. We must be absolutely clear on that. Is what you used to tell me about pre-paid telephones still true?"

"What about them?"

"I'm getting one with the international option. You'll receive a number. I want you to call it in a manner respecting our privacy. As her parents, we deserve that much."

"News-ghouls after you too?"

"One never knows, does one?"

"Message received. No problem."

"Another thing. I need you to listen and remain calm."

"What?"

"Xan Hicks is innocent and I don't care who hears me say it. Who's the best criminal defender—"

"Wait a goddamned minute." *She wants him to defend the murdering bastard?*

"Listen to me."

"They caught him at the scene."

"Remember what I used to tell you about magickal powers? Scrying, for instance? The ability to see remotely or communicate with spirits? That's how I know Xan's innocent. Listen carefully. I learned it from a voice as real as the one you're hearing. Xan wasn't present at the murder. There may not be much we can do for Caitlin. But you *can* help me get the love of her life out of jail. We can grant her that peace."

"For crying out loud."

"There's no time, Wally. If you don't believe me, give me the attorney's name. I'll make the contact myself."

"You do that. Are you finished?"

"No, the name, please. And be expecting the number I mentioned."

"All right. Just a minute." *What can it hurt?*

disappeared

OstarFX executive Wallace Schmidt, titan father of the Calhoun actress whose burned and mutilated body was discovered Tuesday at Lake Hollister, has become meat for predatory cameras and enterprising microphones. It's his turn to sell cornflakes for cable news but they can go to hell. Laurel Ridge is his bulwark against them. The village guardhouse has redoubled its scrutiny of visitors. He's holed up, failing miserably to distract himself with work or contribute meaningfully to that of his operations team. He hopes they're ignoring all but the most general of his instructions.

Those jokers from three days ago, Doak and Dillingham, had him and Leilani in again yesterday to identify a man security cameras caught breaking the police tape at Caitlin's apartment. He was wearing a winter coat and hat. It could have been anybody. Leilani wanted to know what he took away. Tweedle Doak and Tweedle Dum had no answers.

Today Doak called yet again, requesting a private interview with him alone. But ISA isn't his only option for abuse. He declined the agent's offer of an afternoon kick in the nuts, preferring to go ahead with a conference arranged by Adam Goforth, the attorney Maeve hired.

Goforth's office girl hadn't been ruffled by Wally's hostility on the phone this morning. "Adam respects your feelings and extends his deepest condolences. I'm calling with regard to a matter of immediate concern to *you*. Adam believes it's in your interest to be aware of it. We have an opening at 2:30. Is that convenient?"

Goforth's public persona is latter-day Atticus Finch: light-colored suits, folksy, engaged in good causes but not ostentatiously so. In the courtroom he's reputed to project qualities of empathy and reason that shame grandstanding prosecutors.

The salt-of-the-earth theme carries through to the décor of his offices at the pricey end of lawyers' row. The waiting room is homey. The receptionist could be a favorite aunt. She serves Wally and Leilani good coffee in hand-thrown mugs and has her boss out to greet them before Leilani can assess his taste in waiting room reading material.

Goforth, in jeans and crisp Pendleton plaid, prefers to be addressed as Adam. His private office is a cozy, book-lined den. He seats them in comfortable arm chairs and takes a hard chair behind an antique writing desk for himself, saying it's better for his back.

His reason for requesting this meeting is an inability to locate his client. "The detention center booked Hicks in on Tuesday. We were told he was being held incommunicado pending resolution of a procedural issue the lieutenant in charge declined to divulge."

"Go on."

"Stonewalling like this doesn't occur in criminal cases, regardless of the severity of the charge. I followed up personally and received a similar runaround. Today the story has changed. The jail denies any knowledge of Xan Hicks and apologizes for any prior suggestion to the contrary. This development raises the possibility of extrajudicial intervention."

"Are we supposed to feel sorry for him?" Leilani sniffs.

"Not necessarily, but there may be implications for you folks as well. Have you had dealings with the Integrated Security

Authority since the murder?"

"The Special Agent in Charge had us in twice for questioning," Leilani replies.

Wally wishes she'd let him handle this. He adds, "Doak wants to see me again."

Adam makes a note. "Any idea why ISA is interested?"

"It's the pollution," Leilani says. "Special Agent Doak told us Caitlin went to the lake to collect wastewater samples. I hate Diggers but no company should be allowed to poison my drinking water, regardless of who owns them or a national security designation."

"National security designation?" Adam asks.

Wally touches the arm of her chair. "We've heard that Palomar may have an SDI. Caitlin never said anything about illegal activities."

"Good," Adam says. "An SDI could explain a great deal. Defense counsel is typically excluded from cases alleging threats to national security. Constitutional protections have been ruled inapplicable to so-called 'enemies of the state,' regardless of citizenship. Within the scope of their mandates, DoD and ISA are immune from judicial oversight. Those who contend they've been wronged have no recourse. Wally, you're a software man, pretty high in OstarFX as I understand it. May I inquire what specifically you do?"

Wally recites his unclassified job description, pleased that the lawyer doesn't jot it down.

Adam nods. "Let us assume ISA considers the murder of your daughter to have a national security component. They're aware of your key position in counter-terrorism operations. Might they ask themselves if you're a security risk? Have you retained personal counsel?"

Wally hasn't considered lawyering-up and resents the implication that he should.

"You're in shock," Adam says. "You should be aware ambitious people exploit such vulnerabilities to build careers. A prudent man, a man our country depends on, protects himself."

"I have nothing to hide."

"You may have heard of Barbara deShazer, based in Charlotte? We're fortunate to have an advocate of her caliber practicing in this state."

Leilani butts in. "That irritating woman who represents celebrities?"

"That irritating woman who represents celebrities *and gets them exonerated,*" Adam says. "Barbara's vilified for spoiling too much popular fun. Do us all a favor, Wally. Consult her before meeting again with the police or representatives of ISA." He takes a business card from the holder on his desk, writes on the back and brings it around. "This is her private line."

magick

Leilani doesn't approve of retaining a personal attorney. "That's blood in the water to media sharks. What's the high and mighty Mr. Schmidt hiding? You'll have them sifting our garbage."

Wally's more concerned by the potential for sowing doubt in the minds of OstarFX clients, including DoD. A preliminary opinion from CEO Hank Lundstrom leans toward involving deShazer but a final decision will await a morning video conference with the OstarFX Chief Legal Counsel and the Director of Client Relations.

The night drags on. Leilani went to bed an hour ago. When Wally can muster the energy he'll shred the completed list of action items on his desk and join her. For the umpteenth time today the landline rings.

"Wally?" a woman asks through the answering machine. "I have information for Maeve. If you're still awake I'd—"

Wally picks up the handset. "Have we met?"

"Maxine Bakunas, we were neighbors when Caitlin was small. Your ex and I stay in touch."

"Of course." *Max and her husband lived next door in Calhoun Park.*

"I felt so awful when I heard. I've been meaning to send a card. How are you holding up, poor man?"

"About as you'd expect, Max. And you?"

"We're still in town and have three of the most beautiful grandchildren," she brags. "Oh, I'm sorry."

"Think nothing of it. But perhaps we should move on to the reason for your call."

"Herb never throws anything away. I finally found the serial number for that bike you bought from us. Maeve needs it for a police report. But now I can't seem to reach her. Could you… Do you have a pencil handy?"

Well played, ladies. The Bakunas family didn't ride bicycles. Wally checks his watch. It's not too late to place the call. Maeve's a night owl. He enters the digits Max provided into the prepaid flip phone he bought for cash. It's a burner, intended for destruction after limited use. No records tie him to it. Hopefully none connect Maeve to hers. Amongst the billions of transmissions ISA sweeps up on a daily basis, not even the secret police have the computing capacity to readily connect these dots—unless he's foolish enough to phone from the house. If he does *that*, any bush-league snoop monitoring the nearest cell tower could bust him.

The night air is breezy and sharp when he lowers his window at the village gatehouse. He and the attendant recognize each other. The man waves him on, not bothering to remove his earmuffs to hear Wally's greeting. Driving to town is by no means foolproof. The Lexus has an onboard navigation system. ISA could correlate its location with cell towers and refine the data search to manageable proportions. But security precautions are always a matter of degree. Nothing Maeve has to say could justify the resource expenditure.

He turns onto a side street in an old Calhoun neighborhood without closed circuit cameras on the power poles. In front of a dark house he shuts off the car and enters the number he was given.

"Hello?" Maeve says.

"It's me."

"Are you alone? Is this line secure?"

"Yes and yes. Brilliant misdirection, by the way."

"Max is a peach."

"I suppose I should thank you for the respite from staring at the walls, but you must have another reason for this." He sees approaching headlights and leans over, below dashboard level. After the car passes he uses the steering wheel as a grab bar to right himself.

"There's someone who wants to speak with you," Maeve says. "Here she is."

"Dad?"

"Sweetie?" *It's a vicious stunt.* "What is this?" The background noise on the line shifts. He's been put on speaker. "Maeve?"

Caitlin's voice is more distant. "It's me. I swear."

Maeve says, "It was unwise to tell you before. Now she's where I can protect her."

The voice that broke her mother's favorite vase and hid the pieces behind the loveseat pleads, "I didn't know what you'd do."

"What I'd do?" Her uncertainty is too painful to explore. *But the body…* "Who was at the lake?"

"My friend. You met her. She…" He hears rustling noises and muffled crying.

Maeve speaks; "The person they arrested didn't do it. She thinks it was the rednecks from that fight in the alley."

"I didn't tell Xan where we were going. He wouldn't have approved and I didn't want to argue."

"Sweetie, we thought you were dead. If this is some kind of hoax…" Wally's having a brain crash.

"It's not. It's not. Believe me. Please."

"Get hold of yourself," Maeve orders him. "Any day now they'll realize their mistake. Frankly, I'm surprised it's taken your vaunted secret police this long. She had to get beyond their reach.

We've been totally focused on that."

"You don't have to forgive *me*, Dad, but please. Xan's not political; he never was. I'm the one."

"But you're not a D—"

"Yes, I was. I am. I tried to quit, but we had to do this."

"Oh, god." Wally's nervous system can't take much more. He glances up and down the empty street. His fingers and toes are freezing. For heat he starts the car. The blue face staring from the windshield is haggard, furtive. He dims the dash lights until it disappears. "Tell me what happened."

"They shot her, and Camo Man was after me so I ran and the big one yelled at him because the other one was hurt. He kept chasing me and the big one yelled, 'Come right now; the bitch cut Josh bad.' I kept running up the bank as fast as I could but it was raining and I kept slipping. And then I heard their boat. They shot our canoe in the middle of the lake, and it sank and they gunned the motor over to where they came from. There was blood everywhere and Mari was dead. Her phone didn't work. Dad, are you there?"

He's petrified just listening. "I'm here, sweetie."

"Mari thought she could fight. But Camo Man caught her with a fishhook and they grabbed her when she cut the line. I had the sample bottles and she yelled at me to go on. Then there were screams and I heard a gun. I'm the worst friend in the world."

"Mari wanted you to escape," Maeve says. "She'd have died for nothing if you hadn't got away."

Like Caitlin, Wally is scrambling, overwhelmed. "They'd have killed you."

Maeve's reassurances aren't for him. "You're safe. It's over now. Slow down. As you tell us, pay attention to how you protected yourself."

Since when are you a school counselor? This is our daughter!

"I started up the fire trail because it was getting dark. But the boat came back. And a truck on the trail above me. I had to hide behind a rock. After that there were dogs and searchlights. I crawled into a laurel thicket and lay flat until they went away."

"You stilled yourself so they couldn't find you," Maeve says. "Wise decision. It saved your life. Remember, speak slowly."

"So I waited and then I climbed up to a county road. But I was afraid there might be men on it, so I crossed over and kept climbing. I couldn't see, Dad, and it was freezing. I had to walk all night to stay warm. I kept trying Mari's phone but it was wet."

Wally's seat warmer and climate controls don't reach the chill he's experiencing. "You tried, though. That was smart." *Now Maeve has me doing it.*

"I wasn't thinking," Caitlin says. "I got lost. When I finally got to the landing the sheriff's department was swarming my car. I had to pass on by. Then there were a couple of ladies out walking. I told them my boyfriend dumped me on the road last night. They loaned me a phone."

"You used your acting skills," Maeve remarks.

"Uh huh. I tried Xan, but the man that answered asked who I was. So I hung up and connected with … a person who came and got me. She was going to let me off at the apartment but the police were there too. We didn't know Xan was in jail. You have to help him."

"Your mom's already hired him a lawyer. He thinks Xan's been moved."

Maeve says, "We've heard that as well. What strings can you pull?"

Probably none. "I'll do everything I can. You have my word, sweetie. Maeve, I'll cover the legal fees." *She can't afford Goforth's tab for long.*

"That's good of you, Wally."

Xan Hicks is still a loser. "I take it you aren't in this country?"

"Correct," Maeve says.

"She's not as safe as you might think."

"I've spoken to a man experienced in asylum applications. He'll act for us."

Huh? "Aren't we a bit ahead of ourselves here? When this blows over—"

"But it won't, will it? Your government uses people like our daughter as prison labor. I fear for Xan this very minute. It's not as if Diggers advocate violence. Of course, the same can't be said for the Brotherhood of Sword Swallowers. *That's* the group that ought to be on your banned list."

"We can discuss this another time."

"You brought it up."

"Don't let's fight right now," Wally says. "Please pay attention. If you're where I think you are, the United States has an agreement for the repatriation of fugitives, including politicals. Only high value targets are actively pursued but a traffic ticket could get her detained. She can't risk paper trails either. Sweetie, did you cross the border legally?"

"Mom thought we should."

"Did you bring electronics? Phone, laptop, anything?"

"When I went to get them, there was police tape on the door and our apartment had been searched. My stuff was missing."

"You went in disguise?"

"Uh huh."

The man in the winter coat. "Assume your devices are in unfriendly hands. How much does that complicate things?"

"My laptop runs unlicensed software but everything is heavily encrypted."

Attempted evasion of mandated data collection protocols. Not good. "And if the encryption is broken?"

"When I log off, a sweeper erases things people shouldn't see."

"Anonymizer?"

"Do I have to tell which one?"

She's not just dabbling with subversion. Her computer hides behind a random series of intermediate machines when it sends or receives queries. ISA will immediately recognize what it's dealing with, whether or not it cracks the encryption. He wills himself to remain calm. "You built this system yourself?"

"A friend. He's never been caught."

Or is allowed to remain in place. "Okay. The good news is no incriminating files. But the illegal operating system, software and encryption guarantee ISA interest. Are you using credit cards?"

"No. I borrowed what I could and maxed out the cash machines before I left. My passport was scanned at the border but that's the only other record."

"Smart." He tells himself this isn't a Digger; it's Caitlin. "Avoid electronic and other traceable transactions. Your mother and I will supply you with cash. Have you thought how you'll let the authorities know what happened at the lake?"

"Another topic for later," Maeve says. "We're exhausted."

Wally's running on fumes himself. "Aren't we all. But what are those names again?"

"The Brotherhood of the Fiery Sword," Caitlin says, "a secret society of white supremacists."

"I meant the attackers."

"Camo Man is just what we called him. The one Mari hurt is Josh. We're pretty sure his last name is Rice. We don't have a name for the big guy in the alley."

"Did you say Josh Rice?" *Bobo's groundskeeper?* "Are you positive?"

"I can send pictures of him and Camo Man, taken before the memorial service."

"Use snail mail, sent from a random location to my primary address. Nothing to my computer, mobile devices or landline except in dire emergencies."

"Dad?"

"Sweetie?"

"I never wanted to cause trouble for you. I'm through with politics, I swear. Help me free Xan."

"I'll do my best. And from the bottom of my heart, *thank you* for being alive. When that phone rang the other night and it was the police… Maeve, I apologize for my temper. It's been such a shock."

"Don't thank me, old love; thank magick."

"Whatever," he says.

"Happy Thanksgiving. Blessed be."

Wally hangs up, elated and plunged into fresh torment. *My little girl is an enemy of the state.* He'll be lucky to choke down a bite of turkey.

flight

Caitlin wakes in a bed unaccountably scented with lavender. A hotel room. Canada. The room's aubergine and white colors are dim in the anemic light of northern day. Her pillowcase is lumpy. She finds a lavender sachet and a rock, no, a fossil, a coiled ammonite. These must be her mom's doing. Maeve looks up from the book she's reading in a chair by the window and smiles. "Sleep well?"

The sleep of the heartsick.

They go through the motions of lunch at the downstairs restaurant. Then it's up to the room again. Caitlin would rather not relive the turmoil she's been through but her mom believes it's important, sooner rather than later. They sit at either side of the window, sharing the warmth of the radiator beneath it. Outside, Montreal lies under a frosting of gray snow. It's as if this is a safe house and a spy is being debriefed.

Maeve starts her where she left off last night, with the phone call to Reba Stein.

"Reba picked me up and we—"

"Present tense. See it in your mind like a movie. Tell me in present tense."

"Reba picks me up on the highway and we drive to the apartment, but there are blue shirts. We're afraid it might be the start of a Digger roundup."

She explains that the water samples she and Mari collected are worthless without the address of the German lab Dr. Sigurdsdottir recommended for nanotube testing. Reba circles the block of student ghetto housing where Mari lived. There's no police activity. Caitlin gets out around the corner and approaches on foot. Mari has a spare key on a nail under the stairs to her apartment. Caitlin lets herself in. A thick "Teddy/Palomar" folder lies in plain view, the lab information inside it. She takes the whole folder. On impulse she takes Mari's laptop as well.

"Okay," she admits when her mom praises another wise decision. "But leaving stuff scattered around is sloppy. Mari shouldn't be remembered like that." She dislikes having to invent rationales for unconsidered decisions.

"Give yourself credit. Part of you knew what needed to be done and you trusted it."

The retelling proceeds in this herky-jerky manner through the afternoon. Caitlin recounts Izzy's grim mood, triggering the Digger alarm network, and the three of them deciding to board Gertrude and spend the night at a B & B.

Maeve asks, "Did you try calling Xan again?"

"No. I was afraid his phone was compromised." She tells of nearly losing her mind and Izzy's impromptu therapy session when their fears are confirmed by reports of Xan's arrest. Not until the morning after that sleepless night is she publicly identified as the victim. She wants to set the record straight, but that's a bad idea. The cops would hold Xan hostage and force her to betray activists. She calls her mom, decides against Dad. Canada becomes her destination.

She finds her apartment blocked by police tape and ransacked. The blue shirts overlooked her passport. With Denny's help she duplicates and uploads the video she and Mari shot to document the Palomar samples. By afternoon, the bottles and a thumb drive are off to Bonn.

Denny has decided to visit a brother in Massachusetts until the dust settles. Caitlin accepts his offer to share the driving on a no-stopover marathon in his pickup—flying is out of the question and buses also do ID scans. As a further precaution they travel in congested clumps of interstate traffic. Out-of-state plates attract cops on forfeiture shakedowns but they're worst on state roads. The plan breaks down with overheated wheel bearings near Staunton, Virginia. They lose a day. But the rest they get in a no-questions-asked motel prepares them for the night run to Boston and the bleary-eyed breakfast rendezvous with Maeve at a coffee shop off I-95. Before Denny leaves for his brother's, he agrees to ship Mari's computer to Maeve in Toronto. That's safer than chancing a border inspection.

"Another good choice," her mom observes. "I loved what you told the exit officer who scanned your passport."

"That I had the flu? It's how I felt." Evening is descending on Montreal. Long shadows accentuate a sagginess at the corners of Maeve's mouth. The rolled collar of her stylish sweater doesn't quite hide the cords of loosening skin at her throat. Her mother is tired, beginning to age, trying not to show it. "The crossing must have been stressful for you too."

"I was sure we'd be fine," Maeve says, staring out at the fallen stars of the cityscape, "and scared to death of being wrong. The important thing is that we've arrived at a breathing space. Unresolved psychic trauma has crippling effects. The helplessness I heard in you yesterday is one of them. This afternoon we took steps to root it out. You had so little power available to you at the lake, but you used that tiny bit to survive and complete your water project. You had the wit and courage to protect your friends and get yourself here, where we can afford the luxury of reflection."

The fright *has* receded. Caitlin isn't ungrateful but panic has been replaced by excruciating guilt. "Some of my decisions were disasters. I went behind Xan's back by trying to sneak past the Palomar guards. Mari's dead because of that and ISA is doing terrible things to Xan. I've hurt you and Dad too, especially Dad."

Maeve switches on a reading lamp. The room blazes to cheery color. "Guilt is a lousy fact of life, Caitlin. You've a lot of work ahead of you with Xan, and Wally too. I can't make that disappear; had I the power, I hope I wouldn't use it. But do you recall the first promises you and Xan gave each other at the handfasting?"

"About hurting each other?"

"You conceded you might cause pain. I asked if that would be your intention."

"Never."

"Exactly. You acted without malice. You didn't intend his pain. Did you intend to hurt Mari?"

"Heavens no. I felt sorry for her. She had a crush on me. I didn't encourage it but she was like, patiently waiting her turn. Then Xan came along and it finally registered that she and I weren't going to happen. I wanted to make it up to her somehow."

"You acted out of guilt, intending good things. Hold on to that."

"But she died."

"Motivation doesn't always control outcome. As we're talking I'm asking myself: What if I'd stayed with Wally? Would you and I be here tonight? We came so close to losing you down there." Casual fingers wipe her eyes, as if the tears might escape notice.

Caitlin leaves her chair to kneel at her mom's side. She rests Maeve's head on her shoulder.

"Sweetie?" Maeve says, "when you were young you sometimes slept with us. I've missed that so much. Tonight, for me, would you mind?"

The preacher's sermon takes advantage of Calhoun's recent tragedies. "Last week our church family was beset by terrors and great signs. We mourn the attempt on the life of Deacon Rice and the tragic loss of Caitlin Schmidt, beloved daughter of Wallace Schmidt and Sister Leilani. Wake up Christians! The end times Luke prophesied are upon us."

Wally thinks back to Bobo's tale of the hellion son of a dissolute mother, who rose to respectability as head groundskeeper and church deacon. *What a load of manure.* Caitlin's story meshes with the available facts. Josh Rice was admitted to Lumet Regional on the evening of the murder. He'd supposedly been mugged at a roadhouse near Lake Hollister. Wally's research also revealed that Leilani's gossip mills have a better handle on Palomar than do mainstream media outlets—Diggers don't suspect OstarFX of having a presence in their darknet, but it does. The evidence compiled at PeoplesWiki includes autopsy findings on Theodore Arnold, water test reports and details of a broad-spectrum campaign of repression against Palomar opponents. Supporting evidence includes links to photographs of the memorial service assailants. The driver of the truck with the flaming sword placard is definitely Rice. These photos were uploaded by "ShakenIt"— *Lord help us, Caitlin.* Dollars to donuts, these are the pictures she promised to mail.

Wally isn't in church today for spiritual support. Several prayers have already been answered. Caitlin's alive—Leilani will hear the good news, as he'll pretend to, soon enough. Secondly, the OstarFX VP for Client Relations was up against a tee time with the Secretary of the Army and an undersecretary from State. Wally's go ahead to contact DeShazer was swift and painless. Finally, Bobo occupies one of the gilded chairs flanking the preacher. Wally has a few questions for him before flying out.

While the church ladies descend on Leilani at the end of the service, he joins the gaggle around Bobo, who's graciously accepting best wishes for the deacon's recovery. Wally offers his through gritted teeth.

"Our trials are as nothing compared to yours," Bobo tells him. "Lucy's and my heart go out. Your daughter was such a beautiful lady."

"Thank you." *Burn in hell.* "How's Josh doing?"

"He'll mend, Lord willing. Lost a lot of blood though, a lot."

"I'm ashamed to say I haven't followed the news as closely as I might. Was he shot?"

Bobo shakes his head. "Darkie with a knife jumped him outside a watering hole on Highway 7. Slashed him across the face and tried to gut him."

"The Lucky Seven?"

"You know the place?" Bobo's surprised. "Josh and a man on his crew stopped in to wet their whistles after goose hunting. Another act of random violence in this God-forsaken burg."

"Did they catch the perp?"

"Still out there," Bobo sighs. "Josh and Tigger say they never saw him before, but who can tell one spade from another after sundown?"

brass balls

Barbara DeShazer's receptionist tells Wally the pair of brass tennis balls on the walnut stand in the outer office was a gift from Billie Jean King. The tops of the balls are burnished to a shine.

"Clients rub them for luck," the woman says with practiced flirtatiousness. "You may if you like."

He restrains himself. The waiting room is an orgy of self-promotion. Mixed in with the autographed celebrity photos are others showing a woman, DeShazer no doubt, posing through the years with the cream of society—Bobo Huskins isn't represented. She must have been a teenager in the chummy shot with President Kennedy.

Her self-possession is the thing Wally most notices when she fetches him. She's tall, thin, dressed in brown tweed, platinum hair in a French roll. Reading glasses dangle from a rope of pearls. Her face is deeply lined. Somehow her smile doesn't splinter it. Although he couldn't have dredged the gravel voice up from memory, he recognizes it from televised interviews. "Mr. Schmidt?" she rasps. "Glad to meet you. Call me Barb."

He extends his hand. "Thanks for squeezing me in during a holiday week. I wasn't optimistic."

"I wish I'd been available sooner. How can I be of service?"

"Quite a story," she says. "The murder was when again, a week ago Monday? Nine days. Have you been notified of the mistaken identity?"

"It's probably not at the top of Dillingham's to-do list. Per your advice, I declined further interviews with him and Doak."

"Excellent. Don't discuss the matter with anyone and refer all requests for information to me. Were you given a time frame for the DNA tests?"

"One to two weeks. But they should already be aware that my daughter is alive."

"Oh?"

"She uploaded a series of YouTubes. The first of them begins, 'My name is Caitlin Schmidt. According to the cops I'm dead.'"

Barb tilts back in her chair. "Dramatic."

"She's an actress." *Why couldn't she be a housewife with three kids?* "She lays out the pollution case against Palomar and retaliations against opponents of the plant. The second clip shows the murdered girl collecting samples at Palomar on the day of her death. Clip three is Caitlin's account of that trip, including the murder. The fourth eulogizes Mari and appeals for the release of Xan Hicks and a radio journalist."

"Oh my."

"We—Leilani and I—found out last night when reporters started calling us again."

"Your daughter is in a safe place, or thinks she is?"

"The latter. She masked her location with a neutral backdrop and apparently has friends with IT skills. They'll have covered her tracks." Barb's forehead wrinkles. "Details aren't important," he continues, "except that the evasion techniques they used are standard procedure for enemies of the state. I heard from the dead girl's father last night too. That was gut-wrenching. I couldn't fob him off entirely."

"What did you say?"

"That Caitlin and Mari were friends. That I'll be eternally

grateful to her for saving my daughter's life."

"Have there been any admissions of membership in banned organizations?"

"To the best of my limited knowledge, no. But ISA can read between the lines. They apparently have her laptop. The operating system and software are illegal, designed to avoid monitoring. She tells me the data is strongly encrypted. It's a Digger machine."

"Extremist groups aren't my usual fare. Care to educate me?"

Fresh from his own review of free market resistance groups, he tells her the original Diggers were a pre-industrial English sect suppressed for appropriating and farming unused land. The name was revived in the 1960s by an anarchist theater troupe in San Francisco; it engaged in hippie service projects. The current incarnation originated during the 2005-2006 labor reform protests. "People call them communists but they're too anarchic for that. A Digger cell might launch an alternative currency, attack corporate interests with malware or sponsor an underground school system. To the extent coordination exists, it seems to be person-to-person or via an elaborate darknet."

"Explain darknet."

"Darknets are heavily encrypted versions of the private digital networks businesses use for in-house communications. Access to members only—at least in theory. Your office may use one."

"It does," she says. "My practice depends on privacy. But do I detect skepticism in your voice?"

"Commercially available encryption and private network packages aren't worth much against a well-resourced opponent. Even the best open-source systems can be hacked eventually. Privacy is a relative term."

"This is your line of work?"

"It's related. Our primary concerns are state actors and unfriendly international movements, not attorney offices. But, as my wife frequently reminds me, all manner of predators swim the digital waters."

"Including the press."

"Right. It's an OstarFX priority to limit exposure in this matter." He takes a flash drive from his pocket. "Which reminds me, you could assist me in the anonymity department. I told Caitlin I'd do what I can for her boyfriend. She had the sense not to accuse the killers by name in her videos, but she gave a name to me, a protégé of Bobo Huskins. You've heard of Bobo?"

"Of course."

Wally passes the drive across the desk. "This contains the YouTubes and information I've assembled on the murderers. Familiarize yourself, then please get the drive to Adam Goforth in a manner ensuring it'll be taken seriously, despite the anonymous source."

"You've considered FedEx and an assumed name?"

"He must receive a lot of crackpot mail."

"Your name will pop first to his mind."

"Unless unsupported suspicion is admissible in court these days that's not a problem. Adam seems smart enough to understand that."

"I'll see that he does."

"One last thing," Wally says. "Whatever these kids stumbled across at Palomar rang alarm bells at ISA. Expect your office, files, electronic devices and communications to be searched or monitored without warrant or warning."

Barb shows the face-cracking smile again. "No offense intended, Mr. Schmidt, but government snoops could take lessons from some of the operatives hired by opposing counsel. My people are highly experienced in counter-espionage. If they weren't, my practice would long since have deteriorated to wills and trusts."

Wally isn't in the habit of hosting Hank Lundstrom at the University of the Potomac for what his appointment book calls a scouting report on students with OstarFX potential. The CEO occasionally leaves his office for lunch with his wife but everyone else assumes the role of Muhammad to Hank's mountain. Though he's been a mentor and friend since Wally's first anti-virus bootblock for the AmigaOS, the hair on Wally's neck stands when Hank suggests an outdoor stroll. It's a blustery day, blowing drizzle and sleet. Wally imagines himself as Rex, the beloved and decrepit mutt of his childhood, being loaded into the Studebaker for a final visit to the Vermont countryside.

Hank's demeanor is reassuring—but wouldn't it be?—as he inquires about the war games underway between Wally's in-house group and a team of elite cyber-warriors from the Army. Should the political situation in the socialist nations of the south continue to deteriorate, cutting edge OstarFX software is expected to play a major role in America's covert support for regime change operations. With the company's reputation riding on the outcome, it's critical that OstarFX, not Pentagon personnel, man the controls.

Wally assesses the street for surveillance threats. The few other pedestrians in the vicinity are hunched and in a hurry, watching their feet. Anyone attempting to monitor this conversation with fixed or mobile devices would have a beast of a time in these weather conditions.

"We're kicking butt," he says. "The Army kids are bright enough, but can't think on their feet. They're like an orchestra being asked to play improvisational jazz. The agile development process throws them, and their command staff sees it. Unless the fix is in somewhere, we'll have the driver's seat."

"Then all we have to do is deliver the goods as promised. Can we?"

"With high confidence. Our guys and gals are handling every challenge the Army throws at them. We won't let you down."

"I know you won't," Hank says as they cross a park road to avoid a busload of tourists unloading at the Iwo Jima Memorial. "Now, catch me up on your daughter and this Digger business."

"I had no idea she was involved. I should have."

Hank exhales twin jets of steam. "Kids. God bless them."

"The groundskeeper is out of the hospital. I hear the attorney for Caitlin's boyfriend has names for all three killers now, and a friend at the police department. Supposedly a man who plays it straight."

In the near distance the gray steel columns of the Netherlands Carillon rise from the woods. Hank says, "It's years since I've been in the tower. How about you?"

"Sure." The sleet is at their backs. Wally flips up the collar of his overcoat. The climb to the viewing platform is wet, not icy. They have the place to themselves. It's windy but dry at the rail overlooking the ranks of headstones in Arlington. They survey the history of American warfare lying before them—Wally reminded again of Rex—and the Mall across the river. Sleet blurs the Lincoln Memorial and Washington Monument. The Capitol Building is whited out.

"Let's suppose," Hank says, "that a connected sugar daddy

owns an outdated factory in his home town. He'd rather not close it. Somebody pitches him a process to convert plastic bags to a film that bends radar waves. It makes things disappear. Maybe, in time, it'll work in the visible spectrum too. He takes the idea to Defense and scores a fat R&D contract. Trouble is, his product doesn't meet quality specs. He keeps tinkering, getting extensions. Defense eventually loses patience and shops elsewhere but Sugar Daddy is too plugged in to cut loose. So they go the lemonade route. Let the Red Team think Sugar Daddy's crap is the best we have. His junk hides the existence of the stuff really used to cloak weapons. You follow?"

Wally does.

"The scam worked for a while but the Chinese sniffed it out. Now Sugar Daddy's product is truly worthless. Defense tires of being bled. They're behind the scenes duking it out with him and his allies on the Hill when a radical group raises Cain over wastewater from the factory. Sugar Daddy wants an end to the agitation, but the rabble-rousers don't take the hint. So he turns screws in Washington, claiming he's the victim of an enemy propaganda campaign. Weak sisters in the Pentagon are falling for it, threatening the jobs of folks at home, and so on."

The sleet is changing to snow. "To date, ISA has Sugar Daddy's back," Hank says. "If it should switch sides and green-light the pollution card, Defense's version of the truth gets a boost in the contract dispute, probably a decisive one. But who's going to risk his career over a peanuts contract in Podunk if Sugar Daddy's still standing at the end of the day? Without high confidence that he'll be in no position to kick ass, ISA stands pat."

"It wants to make the switch?"

Hank studies the whitening fields of the dead on Robert E. Lee's former estate. "Ever wonder if the back-stabbings of yesteryear were more honorable?"

"You're out on a limb, reading me in on this."

"Be careful, Wally. Caitlin's your heart and soul. OstarFX is mine."

The price for Caitlin, maybe me too, is Bobo's head on a silver platter, delivered without fingerprints.

*P*romise me you'll stop."
"Hmm?"
"Promise you'll stop."
"Stop what?"
"Taking so many risks."

rhythms on a flaming drum

I can't stop, Dad," Caitlin says. "The press is finally showcasing Xan's disappearance and the official non-answers. This is the moment to ratchet up the pressure. Where are you, anyway? What's that noise?"

"Intermission at Strathmore. Leilani can't have Christmas without *The Nutcracker*. She's off to the ladies room. Please, sweetie, be patient. Bureaucracies are aircraft carriers, not ballerinas. It's only been two weeks since your YouTubes, less than that since Xan's attorney had a word with Calhoun PD. Things take time." He hopes he doesn't sound as shouty to her as he does to himself. He's having to cover his free ear to hear. This is his fourth call on the burner, and the fourth location.

"Don't you realize what happens to the disappeared? They're tortured. Some die. Others are never the same after. If naming Josh Rice could get Xan released a day sooner, I'll take that risk."

Dangerous and dumb. "Think before you do. Game it out with me. You publish an accusation against Rice. Reporters descend on all involved. What happens next? Rice and his pals lie low or skedaddle, and Bobo attacks. He'll accuse you of industrial sabotage—you've admitted to stealing water samples and sending them to Germany. Are you spying for them, for the Soviets, the Chinese? He'll play American distrust of foreign meddling for all it's worth. And what about Rice? Unless he's convicted—and realistically, with Bobo's leverage, what are the chances?—he slaps you with a libel suit. You'd have to appear in an American court to defend against it. If you don't, the judge automatically rules against you. Goodbye trust fund. You're broke. But if you do return, you're subject to detention under the Espionage Act and find yourself in the same fix as Xan."

"Dad, he's not just some hottie drummer."

No, he also cuts grass.

"Once upon a time you and this country were in awe of him. Remember me saying I met John Henry in Memphis? That I loaned him my jacket and never got it back?"

"Vaguely." *That kid who had us believing in cowboys for a day or two?*

"I never expected to see him again. Then, last spring, there he was, busking at the Xchange Mart. Xan trusted me. And because he did, he's in prison. I can't abandon him regardless of the cost."

"I'm being told what, Xan Hicks is John Henry?"

"He never told anyone and neither have I, until now."

Even a credulous idiot like me can't swallow that whopper. "Sweetie, that's wonderful but he could be the Second Coming and it wouldn't matter. If he's released, John Henry or innocence won't factor into the calculation. It'll be because ISA determines he's more useful to them on the street. That's the hard truth."

"You're *admitting* the system is totally corrupt? Nobody worth a flying flip cares about right and wrong anymore?"

Wally flares. "Don't go there. They care. I care. Get this through your head: It's not so simple. There are other stakeholders, other considerations. What I'm saying is that the key to his release is convincing ISA they're better off without him in jail. That's the challenge. If we solve it, he walks."

"So what do you suggest? I haven't had your practice negotiating with secret police."

"I should be ashamed of saving your bacon in college? As I told you before, I'm working on it."

"I'm sorry. I didn't mean that like it sounded."

"Apology accepted. So, how are *you* doing?"

"It's way cold here. We found a little apartment. I move in this weekend."

Leilani's crossing the lobby toward him. "Got to go, sweetie. Remember, you're not in this alone. We'll think of something."

He wasn't quick enough with the goodbyes. "Who's that?" Leilani asks.

Wally mouths, "Caitlin."

"Really? Where is she? How is she? Let me speak to her."

If surreptitious phone calls are the new normal, this is as good an opportunity as any to bring her up to speed. "Leilani wants to say hello."

"Okay." Caitlin doesn't sound enthused.

Leilani doesn't recognize the phone she's handed.

"I'll tell you later," he says.

"Caitlin? Your father and I have been so worried. Where are you calling from?"

"No," Wally says, loud so Caitlin hears. "That's not a question she can answer."

"But dear," the social secretary of the Schmidt household replies, "we need an address for her Christmas card."

"No, we don't. The only thing she wants for Christmas is her boyfriend." *That's it! Bless you, Leilani. That's my line of attack. We'll send Bobo a Christmas card.*

rhythms on a flaming drum

Wally initially blames himself for the deleted call log in the burner phone. Perhaps he did it by mistake though he knows perfectly well he didn't. He borrows a SIM card reader from the OstarFX lab and does the data recovery upstairs in the privacy of his office suite. The list of calls sent and received from Maeve and Caitlin is followed by a number he doesn't recognize, dialed the morning after the ballet. Perhaps Leilani found the phone by accident, accidentally used it despite his warning not to, then erased the log from embarrassment.

The test of his belief in this theory would be redialing that call. He stalls, consulting publicly available reverse directories without luck. Not until he's out of other options does he check the classified place he fears to find it and does; the number is assigned to ISA. If his prepaid network isn't already monitored, it soon will be. He asks himself if she called Doak. *Only if she's a new informant.* It hadn't been long after Caitlin's expulsion from Ruskin and the sedition inquiry against her that he first met Leilani at an unclassified security briefing for ISA officials. He'd been divorced for years, was feeling his oats after promotion to the OstarFX top floor. She was young, eager, exotically pretty, supposedly a public relations functionary. How could he not be flattered by the attention?

His experience with ISA's operational side about Caitlin's predicament had been wholly different. He'd recognized early on that negotiating with the field office conducting her interrogation was a weak play. A bit of research led him to their boss's boss, the special agent in charge of ISA Region 2 in Philadelphia, a martinet whose name eludes him. One of the man's children had avoided a DUI conviction the old-fashioned way, by joining the Army. Wally cold-called Hauser—*that's the name*—Garland T. Hauser, and proposed a father-to-father discussion of Caitlin's situation, letting slip his awareness of the son's enlistment. Hauser suggested a ritzy gasthaus restaurant with an extensive wine list.

He'd met Wally there with a shark-tooth grin and dainty ears like pull tabs projecting from the white sidewalls of his temples. Wally's Prussian roots took instant offense at the caricature of Aryan precision evident in Hauser's appearance and humorless mannerisms. The man expected to be regarded as a minor deity and wine connoisseur. In West Germany his self-presentation might have been grounds for arrest on charges of cultural defamation.

Wally listened attentively to a lecture on Rieslings and flattered Hauser's ego with tales of thwarting internet bad guys. The jockeying for dominance persisted until Wally dropped a reference to another of Hauser's personal travails: his wife's secret dependence on narcotics. Terms for ending the ISA witch hunt were indirectly negotiated over glasses of a rare dessert wine produced, Hauser said, from rotten grapes. He agreed to terminate the inquiry into Caitlin's "petulant feminist demands" in return for an exclusive cybersecurity presentation to Region 2 staff. Victory had tasted cloyingly sweet, with lingering hints of kerosene, a lot like the wine.

He's sickened to imagine that Leilani's attraction to him might have been professional. But why assume otherwise? From ISA's perspective he was an unknown quantity with a leftie daughter and his fingers on important security infrastructure. They set a honey trap; he swaggered into it. Her religiosity was the perfect finishing touch. Who'd suspect a devout Dominionist? Not Wally Schmidt, he married her. Hauser and his cronies must have laughed their asses off.

That's not important now. He repeats it again and again as a mantra to keep him afloat in a scalding broth of humiliation. If ISA ever had a legitimate loyalty concern, he laid it to rest years ago. Other than failing to adopt Leilani's Dominionist opinions, he's denied her nothing. She enjoys a titan lifestyle, the envy of her family, former co-workers and 99.9% of Americans. Yet she doesn't hesitate to expose Caitlin, whose loss she so lately pretended to mourn. He imagines roasting ISA's whore with a flamethrower, blasting away until the stench of her existence is a cinder no more recognizable than Caitlin's friend. How will he prevent himself at dinner from pinning his wife's disloyal hand to the table with a carving knife? How not strangle her in her vile sleep or assist her to fall down the stairs? *Maybe she won't die. Let her slobber in a nursing home, fed gruel through a stomach tube.*

That's not important now. He'll return the compromised phone to the drawer where she found it. His customary aloofness will conceal his feelings until the business with Bobo is resolved. Then he'll kick her butt so hard she'll land on the curb across the street.

That's not important now. The phones he, Maeve and Caitlin use are insecure. He'll buy replacements, overnight two phones and a handwritten explanation to Maeve, trust her to have a safe means of contacting Caitlin.

Modifications to the Chinese government worm he's secreting in Bobo's online Christmas card are nearly complete. Time is of the essence. Bobo's only likely to ignore the standard warning against opening images from untrusted sources until ISA alerts him to Wally's illicit phone network.

Two junior associates seldom seen on the OstarFX top floor join

Wally for the elevator ride to the lobby. One is a former student named Kenneth. The other is running off at the mouth. "Chagas hasn't got the balls to nationalize ethanol production. He does and we pull the plug on his command and control, take down Brazilian TV—"

"Garrett," Kenneth interrupts, "I don't believe you've met Director Schmidt."

Garrett droops like a boy caught using profanity within earshot of the principal. "Director Schmidt?"

"I haven't had the pleasure," Wally says, "Garrett…?"

"Lombard, sir." The kid offers to shake hands. "Garrett Lombard."

Wally directs Garrett's attention to the closed circuit camera in the upper corner of the car. "Smile; a clear image simplifies disciplinary proceedings."

Garrett bows his head and says, "It'll never happen again, sir."

The elevator door opens. Wally lays a fatherly hand on Garrett's shoulder as the kid prepares to bolt. "Once upon a time we had a saying: 'Loose lips sink ships.' It's still true."

"Thank you, yes," Garrett stammers. "I will. This … we've got to … it's our floor."

"Nice to see you again, Kenneth," Wally calls after them. He hopes Internal Security goes easy on Garrett's youthful exuberance. It's a better excuse than Wally can offer for his own stupidity.

The lobby is never busy, even at lunch hour. As he leaves to round up the cash he'll need for replacement phones, he acknowledges Supervisor O'Brien at the screening station. O'Brien's training a new hire, a woman who undoubtedly dreams of breaking through the glass ceiling to management level. He'll lead her on, then break her as he has the others.

That's not important now. Wally reviews his game plan. Leilani will be told he's working late and not to hold dinner. When he does get home he'll plead the press of work and closet himself in the office. The family photo he's using to deliver the worm to Bobo was shot at Caitlin's handfasting. She and Xan smile with an innocence they'll never recapture. The picture also includes Leilani, revolting as her face has become. *That's not important now.* He'll tweak the worm, test and test again. When it's right he'll launch it. The process might take half the night. No risk of getting to bed before she's asleep.

rhythms on a flaming drum

BasqueGoddess: Lab confirms nanotubes. Pub strategy? Xena's ghost ready for dirt docs if/when available.

Wraith: bg handle so weird 2 c. 16k docs w8ting in filecab. consensus 2 release lab report & dirty docs together. ma&pa say press hot 4 smokin guns. good hunting

Way to go, Denny! Sixteen thousand files, wow! Like it's nothing for him to raid Palomar's computer network. Caitlin's eager for the challenge. Her dinky apartment in Toronto is strictly utilitarian, belying the gay Victorian exterior of the house. The Portuguese family downstairs only slightly enlivens the white interior walls and generic furnishings. She has no Portuguese and the parents struggle with English. Conversations are a mix of sign language and translation provided by the couple's young son. She's been discharging her impatient energy with walks. Although she's better dressed for the weather now, the biting cold quickly chases her indoors again.

Restlessness aside, her mom's coaching sessions in Montreal are paying dividends. Caitlin trusts herself better than she imagined possible. Her instincts *had* been good during the days of flight, not least the decision to grab Mari's laptop. Thanks to Mari's obsession with the TV fantasy *Xena: Warrior Princess* and an appallingly obvious login, Denny was able to restore the laptop to Digger functionality and improve its resistance to intrusion during the Virginia layover. He had BasqueGoddess online again before his truck was fixed. Without the laptop, Caitlin realizes, she'd truly be languishing in the frozen north.

BasqueGoddess: Congrats, Wraith! Glad you're on our side. If there's a smoking gun we'll find it.

His weirded-out reaction to new chat room messages from BasqueGoddess is understandable but he was the one who thought it best to retain Mari's handle for confusion value, in case ISA has hacked the darknet.

Reba, the "Ma" of "Ma&Pa," hinted at her own discontents in a veiled account of Mari's memorial service. They'd held it at the Living Spirit Fellowship Hall, the indomitable Mother Prentiss— free pending trial—officiating. Thankfully, the Palomar thugs stayed home. Poitier, aka Tijon, led an *a cappella* version of "Let Your Hammer Ring." Reba wrote, "ShakenIt should have been here to lay her to rest."

Caitlin read this as an accusation. The consequences of setting foot in Calhoun should be obvious to Reba but hearts don't listen to reason. She crosses her fingers that the Street Artists will see wisdom in the grassroots idea she's setting into motion.

john henry

Caitlin's call for a "Free John Henry" campaign yields a response both gratifying and curious. The chat room Diggers are happy to spread the word but Xan's friends reply with a wink and nod. This despite the famous archival news clip at the Barboro Hotel. John Henry was clean-shaven, his face grimy and obscured by hair, but it's obviously Xan. The voice alone should convince his friends. Why is it harder to believe John Henry and Xan are the same than that his percussion solo at Teddy's benefit was an act of imagination? Tijon, Denny, Izzy and Reba discount the evidence of their own eyes and ears. To them, Caitlin's proposal is an entertaining scam.

Ma&Pa: Have you considered the downside of him having to live down a legend?

BasqueGoddess: It's better than torture.

Poitier: Dam str8.

Wraith: u no he may b a judas rat?

BasqueGoddess: What????

Wraith: have a loc8r implant. judas rats xpose friends 2 black meanies

BasqueGoddess: OMFG!

Ma&Pa: Meanies won't decide that based on who we say he is.

Poitier: Never underestimate Massa's sick mind.

Wraith: i say go 4 it. bet yr man does 2

Poitier: Me 3. BG?

BasqueGoddess: We have to get him free.

Ma&Pa: Okay. So, the online petition drive begins Monday?

BasqueGoddess: Yes, before New Year's.

Ma&Pa: We'll handle posters. Maybe somebody will retitle the music video to demand his release? Wouldn't that be a great touch? The media frenzy could be fun. Happy holidays from Ma and me.

Poitier: If Sandy Claws has his act together, gr8 things bound 2 happen. Glad ur back in the fight, sister. The Palomar package is killer. Bobo the clown is in 4 a shit storm.

diminished in her eyes

I'm so sorry," Caitlin says. "Christmas with Leilani must have been a bummer."

"I've had better," Wally admits. He's speaking from his car in the half-empty OstarFX lot. It's been dark for hours. Minutes ago closed circuit cameras watched him egress the building and get into the Lexus. They'll soon observe him leave the car, re-enter corporate headquarters and return to his office. The cameras won't see that that's where he stores the new burner phone. On the whole, OstarFX security measures do him a favor. Mobile communications in the vicinity of the building aren't handled by commercial towers. It's safer to place multiple calls from this single, convenient location.

He doesn't tell Caitlin that self-judgment is more galling than a disloyal wife. How does a man who deals in conspiracies for a living fail to comprehend that his openly leftist daughter is a Digger? That Leilani's an ISA plant tasked to spy on him? A competent security expert doesn't. This incompetent one marinates, very privately, in his own bitter juices and skulks to his car for phone calls.

The modified Chinese worm he sent Bobo for Christmas is in place and undetected. But the plan for ongoing access to Bobo's computer network has hit a bump. Another hacker, one with Digger ties, exploited a default password in the Palomar subsystem to steal internal documents. The company's systems analysts are in crisis mode. Bobo's entire global network, RL&H Group, is under review. Enhanced monitoring protocols have boosted sensitivity to nonstandard activity patterns.

While Wally's worm is unlikely to be discovered, communications with the network are potentially more vulnerable. He should be separated from RL&H by several intermediate shells of international servers. The relay server selected at each layer should randomly choose its successor in the adjacent shell, send the packet, then forget what happened. Any attempt to trace a message to its source would, in essence, have to precisely recreate a path through a digital onion in which layers of forgetful servers rotate independently relative to each other. High quality onion router setups are costly, time-consuming and a prerequisite for durable success in the big leagues. OstarFX routinely employs them. While Wally's messages are strongly encrypted, his jerry-rigged routing system more closely resembles layers of disposable gloves than whirling shells of onion skin. From a countermeasures perspective, each packet he sends or receives is a data point in an uncomfortably small puzzle.

Taken together with his personal failures, the bad luck of the RL&H security upgrade has Wally second-guessing himself. Here he sits, receiving condolences from the daughter his naïveté allowed to wander unchecked into radicalism. They both know he's diminished in her eyes. Should he confess that he's slipping? He's beginning to understand why his own aging parents prefer not to discuss infirmities. The omission conserves dignity.

"I see Palomar's under the media gun," he tells Caitlin. "Please, be careful. Leaks of proprietary information are punishable under the Espionage Act." Curiously, to date, the Justice Department, normally a vocal attack dog in such matters, has been silent. Palomar's terse, written statement of compliance with relevant laws stands alone, a state of affairs the leftist press interprets as a green light to hype the allegations of pollution and cover-up.

"Isn't it wonderful we're finally being taken seriously?"

Did she hear what I said? Does she care?

"Dad, it's so strange, you and I talking politics, but also good. I hope it's the same for you. If you're willing, I thought of something you can do for Xan."

"What might that be?"

"You said ISA has to decide he's more useful out of jail?"

"Go on."

"There's a campaign to free John Henry."

"Oh?"

The PR offensive Caitlin outlines is a blend of emotional and moral appeals, standard populist crap. But ISA *might* be convinced that the reappearance of a sponger demigod would draw adoring activists into the open. She doesn't mention how she'll neutralize that risk to her associates.

"Do you have access to the Total Awareness Matrix?" she asks.

She's inviting me to be a Digger agent? "Sweetie…"

"Hear me out. I can't prove to certain people that Xan lived in Memphis during the quake. You could."

"Even if it were true, I can't reveal classified information."

"No need to. If an ISA informant sees it and passes it on, mission accomplished."

Wally perks up in the driver's seat. "A note on a desk?"

"Perfect."

She's throwing her old man a life preserver? Yes, sweetie, a thousand times yes. Nothing would give me greater pleasure than giving Mrs. Schmidt an opportunity to earn her keep.

new year's eve

Leilani sweeps into Wally's home office in a backless gown. It's black, slinky, studded with sequins complementing the diamonds in her ears and around her neck. The wife of Lieutenant General So and So is throwing a New Year's Eve party. He's away on a tour of various hotspots and Mrs. Lieutenant General is lonely. Leilani's sympathy goes only so far though. She's taking no prisoners in the competition for best dressed socialite.

"Before we go," she says, "we ought to call Caitlin and wish her Happy New Year. Why aren't you dressed?"

"I'm working," he says, "not going out tonight. Enjoy yourself." He's reviewing his first and, so far, only harvest of files from the RL&H Group network. He'd hoped to finish days ago but business intervened. *Damned Latin Americans; why do they insist on electing hard-ons like Chagas?* He's nostalgic for the good old days when profits from South American commodity exports took the first boat north. With that money staying at home, members of the *Alianza Bolivariana*, as the socialist presidents term their anti-American cabal, can afford to staff critical digital infrastructure positions with technical talent from South Asia and the Far East. It's an ongoing battle for Wally's people to maintain OstarFX's hidden presence on the levers of those economies. He's been ensuring that the United States stands ready, as the elevator blabbermouth claimed, to turn off some lights.

"Nonsense," Leilani says. "All you do is work. Shut that down and get dressed."

Wally looks up from his monitor. "The world doesn't stop for parties."

"You have people under you to do whatever it is that's so important."

"Leilani, don't nag. Go on. Enjoy yourself."

"You haven't said how you like my dress."

"It's fine. Now please…"

Her cheeks color. She's half-past irritated, steaming toward pissed. She leans across the desk, hands on hips. "If you insist on being a party pooper, let's at least call Caitlin before *she* goes out for the evening."

Wally doesn't merely hate his wife; he loathes her. For a second she's blotted out by a red flash. The occurrence of this cliché in real life startles him. He rubs his eyes. "I don't call her. She calls me."

"This really is too much," Leilani snaps. "You bend over backwards for her and her violent boyfriend and she lies to your face. I saw the note on your desk. You can't spare time for me but have plenty to waste on him? Who cares where he lived years ago? Today he's where he belongs. What did I tell you months ago? His name *is* Alexander."

"Leilani, go before you say anything else you'll regret. Stay out as long as you want."

Like Alexander Dawson Hicks, who paid rent in Memphis during the months preceding the earthquake, Leilani is a percussionist. The doors she slams are music to Wally's ears. If she's as good at her day job, ISA is aware that the John Henry scenario passes a preliminary sniff test.

But he sets that question aside to concentrate on the RL&H files. Bobo is concerned, first and foremost, with return on investment.

He has no patience for executives who excuse underperforming results with tales of production glitches, labor issues or research and development delays. He's as crudely spoken in writing as in person. But for a translator's purposefully inaccurate rendering of a diatribe against a Bangladeshi official, an advisor there warns, the Honorable Huskins might be subject to an Islamic death sentence. Bobo's reply? "Remind me to throw you a bone for Ramadan. We can't have a fatwah screwing our pooches in Chittagong."

The Southern Mountain Alliance folder Wally copied from Bobo's personal directory is replete with huckster pragmatism and snake oil pitches, little else. Sent Messages to Administrator Hufnagel and others in the Calhoun/Lumet County power structure applaud the stern approach to anti-Palomar "terrorists." The insensitivity to environmental health concerns expressed in those messages would have been pay dirt if the most egregious examples weren't already posted online, courtesy of the other Palomar hacker.

On the chance that media interest surrounding those leaks stirred the pot, Wally takes a second dip into the RL&H Group network. A new message from the Director of Systems Analysis assures Bobo that network vulnerabilities have been corrected. Wally's glad of it. The Chief Financial Officer has prepared an annotated spreadsheet of past campaign contributions and results—with a General Election on the horizon and the Presidency up for grabs, Bobo is evidently ready to consider investment options for the upcoming cycle. It's an impressive list of beneficiaries and sums. According to the annotations, chairmen and ranking minority members of relevant Congressional committees are Palomar allies in the DoD contract dispute. Bribery or commonality of interest? Either way, the paid help won't buck his wishes unless he jeopardizes their places at a larger money trough. *But what if he does? Why not?*

Wally's worm affords him an opportunity to impersonate Bobo online. He can threaten politicians who don't redouble efforts on Palomar's behalf. Given Bobo's personality, who'd doubt the authenticity of such messages? The RL&H network will store them as though they originated with him. Short of being dead in front of witnesses when the emails are sent, he'll be hard pressed to prove the vitriol isn't his.

The challenge of imitating him in print is simpler than Wally could have hoped. Bobo has contacted several movers and shakers recently, including those Wally seeks to spook. His writing style tutorial begins with a complaint Bobo sent to the private address of the Chairman of the Senate Armed Services Committee.

Joe,

I realize you people don't celebrate Christmas but I hope you had a good one anyway. Say, you have a lot going on and everything but you must have heard THE PALOMAR CONTRACT EXTENTION IS STILL HANGING FIRE. My people have been talking to your people or they say they have for more than a year. I can't see how it's done a bit of good. That beaner Procurement saddled us with doesn't have the sense God gave a tamale. You probly missed it but Mendoza's waving bad press in our face from a bunch of tree hugger commies. One of them damn near cut the gizzard out of my man. Would have done it too if he didn't have his buddies along to blow the cunt's head off. They were defending my private property at Palomar. You helped us get the Secure Defense Industry designation for it. So where's MY security? Sure as hell not on the ground where it needs to be. Not in the goddamned Pentagon. And what does Josh get for his troubles besides a hundred stitches and having to hold his guts in on the way to the hospital? I'll tell you. The police on his ass.

This harassment must stop, here and now. I've been

good to you. You said so yourself. I'm ready to be good again in the 5 figures range for starters but you have to damn well do your job. Elections are ugly. Don't make me look elsewhere. I NEED TO HEAR WHAT YOU'RE DOING FOR ME. Phone is alright if you prefer.
Respectfully,

The incorrect spelling of probably is consistent throughout the collection of cut-and-paste variations Bobo fired off to other minions on K Street and Capitol Hill. Wally's scheme is redundant. More remarkable still, the Chair of the House Defense Appropriations Subcommittee replied.

Dear Bobo,

Thank you so much for your holiday greeting. The Lord bless and keep you and yours during this Holy season. My prayers go out to your injured man. I've been apprised of the headwind you're coping with and am doing all in my power to assist. If it takes a special appropriation, so be it.

My best to Lucy,

Terry
Congressman Terrence L. Jakkola
Proudly serving Minnesota's 9th District

Bobo has beaten him to the punch with legitimate fire and brimstone threats. How many other recipients are as servile as Congressman Jakkola? Wally will check back in a few days to see. Absent evidence of rebellion in officialdom he'll, indirectly, pass the donation spreadsheet and incriminating emails to the media. Unless Caitlin's security consciousness has drastically increased she'll have given her new address to Digger friends. Who can say who *they* gave it to? He can anonymously FedEx a flash drive to her from Atlanta while he's in town for classified interagency briefings next week. Apart from fellow attendees representing DoD, State and the uniformed services, nobody outside OstarFX will know he was in Georgia.

limbo

Caitlin is far away, scarcely louder than a whisper. "Xan, is that you? I need help. Where are you?"

At the moment, he can't say. He's too groggy to move. Has a fierce pain in the belly.

"You gut-shot, white meat?" Lightning asks. "It a sorry way to go if you is."

The shock belt prevents Xan from touching where it hurts. He hears the warning tone. Lights flicker. He flings his arms from the belt, barks his knuckles on a wall.

He can't dislodge the Texan from his ear. "Gentlemen, allow me to introduce the great John Henry. Doesn't look like much, does he? Nothing like the people's hero you'd imagine."

The bean slot squeaks open. It's a struggle to sit up but the consequences for failing to do so are pitiless. The ration cake waits on its toilet paper napkin. Beside it a tiny cup containing a speckled capsule, white tablet and football-shaped horse pill. He's seen them before, or thinks he has. Perhaps he dreamed it. Caitlin's voice is a bad dream. He can't find her. Only sledgehammer on bone. He collects the food and pill cup from the bean slot, slides along the steel bench toward the sink and toilet. *Wasn't there an exercise yard?* The rear of the cell is solid concrete. He empties the cup into his mouth, bends for water. The white pill falls from between his teeth and washes down the drain. He quickly cups his hand under the tepid stream, drinks. The cell didn't see what happened. He bites into the cake, drinks again.

He and Mr. Schmidt stand on a rocky mountaintop. Wally shakes a stick at him, sounding like the Texan. "This is the greatest country in the world. The greatest there's ever been. What are you, an anarchist? Communist? Digger?"

Police insist on inspecting the theater. One carries a camera. Another orders Caitlin to hand over her keys.

Xan volunteers to show the cops around.

"We'll start in the backstage areas," a blue shirt says.

"That's not where the damage is."

The cop points to the janitorial closet. "Open it."

"You want to see cleaning supplies?"

"Show me."

It's a blessing Mari went home. She'd punch a cop for less. But the Texan says she didn't go home. She's dead.

"They runnin' a shazam on you," Lightning warns.

The blue shirt rummages through the closet. His buddy films the sink, shelves, the mop bucket.

"What are you, an anarchist? Communist? Digger?"

"It's a capitalist mop, officer. I swear to you. From our last show. My girlfriend danced with it."

"We'll be the judge of that. What's this room here?"

"Wardrobe." Xan pushes the door open, stands aside.

The camera cop peeks in. "Get a load of this," he laughs. "Grade school chicken outfits. Sums things up pretty well, I'd say."

"Xan, is that you? I need help. Where are you?"

immunity

It's an Arctic blast of a lunch hour in the parking lot alongside the smoked glass cube of OstarFX headquarters. The Director of Human Resources, head turtled between his shoulders, quick-steps by. Wally has the Lexus idling, the seat heater adjusted. He may as well be physically comfortable during illegal phone conversations.

"How could I trust the government to keep its word?" Caitlin asks.

He has just informed her that, according to Barb DeShazer, the U.S. Attorney based in Charlotte is prepared to discuss federal immunity if Caitlin will testify against Mari's killers before a secret grand jury and any follow-up proceedings.

"Barb's friendly with the prosecutor. He has an honest reputation and she's willing to represent you in the negotiations. You could ask Adam's opinion too."

"They'd have to release Xan first."

"Give it a shot, why not? You'll also be interested in what else she said. Murder is a state crime. To prosecute this case the feds would have to dust off an obscure fifty-year-old law from the failed civil rights push of the 1960s and claim that killing Mari violated her civil rights. That's almost unheard of. Second, grand juries for Western North Carolina are normally convened in Calhoun, not Charlotte. Barb thinks the unusual venue and different U.S. Attorney could signal more than an attempt to limit Bobo's ability to protect Josh Rice. Rice looks to her like a small fish."

"Murder is small fish?"

"Potentially, yes. The feds don't ride to the rescue just because a state refuses to pursue a criminal charge. Justice may think it can get Rice to rat on his boss. Bringing Bobo down would be a very big deal."

"He's been poisoning people for years."

"If Barb's right, Justice will play nice with you. Prosecutorial failure anywhere along the line would mean heads in high places roll; Bobo would see to it. She thinks Justice will telegraph its hand during immunity negotiations. If they're after him they won't require you to inform on friends."

"I wouldn't do that."

"Talk it over with her. Forget the celebrity reputation. She's sharp and well-connected. What else is new up your way?"

"Not sure. I received an anonymous package. Nobody but you, Mom and a computer friend should have my address. That's worrying."

"Did you open it?"

"It's fabulous information if the contents are genuine and the source is on our side." She pauses for a response Wally doesn't provide. "But how can I be sure I'm not walking into an ISA trap?"

Wally cringes in his seat. "You wouldn't be the first, sweetie. But ask yourself what ISA purpose is served. If there's no good answer, I'd take my chances and go with it."

The hypocritical aspect of hiring a notorious titan attorney almost prevented Caitlin from accepting her dad's advice to consult Barb DeShazer. Now she's very glad she did. Barb's voice isn't at all motherly—it reminds her of Mrs. Jaeger, a fearsome soccer coach from middle school—but the sheltering aura it projects is a match for Maeve's. Negotiations with the U.S. Attorney are underway and Barb's optimistic. She's also great with the media. Her office organized an afternoon of interviews at a location that won't be disclosed to reporters until the last minute. She and an assistant are up from Charlotte to oversee the event.

It doesn't seem possible that Barb's ancient, slender frame can withstand the pace she demands of it. This morning has been non-stop interview preparation in the motel room they'll use. There's to be no mention of Bobo Huskins or any new detail on the killers. Caitlin isn't to discuss legal proceedings or impugn ISA while Xan remains incarcerated. "Deflect questions on organized political resistance. The campaign against Palomar was a spontaneous community development. Period."

That's sort of true.

"We screened out reporters with obvious political agendas but expect awkward questions. Consider this afternoon as a deposition. Anything you say can be used against you. The opposition will study every word; count on it."

"But I want sympathetic reporters."

"They're the most dangerous. You might lower your guard."

Barb takes her through a list of possible questions. They craft safe answers. When Caitlin has them firmly in mind her attention shifts to production values. "Camera operators will want better lighting than a window and table lamps. What can we do for them?"

"Honey," Barb croaks, "we're not peddling your latest film. Today you're playing a wife who needs her loving husband. Unflattering shadows are your friend. And pull your hair back. We want the girl next door, not a magazine cover."

TV media have twenty-minute, one-on-one time slots, no extensions. First up is a former war correspondent interested in a survivor's account of Mari's murder. Caitlin's ready for him. Barb doesn't intervene until he compares Bobo Huskins' power to that of a tribal warlord and asks Caitlin to agree.

The second and third reporters take a human interest approach. How is Caitlin coping? Is Xan really John Henry? When she says yes, they move on to questions of love and longing.

Fourth in line is Francine Henry, who passes for the investigative journalist at NewsStooge. Caitlin supposes she should be honored that the station ponied up for travel expenses. Francine delves into the pollution allegations and the courage it takes to fight City Hall, a refreshing but dicey line of questions Barb warned about.

Caitlin describes Mari as a theater co-worker devoted to Teddy Arnold. "She felt bound to complete his work. I tried to do the same for her." Off-camera, Barb nods approval.

It was Caitlin's idea to save Sonia Crockett for the last of the televised sessions. Her primetime show has the largest audience. She's also the reporter Xan eluded at the Barboro, an embarrassing historical footnote sure to be raised. But her breezy hello doesn't give away what she'll do with it. She places two cameramen with directorial efficiency—there'll be no time wasted on reshoots for a different camera angle.

With cameras rolling she transforms herself into a girlfriend eager to catch up on the latest. Her opening questions establish context. Caitlin answers concisely. They both understand where this interview is headed and share a desire to get on with it.

"You've made the rather sensational claim that your missing fiancé is the man we knew as John Henry after the Great Memphis Quake. That it was Xan Hicks who rescued Albert Griles and his daughters from the collapsed hotel."

"When you tried to talk to him that night I was standing maybe fifteen feet away."

This is not what Sonia expected to hear but she stumbles like a pro. "You were there? Were you and he already acquainted?"

"I was a Direct Action Now volunteer. I saw him leave you and was concerned about his condition. So I chased him down. That's how we first met."

"And you kept his secret all these years?" The question drips with doubt.

Caitlin smiles. *My turn, girlfriend.* "He didn't treat me much better than you. A few blocks from the hotel he asked to borrow my windbreaker. I loaned it to him. He didn't tell me his name or where he lived. He was supposed to return the jacket but I didn't see him again until last spring, at an outdoor market in Calhoun. I thought it couldn't be. I mean, what are the odds? Later, I had to confront him before he admitted who he was."

"But why? Who runs away from heroism?"

Caitlin shrugs. "I only know Memphis gave him nightmares and that he hates it when people say, 'All is lost.' He wants nothing to do with John Henry. He didn't play 'Let Your Hammer Ring' until the band insisted at the fundraiser."

"I've watched that video. Amazing. All of you. You have a

quarter million views."

"He and Tijon were really into it. Xan's a genius percussionist. But that didn't prevent him from being disappeared for a crime he didn't commit."

Barb silently, vehemently objects to the word "disappeared."

Caitlin dials it down a notch. "He didn't do what he did in Memphis to become famous. He just believes people should help each other out of bad spots. Now he's depending on us to do the same for him."

Caitlin and Barb exit the motel by a side entrance while the last print journalist packs up under the watchful eye of Barb's assistant. The performance critique waits until they're snug in a booth at a busy neighborhood restaurant.

"Overall, you handled yourself well," Barb begins. "One major flaw: the use of radical terminology."

"I'll be careful."

"That's a must," Barb says. "Something else to consider: this afternoon you controlled interviews by expanding on answers. In court the rule for witnesses is exactly opposite. Do not elaborate. Answers should be as brief, factual and narrow as possible. Fewer words leave attorneys less to exploit."

Caitlin suggests the green Thai curry. Barb orders the beef version. Caitlin, who has strayed from vegetarianism, opts for chicken. "What about Xan?" she asks. "Are they willing to let him go?"

"The leaked Huskins documents destroy the prosecution's case. Eric's still dangling Xan but the Calhoun district attorney must be complaining as loudly as we are. He's the public face of the proceeding. Popular opinion isn't kind to prosecutors perceived as corrupt. Believe it or not the same holds true in Washington. As soon as microphones appear under the proper noses, expect your fiancé on the next bus home. Our main sticking point is the prosecutorial tradition of unlimited cooperation in return for immunity."

"I won't inform." The soup is served, coconut-scented springtime in a bowl.

"Eric's more resistant than I anticipated. Are there vulnerabilities in your past of which I'm unaware?"

"Such as?"

"Have you acted as an agent of a foreign power, participated in a kidnapping, armed robbery, bombing, peddled drugs, those sorts of things?"

"Am I the red peril?" Caitlin laughs. "Not hardly."

Barb's not satisfied. "In my circles Diggers are classed with communists, jihadists, Bolivarians and other worshippers of evil."

"That's filet of Christian child in your soup."

Barb glares from behind a portcullis of wrinkles. "Don't toy with me."

"I should confess my crimes to you?"

"If I'm to adequately represent your interests, yes, but with circumspection."

Caitlin counts the transgressions on her fingers. "Drug dealing: I supplied women with contraceptives and assisted others to access abortion services. I stenciled graffiti on the walls of oppressor institutions. I handled information illegally obtained by others. I covertly distributed fliers. That's the list. I never worked on behalf of a foreign power. My rejection of the Darwinian social model is strictly nonviolent. Violent cultures are oppressor cultures, regardless of ideology."

"Anything else?"

"No, Barb. Diggers don't carry more than their share of dread diseases or raise demons from the crypt."

"I'm to believe you're a victim of an oppressor culture?"

"Less so than most people. That's why I'm in a better position to act. The average family has all it can do to cope with day-to-day necessities. They may not accept the propaganda the free market shoves down their throats but it doesn't matter because they can't afford to resist. I admire the few people in those circumstances who are willing to put themselves on the line anyway. My friend Mari acted without the safety nets and influence available to me. The least I can do is use my privilege to support her courage. Is that an acceptable answer?"

"For court, certainly not. For me, I'll take it under advisement."

"So what's next? What should I be doing?"

"Eric is pitting your anxiety for Xan's release against your reluctance to serve as a government informant. Carefully managed publicity is your strong suit. We'll continue to exploit it but there can be no wavering or weakness. Trust me on this point. I'm a bloodthirsty Darwinian and a hell of a poker player."

loose in the free territories

In the dead of night Xan waits at a sidewalk bench, freezing. A streetlamp lights the sign in a curtained window.

ADMISSION HOURS 5PM-9PM DAILY

RING BELL FOR SERVICE

He's tired, dizzy, but he's used to that hangover from Prison World. He searches for his memory, for what happened before. Can't find either thing. He walks, tries to, staggers more like.

A bright line suddenly stripes the sidewalk. He stops, fearing to cross. Behind him a creaking noise. He's trapped.

"Hey, buddy. Did you ring?"

He turns, loses balance, catches himself. A wider puddle of brightness spills from a doorway. In it, a curly-headed man in a parka. The accent isn't Texan.

"You look shaky," the man says. "I can't offer you a bed at this hour but you could sleep in the lobby."

Xan retraces his steps, is invited into the light. It's warm. There are tables and plastic chairs. The man sets a lock, sends a shiver snicking down Xan's spine. Prison World must be close.

"No," Xan begs. "Please. I've got to go. Let me out."

"Ah," the man nods. "What if I open the bolt and set the

security chain? Nobody's trying to keep you here. If you stay, you and I will be awake for a while yet. Between the two of us we can keep the wrong people out. How's this?" The lock clicks open.

Indecision renders Xan immobile.

"Take a load off," the man says, indicating a seat at a painted table. "Like something to warm up? I can nuke you a hot drink."

Xan's mouth has been less dry since he began spitting out pills, but he's very dry now. "Water," he says. The bible on the table is ragged. He's wearing someone else's gray hoodie.

The dude brings a paper cup and clipboard. "My name's Ethan," he says. "What's yours?"

"Xan." The water burns his teeth with cold.

Ethan writes on the clipboard. "Mind if I ask a few questions? Part of the drill," he sighs. "How you feeling?"

"Shit-faced, but I don't think I'm drunk. Am I drunk?"

"Doesn't smell like it. Pills maybe?"

"I spit them down the drain." *Oh, no.* The lights don't flicker. He braces for a shock. Hesitantly fingers his stomach, is bewildered by soft flesh.

"Where is this?"

"Calhoun, North Carolina. The lobby of the Evangel Mission on Front Street. Today is Ash Wednesday, nigh on two in the morning."

"When again?"

Ethan grins, "February tenth. What's your last name, Xan?"

Voices. His arms are dead from slumping over the table, book for a pillow. This sparring sounds familiar. He heard it at the Barboro. *Am I in Memphis? It was Calhoun. A man there called me John Henry. Caitlin might be in Calhoun. She's dead. So is Lightning. What if I am too?* Deep shadows shape the darkness. He stands cautiously, his arms tingling tubes of uselessness. The legs are better, head not as swimmy. *This isn't the Barboro.* Concrete floor. Large cross on the wall. A framed picture and loaded bulletin board. Men at a table. They stop talking.

"Fellas," he asks, "where are we?"

"I'm in the Front Street Mission. Where are you?" a man laughs derisively.

Another says, "We'll have coffee and oatmeal soon."

The thought of food knots Xan's stomach. "My girlfriend's waiting for me. I think she is. I have to go."

Day breaks on the trudge down toward the river from Front Street. He passes the Harlequin Theater. Closed. No show posters in the cases. He checks a front pocket for keys. The other one. *Hallelujah*. Keys and dead cellphone. The billfold in his hip pocket contains money, a credit card and driver's license.

At the sight of Caitlin's apartment building he breaks into a bone-rattling trot. He warns himself not to be disappointed if her car's gone, but he is anyway. Their names are beside the Suite C button. He pushes it. No response. He enters his key code. The door buzzes. Up stairs and up stairs again, legs shaking, out of breath. On the third floor landing, a whiff of garbage. His key fits the lock. The Free Territories have never allowed him to get this close.

Caitlin's overturned couch rests on its cushions. Stuffing protrudes from torn upholstery. The kitchen sink is full of silverware, junk drawer contents, dry rice, beans, what might have been flour. Her philodendron in the window hangs dry and brown. The guestroom/office was looted. Laptops, printer, file drawers, all missing. The bedroom is a wreck as well. The mattress and box springs lie askew in the bedstead. More dumped drawers. Scattered clothing. Only the bedside table was spared; the reading lamp and chargers are where they belong. He connects his phone, gets a lighted screen. Tries Caitlin's number, hears an out-of-service recording. He fixes the bed and crashes fully dressed.

Her phone is still out of service in the afternoon. He changes into a shirt and pants resembling his. Way, way too big. The man in the bathroom mirror is shaggy, gaunt. His stomach hurts. Perhaps he's hungry. He goes to the kitchen, opens the fridge. This is where the rotten smell lives. Containers are fleecy with mold. He fills a trash bag. The bag bumps along the stairs with him as he sets off for the food co-op. There's a vicious canine squeak on the second-floor landing.

"Who are you and what are you doing?" Mrs. Letourneau shouts, as frightened as her dog.

"It's Xan. Sorry to scare you. Just taking out the garbage."

She drops Bitsy's leash, clutches her chest. "Oh, my lord," she gasps. "Aren't you supposed to be in jail?"

Bitsy launches at Xan's crotch. He deflects the attack. The dog bounces off the wall of the stairwell.

"Bitsy, come! This instant." The old lady fumbles with her door, disappears inside, the dog scooting between her legs. He hears a strangled yip. The door cracks open. She pulls the leash inside, shuts the door again. "I'm calling the police."

"Can you tell me where Caitlin is?"

"I'm dialing 911."

"Please, I have to know."

"She hasn't been here since they said you killed her. Go away."

"She calls me for help."

"I told you I haven't seen her. Will you please leave?"

"Wait. They *said* she was killed?"

"Later they said it was somebody else. Go away!"

Xan's ecstatic. "I told you, Lightning. I told you."

A feeble voice in the apartment asks Mabel who she's yelling at.

"That man they arrested. He escaped."

"It's me, Mr. Letourneau. Have you seen Caitlin?"

"How am *I* supposed to see her? I never leave this goddamned apartment."

Mrs. Letourneau tells him to bring the telephone.

"No need," Xan says. "I'm going."

The co-op declines his credit card. Twenty-three dollars in cash buys sausages, bread, cheese and oranges. On the way home he notices Janet's car in the theater lot. He fishes for his keys, unlocks the front door and lets himself in.

She pokes her head out of the business office. "Who is it?"

"I'm looking for Caitlin."

She rushes him, nearly knocks him over with a shrieking embrace. It's brief. She retreats, nose wrinkling. "We've been so worried. You look awful."

"Hi, Janet. Have you seen Caitlin?"

"I wish she were here. I'll never master this tax stuff."

"Is she okay?"

"According to Reba, she's in Canada."

"What? At her mom's?"

"We can call Reba and ask."

"Izzy?"

"Xan?" The line goes silent. "Xan, is that you?"

"I'm at the theater. Where's Caitlin?"

"Stay where you are. I'll be there in ten minutes."

rhythms on a flaming drum

quid pro quo

The immunity offer Barb negotiated is a thicket of legalese. As Caitlin understands it from the draft and explanatory notes her mom received by overnight mail, in return for testifying truthfully before the grand jury and any subsequent federal proceeding against those charged in connection with the violation of Mari's civil rights by homicide, the United States grants immunity from prosecution arising from said testimony and also for a list of specific offenses, including espionage, which may have been perpetrated … blah, blah, blah, blah.

The notes urge Caitlin to accept the draft as written. Barb will bring the paperwork to Toronto for signature. Then they'll fly to Charlotte together, reducing the chance of complications with Customs and Border Protection. Caitlin's grand jury appearance would be scheduled for the next day. After that she can go wherever she likes.

Though Xan isn't mentioned in the draft, Barb still thinks his freedom is imminent. Media pressure on government officials is mounting. Sonia Crockett's network is assembling a primetime special. John Henry questions chased the Attorney General from the lectern at a press briefing called to announce a Department of Justice push to limit favoritism in government contracts. A Sunday morning news show discussing British allegations of

American involvement in South American unrest digressed to ambush a member of the Senate Intelligence Committee with evidence of sizeable campaign contributions from Bobo Huskins and asked the senator to explain his ties to the influence-buying financier.

"A juicy scandal might better serve the national interest than exploring the rise of anti-Bolivarian movements. Nevertheless, distractions often develop their own momentum. We're well-positioned for Xan's release," Barb writes.

This cynical assessment could be a hundred percent accurate but the lack of a written guarantee is a deal-breaker for Caitlin. The prospect of returning to the United States worries her mom but she's trying to reconcile herself to it.

"The past pushes; the future pulls," Maeve said at the restaurant where Caitlin was being introduced to British teatime. "It doesn't take a tarot reading to grasp the direction of the forces at play."

"I won't sign unless Xan's free."

"Nor should you. It's important to feel empowered before taking an irrevocable decision."

"*Feel* empowered? That's so condescending."

"On the astral plane," Maeve said. "We can't be certain whether actions cause effects or merely precede them. Maybe what happens is always and forever what happens, like the events in a book. Maybe we're elements of a pattern vibrating in more dimensions than we're able to appreciate. But we need to *feel* as though we make a difference. And if only in the conjuries of understanding, we do. We align ourselves with the past and what lies ahead. That's a magick as vital to human wellbeing as material conditions. I'll have amulets ready for you and Xan before you go. Don't leave without them."

It's been that kind of day. One incomprehensibility after another. The task of plowing through the verbiage in the immunity document isn't high on Caitlin's list of preferred activities tonight but it has to be done. Her questions are multiplying. She welcomes the ring of the burner phone.

It's her mom again. "Your friend Reba tells me Xan's in Calhoun, asking for you. Do you have her number?"

Caitlin's heart races with a relief her mind is unready to trust. "Is she sure? Has she seen him?"

"I gather he's with them," Maeve says. "How will you contact her? Is it safe to telephone?"

"Can you call her back and say I'll meet her in PhoneBooth?"

"She has a phone booth?"

"It's complicated. I can explain later."

Reba's smiling broadly. Her greeting rises and falls like a birdcall. "He-llloo-uuuu. So good to see you, dear." The shape of her mouth jumps through the words, pauses a second time at the smile, then goes jerky again. "Xan's downstairs having a bite to eat."

"How is he?"

"Other than looking like Jean Valjean fresh from the Bagne? Izzy says he's been drugged but that should pass. Look away from your screen while Gertrude and I go downstairs."

"How's Gertrude?"

"She misses you. We all do. The collective has been such a struggle. Almost there. Xan, I have her. Here she is."

The picture stabilizes in the Stein's dining room. Xan's face careens into view. It's alarming, all bones and sunken eyes. "Caitlin?" His beautiful baritone is thready, distant.

"It's me, Xan. I'm here."

"Is it really? I found your sea charm in the mud but you keep calling me. Lightning says you're a trick to get me to talk."

"Who's Lightning?"

"He's in Prison World with me. He's dead so the Texan can't keep him out."

"I don't understand."

"I didn't want to kill him but he lost his pistol."

He's out of his head. "You're not in prison, babe, not anymore. I'll be home as soon as I can." *There'll be flights tomorrow. But if they disappear me at the airport I'll never get to him. Can ISA be that cruel? Barb warned me.*

"Where are you?"

"In Toronto, only for a few more days."

"Can I come there? In the Free Territories I can change where I am but can't stay long."

Caitlin struggles, for his sake, to contain her panic. "How do you mean?"

"I wake up in Prison World."

"You're safe now, with Reba and Izzy."

"But sooner or later I wake up."

"Baby, what did they do to you?"

"They have lights and a shock belt. I'm supposed to take pills. And there are needles, I think. I have to eat but it's hard."

"Why?"

"They kicked me in the stomach. When can I see you for real?"

"In a few days, very few."

"Our apartment is a mess. I scared Mrs. Letourneau."

"Please, Xan, this is important. Reba, Izzy, are you listening?"

She hears yesses in the background.

"Keep him away from the apartment. It'll be staked out by news crews. He's in no condition for that."

Xan says, "Why? Mrs. Letourneau said I escaped. But I didn't."

"I had to tell them about John Henry to get you released."

"You told? That's how he knew."

"Who?"

"The Texan. The guards kicked me when he found out. And the man at the Mission called me that. Did you tell him too?"

freakshow

I t's good news and bad news, Mr. Henry," the financial responsibility clerk at Urgent Care says, sliding again into her seat behind the bulletproof glass. "Mr. *Hicks*. Please forgive me. Dr. Glanville will be on duty at Southside tomorrow. No one else is authorized to see you." To reinforce the rejection of Xan's treatment application, security officers have taken positions behind his intake cubicle.

Bouncers? His hair and beard are presentable today. His head is better. This isn't the Free Territories. He knows that now. It's the real world, but different. The friends who drop by Izzy and Reba's behave strangely. Adam, the lawyer Caitlin's family hired, treats him like a war hero. Their trip to the cop shop to reclaim the van dragged on for hours. He was a freak on display. Admin could have sold tickets.

His digestion is all wrong too. It wasn't just the crap food in Prison World. Reba's a decent cook but the more he eats, the worse he hurts. He thanked Izzy for volunteering to bring him to the clinic, but there's such a thing as too much handholding.

"I'm good for the money," he tells the clerk. He has explained the cancellation of his credit card. It's not his fault he hasn't made payments since October.

"At first I thought that was it," she says. "The business office has to approve first-party payers. But they overrode the payment exclusion and still couldn't get your application to process. It's very unusual. Only federally qualified physicians are permitted to treat you. Dr. Glanville will be at Southside, tomorrow."

"Doc's a good man," the male guard behind him says.

The female officer hands Xan a sheet of health tips. One side concerns home treatment of diarrhea, the other, constipation. "We wish we could do more for you today," she says. "I'm so honored to meet you, Mr. Henry. My boys have looked up to you since forever. They'd flip over your autograph. The names are Brett and Chandler."

He signs both sides of the paper, returns it to her.

The Steins aren't surprised by the runaround. At dinner—chicken soup—Izzy asks Xan if he had medical treatment in prison.

Pills and shots, though he wasn't told what for.

"And the pain began after you were kicked? Only in the stomach?"

"No, but worst there. Probably from the shock belt."

"After dinner could you pull up your shirt and let me look?" Izzy asks. "We might get a better idea what's bothering you."

This is no weirder than anything else. Xan pushes away from the table. Gertrude raises her head from the mat in the corner. The houseguest is a reliable source of people food.

"It can wait," Izzy says.

Xan gets up, displays scrawny abs under a fat-free covering of prison pallor.

Reba says, "I'll step out."

Izzy stops her. "Won't be necessary, dear. I can see it from here."

"See what?" Xan looks down, stretches the skin this way and that, though it aggravates the cramps. A small pink scar is tucked into the fold of skin above his navel.

"New scar?" Izzy asks.

"I didn't have this."

"You may be bugged."

Reba says, "Dear god."

Xan wishes somebody would explain.

Izzy elects himself. "The Judas Rat program. ISA doesn't rely on ID chips, cellphones or ankle bracelets to covertly track former detainees. They implant GPS units. A sufficiently abused and drugged prisoner won't remember the surgery. You've heard of the python hunts in Florida? The Wildlife Service keeps a few females alive, puts trackers in them and turns them loose to attract males during breeding season. Then it's curtains for her and all her boyfriends. That may be what ISA has planned for you."

Reba objects, "Must you use such a vile analogy?"

"He needs to be aware, Reba. We all do. The 'special' doctor at Urgent Care will either tell you you're fine or diagnose appendicitis and operate if he thinks there's a malfunction with the GPS."

"I told the Texan I'm not political."

Reba says, "Some of your friends are Diggers. They're trying to learn which."

"The Texan said I'd lead him to Caitlin. She can't come here."

"Slow down," Izzy says. "They don't need you to find her. She's protected by an immunity deal. But try this on for size. If ISA believes you're John Henry, they may think Diggers will flock to you."

"The Texan said Caitlin."

Izzy chuckles, "A wise government official once told me the world is run by C students. The schemes they concoct to get ahead trip all over each other. Maybe your Texan didn't get the memo from the Justice Department."

"Caitlin can't risk it. You shouldn't either. They'll suspect you. I should leave."

Reba's voice pinches. She shakes her head. "No one is safe anywhere. If they put this … thing in you, we'll do something about it. Caitlin must be told, of course, as soon as she arrives. But don't bring it up tonight when we're on PhoneBooth with her. The grand jury testimony requires her total focus."

"In the meantime," Izzy says, "I'll contact a few people; see what we can do to establish a firm diagnosis. Would you be willing to have an X-ray? There's a vet in town with a machine accommodating animals as large as Gertrude."

shrapnel in the gut

The cinder at the lake won't loosen her grip on Xan until he's with Caitlin in the flesh. He has brought the van to Charlotte, to meet her after the grand jury. She's registered at a motor inn near the airport, the sort of anonymous rendezvous prone to shady characters. Management and the blue shirts might or might not be on friendly terms. The deskman runs a thorough ID check before issuing Xan a keycard.

Caitlin's second floor room, what's supposed to be her room, has a view of cars and asphalt. Unfamiliar women's clothes hang in the closet; others spill from an unfamiliar suitcase on a queen-size bed—unmade—the first hopeful sign of Caitlin. Next to the clock radio is a heart-shaped box of chocolates and a note. Her writing. She loves him, misses him. Don't expect her until evening. Happy late Valentine's Day.

The clock jogs his memory. He should eat, a misery dictated by hours, not hunger. Hunger's a constant. So are the cramps. The more he eats, it doesn't matter what, the worse the twisting misery. The animal hospital X-rays showed a device the size of a cigarette lighter lodged like shrapnel in his gut. The vet thinks it's caught in the membranes.

Xan rings the desk for lunch recommendations. The man hasn't heard of Xchange credits and has no idea which establishments accept them. The nearest "hippie" supermarket is miles away. Xan copies the directions, adds a line to Caitlin's note, telling her that he's here.

The grocery store doesn't accept credits, which sucks, but it has a food bar. He's placing his order when the shoplift alarm at the entrance sounds. The pulsing tone buckles him. He clutches his stomach. A store patron decides he's having a heart attack and screams, "Call 911."

"Don't!" he says. "I'm okay." He gets off the floor, apologizes for creating a scene. "Drop attacks run in my family." Where he pulled that excuse from, he can't guess.

The spectacle unnerves the server preparing his plate, who asks, "Sir, would you rather have a box to go?"

He would.

He pokes down the chicken salad in the van.

The antics of Charlotte drivers distract him from his guts and the supermarket debacle. He circles the hulking mausoleum of a courthouse where the grand jury meets. Decides against going in. Doesn't trust himself if he's groped by security. On the sidewalk around the corner, riot cops outnumber a gaggle of demonstrators whose signs accuse the United States of causing public service outages in Brazil and Venezuela. He continues west until he finds a convenience store that sells gas priced for locals. Cash is in short supply.

The worst of the stomachache is over as he closes the curtains in Caitlin's room. He relaxes to the hum of highway traffic. Takes Izzy's advice about calming breaths. Takes a nap.

"Xan!"

He swings and misses at the weight diving into bed with him.

"Baby, don't hit. It's me."

Caitlin's voice. The weight smothers his punching power. He opens his eyes, rolls onto the floor, onto his feet. It *is* her.

Mortified with himself, he sits on the bed, at a distance, giving her space. She's scared. Her next approach is gradual, the touch on his shoulder tender. He wraps his arms around her, imprinting her, every square inch, every tremor, the smell of her hair, the wetness where she nestles against his neck. Together, they lie down.

"What have they done to you?" she whispers.

His head clogs with a snarl of moments too immense to fit through his mouth. If there's a tag end, an answer that might unravel, he can't find it. He could as easily reach down his throat and jerk out the tracking device.

"They bugged me," he says at last. "There's a GPS in my stomach." He shows her the scar. "I'm being watched. It's why I can't eat. People should stay away."

This is the first she's heard of the tracker. But, like the Steins, she seems less surprised than resigned. She touches the place with her finger. Tears course down her cheeks.

"Gertrude's vet found it on an x-ray. He thinks it can be removed."

She wipes her face, motions for a Kleenex from the bedside table. "Dr. Wachowski?"

Xan passes her the box. "Yeah, the vet from your birthday party. Since when do they have hi-tech operating rooms?"

She blows her nose. "His practice is special. Women in trouble have gone to him for years. Did he say he'd do the surgery? I'll pay him anything."

"He said he'd consider it. If things go wrong, don't blame him."

"No." She slaps the bedspread. "I'm not hearing that. Don't say such things."

Beautiful sentiments. Sweet and thin as air.

"My attorney has good news for you on the financial end. We'll see her tomorrow, before going home."

rhythms on a flaming drum

The society lawyer's paralegal asks Xan if he'd like to rub a pair of brass tennis balls for luck. He can't believe it. Caitlin and the lawyer want him to do press interviews, especially with the cable lady he ducked in Memphis. Sonia Crockett proposes to stage a live reunion show with the Griles family. There's money in it. The attorney says there'll be more, possibly a lot more, if he sells the rights to his story—she's not an agent but has friends who are. She advises him to build a brand while he's hot.

"Take the money, white meat," Lightning cackles, out of the women's hearing. "The gravy train don't come around too often."

"Of course we don't *have* to," Caitlin says. "I don't like it either, but without the press you'd still be in that hell hole."

"So we let them exploit us?"

"We're exploiting *them*," she says. "John Henry shows it's still possible for regular people to look out for one other. The free market will pay us to undermine its brainwashing."

Barb, the wicked queen in the business suit, grinds out words like a pepper mill. "If money offends you, give it to charity. Use it to pay my fee."

"Or medical expenses," Caitlin suggests, "to rebuild your strength."

Barb says, "That is top priority. People identify with heroes, not victims of the prison system. You'll require a competent makeup artist. I can arrange it."

"Not necessary," Caitlin says. "We're in the theater."

He's on the verge of walking out when Lightning stops him. "Chill, man. Everybody turn a trick now and again. Hold it back about you and me though. Don't tell that. Our business not they business."

"If you agree to an exclusive with Sonia," Caitlin says, "you wouldn't have to talk to the others until we're old news. Most of them will leave us alone."

"An exclusive pays better as well," Barb says.

The deck is stacked. All is lost, but when hasn't it been? He hangs his head. "How soon?"

Caitlin strokes his hand. "You won't regret it." She squeezes his fingers. "We'll be fine. I promise."

damned hackers

Cyber-operations in Brazil, Venezuela, Argentina and Chile are proceeding on schedule; the OstarFX Whirlwind G-3 toolkit has crashed enemy command and control systems, blacked-out strategic power grids and rendered telecommunications networks selectively inoperative. Inevitably, bumps on the road to regime change are cropping up. Accusations of U.S. responsibility for the digital sabotage were factored into the offensive equation, but State Department cheerleading for the accompanying military uprisings lends these rumors undue credence. More troublesome for OstarFX are British and German press reports that European intelligence services obtained malware code implicated in the disruptions of service. If true, Wally's baby has been compromised.

At this stage he has little definite to report to Hank Lundstrom other than the fact that Whirlwind remains operational throughout the theater of battle. Press accounts might be inaccurate. Perhaps a network analyst sniffed out a module of encrypted code but failed to realize that Whirlwind automatically reinstalls on repaired or replaced equipment. An intentional security breach hasn't been ruled out either; coordinated action on a continental scale involved a cadre of middlemen with partial awareness of the toolkit. In any event, Wally's confident that the source of any actual fault, whether in code or personnel, will be exposed.

"Put your best talent on it," Hank says. "God, I hate this. We'll have alphabet agencies all over us."

As protective as Wally is of his people and his code—Whirlwind is a cyber-warrior's wet dream—that's not the only thing on his mind today. He's been debating what to tell Hank about Leilani. The alphabet agency remark settles the question. "May I speak freely?"

The stilted formality catches Hank off guard. "Proceed."

"Remember that situation with Caitlin? She's home now, out of the woods as best we can determine. Her boyfriend's been released too, not in the best of shape from what I understand, but out. These facts are likely to surface in security reviews."

"That's manageable," Hank says. "I hear ISA is investigating defense contracts and hazardous waste discharges down there. It seems your daughter may have performed a valuable public service."

Where doesn't he have an ear?

Hank continues, "I won't be surprised if Bobo Huskins buttonholes you for advice on network security. Hackers keep depantsing him for the news media. Excellent advertising for us. Marketing reports a significant uptick in inquiries from public and private officials."

"Damned hackers," Wally says. "Bobo probably won't bother with me. He likes to go straight to the top."

"He'll find OstarFX willing to listen."

Wally takes a deep breath. "As the Caitlin thing unfolded, I uncovered another issue. I strongly suspect that my wife's an ISA informant and that I'm a target for her and her handlers."

The story of the prepaid phone has Hank's full attention. "Was there prior knowledge or any financial connection to Caitlin's political activities? Did you assist her in any manner to leave the country?"

"No, but I've lain awake asking myself how I could have been so oblivious."

"Is Leilani aware of your suspicions?"

"Not yet. But I haven't conducted sensitive business at home since December."

"I should have been informed." *ISA hasn't told you? Really?*

"Until the complication with the toolkit, I judged her to be a private problem."

"Ugly situation." Hank's expression is grim. "You and I have been through a lot together, Wally. I've never doubted your commitment to OstarFX. Give me an honest answer; are you up to the task of the internal reviews?"

"Absolutely. I planned to confront her after the active phase concludes in South America. But it may be better to get it over with."

"That would be prudent. And Caitlin?"

"We've normalized channels of communication. She and her boyfriend are staying at the Laurel Ridge house until media interest abates."

"Quite a story about the boyfriend," Hank says. "Is it true?"

"She believes it."

"They're teasing a TV special on him. My wife and grandson are dying of curiosity. What's he like as a man?"

"Not my idea of a folk legend. If he's a fraud, tomorrow night should tell the tale. The rescued family is scheduled to appear."

rhythms on a flaming drum

give it to the lord

Since taking refuge in Laurel Ridge, Xan's lying low. Caitlin, who has retrieved clothes and other belongings from their apartment, says Mrs. Letourneau and Bitsy are also in hiding from reporters and gawkers. The gated privacy of titan villages has advantages. No press allowed. It's a closely held secret that the interview for *In the Know with Sonia Crockett* is set for the Harlequin Theater. Xan and Caitlin slip through the media gauntlet outside the gatehouse in the back seat of Reba's car.

Sonia's plastic personality hasn't changed. She claims to envy Xan's low weight; says the camera adds pounds. He mumbles false regrets for his behavior at the Barboro. She tells him to save it for the show. "Can you raise your energy level? You're John Henry for Pete's sake."

Albert Griles arrives while Xan, Reba and a cameraman are sorting out the stage lights. Albert's balder, gray at the temples, wearing a suit and tie. Xan recalls the bear hug in the hotel laundry, braces for another. But as they make eye contact, Albert's joyful expression fades.

"John," he says, shaking Xan's hand. "I'm blessed to see you again. Shawna and La-trice send their love. We were hoping they could tell you in person. You should hear them sing your song.

Lord a mercy."

"Great to see you too. But call me Xan. I only played John Henry on TV."

Albert apologizes profusely. He's been practicing and still messed up.

Xan forgives him; "I've been called worse. Sorry your girls aren't here. I was looking forward to them." He notices a cameraman recording the conversation and says under his breath, "We're being filmed."

"Hmm," rumbles Albert.

"Come meet my girlfriend. The TV crew brought snacks and drinks. We'll get you some."

The big man declines, watching his weight. Cameras don't follow them into makeup, where Sonia and Caitlin are doing their faces and hair. Introductions complete, Sonia tells Albert the network did its best to arrange furloughs for his daughters.

"Training school administrators can be so frustrating," she says. "Give Caitlin and me another ten minutes. Then we'll do you." Albert's not wild about makeup. "Just a little powder," he's told.

Xan takes Albert into the property room, clears the bird outfits from a couple of chairs. "What's this training school stuff?"

Albert remains standing. "They took them and I can't seem to get them out." His huge frame sags like melting wax.

"What happened?"

"A gangster kid tried to mess with Shawna and the police wouldn't do anything. My wife wasn't thinking. She saw the boy at a fast food. Caught him in the restroom, cracked his skull against the wall and cut off his business before he came to. She's hot like that sometimes. The judge gave her fifty-four months. Children's Services say I'm unfit because my babies aren't under proper supervision when I work."

The parent's nightmare.

"I go around to the places to prove I'm responsible. Me and my pastor started a ministry for black folk on work release. We arrange places to stay, jobs when there are any. We counsel the men to trust Jesus. I have to do that too." He reaches into his coat, pulls out a studio portrait. "I brought a picture of Shawna and La-trice. Want to see? They came out of that hotel like Daniel from the lion's den. Thought they had the world by the tail."

The twins might be a couple of years older, all smiles and Sunday clothes, beaded cornrows. "Beautiful young ladies, Albert. Let's get this on the show. Publicity worked for me. Maybe it will for them."

"We'd appreciate that," he says. "But John, I can tell you've been treated rough. Did they keep you in the hole?"

"I suppose."

"Thought so. They turn loose of a man's body but the evil stays locked up in him. Give it to the Lord before it eats your soul. You led me from the darkness one time. Let Jesus and the hammer of faith lead *you*."

"It's only a stomach problem."

"Would it be all right if I pray for you?"

"If you want to."

Albert drops to his knees. "Will you join me?" He's done this before. The cadences roll from him. Xan can almost hear the amens from the church choir. He feels like drumming, claps hands on the floor. Albert sings a verse of "Let Your Hammer Ring." *Who has the right if not this man?* They're at the hammer again, the two of them, making chips fly.

The door swings open. Sonia whispers to Caitlin, "Just like Memphis."

"Clap for the Lord," Albert instructs them. "Respect His presence. There's a healing going on."

Sonia's fretting the schedule. "Can't it wait? A-block is live in twenty. We need to get that shine off you."

rhythms on a flaming drum

in the know

Wally's development team has tweaked and fiddled and patched Whirlwind on the fly, extending toolkit capabilities in the heat of battle. This success, in spite of an exposed code module, is silencing Special Ops traditionalists. He hasn't had a full night's sleep in a week and yet, with the end of the Leilani charade in sight, he's at peace. Somewhere along the line he began to believe the mantra provoked by her betrayal. *That's not important now.* Painful feelings, yes, to be acknowledged and suffered through, but only personally relevant. Any direct display of fury would endanger him, Caitlin and OstarFX. Far better, and more self-affirming, to channel it into cold, considered, effective action.

Before the unmasking he wants Leilani to comprehend that Caitlin may be radical and occasionally rash, but in the service of honorable objectives—not to mention being family. With luck, tonight's edition of *In the Know* will demonstrate that character, shaming Leilani's sleaze by comparison. For all the sanctimonious posturing, the fact that her handler is a senior man here in Arlington implies that she's been an ISA asset all along. Her marriage vows were predicated on deceit. Nor has life together revised her loyalties. The laptop he set out to tempt her has repelled numerous login attempts while recording keystrokes and audiovisual evidence of consternation that, in another context, would have been hilarious. Having failed to achieve direct access to the laptop, she next attempted an antiquated malware attack. The cutesy viral slideshow she forwarded to his Inbox was readily traceable to her masters. Her Christmas gift to him, a bugged paperweight, sits on his desk down the hall, in position for ISA to eavesdrop on Mrs. Schmidt's undoing. But that won't be the only electronic witness, should push come to shove. He mixes two seltzers with lime. Tonight's no night for alcohol. For both their sakes he hopes she maintains her cool. He sets one of the drinks on the coffee table in front of her.

In the Know opens with the archival clip of John Henry stepping from the hotel entrance with a large colored man and two kids. Leilani's restless. She goes to pop popcorn.

Several commercials later, Sonia Crockett is live with Xan. He's hollow in the cheeks but smiling as she asks why he shunned the publicity his valor was due. He talks about discovering an injured man in the hotel and flagging down a satellite truck from Sonia's network during a futile search for assistance. The driver said he was there to cover the news, not make it. Xan returned to the victim alone and did what he could until the man died, only to have a strong aftershock block his own escape. While hunting for another he happened upon the Griles family. The four of them eventually hammered their way to safety and Sonia waiting at the hotel entrance. The flatness of the account heightens its impact.

Ms. Crockett might rather have suffered John Henry's sledgehammer than an on-air indictment of her network's callousness. "The producer told us he saw you go in; that's all," she sputters. "Why didn't you come forward sooner?"

"She's lucky he was too tired to throttle her that night," Wally observes while Leilani's mouth is full of popcorn.

"I didn't exactly volunteer to come forward now," Xan says.

Wally wags a finger at the larger-than-life image on the screen. "Now *that* sounds like Xan Hicks."

In the next segment, Albert Griles tells of being trapped in total darkness with twin eight-year-olds, the hotel crumbling around them. He was praying for the Lord to take them swiftly when he heard hammering. Xan's inability to reach them from the kitchen tried Albert's faith almost to the breaking point. For him, the flashlight rays from the laundry room were a spiritual affirmation.

"My babies were supposed to be with me tonight," he says, "but the training school has them." He reaches into his jacket.

Sonia politely cuts him off. "When we return you'll meet the woman who broke the John Henry story. Stay tuned for Caitlin Schmidt."

Wally smiles at the restlessness beside him on the couch.

Sonia's first questions for Caitlin are chummy. Then, from nowhere, "What attracts a woman of privilege to controversial political causes?"

"My resources allow me to combat human misery better than most. Take tonight. We're on your show because I'm a titan, not Shawna Griles, and because John Henry has a following. He didn't when he needed assistance in Memphis."

Sonia tries to interrupt but Caitlin steamrolls her. "Albert isn't as lucky. His daughters and thousands of other nameless kids are having their futures destroyed in training schools. But for an accident of birth they could be you and me."

"We'll be back," Sonia says, straining for composure under fire, "with the inside story of the song John Henry made famous in the Barboro Hotel."

Wally allows himself a handful of popcorn. "That poor woman can't pitch for serving up line drives at the mound."

"Maybe Caitlin hasn't heard of charity. The Southern Mountain Alliance rescues deserving children from those schools."

"I doubt Bobo's goon squad has much use for black girls."

"What 'goon squad'? You don't know that."

"It'd be a fate worse than training school."

"And what do you mean by that?"

He nods at the screen. "Show's on." This segment begins with a clip of Xan, Caitlin and the black singer performing "Let Your Hammer Ring" in the Peacock Courtyard. Wally turns to Leilani. "That afternoon at Paul's party on the roof of the Halloran? This was the noise we heard."

"You advised him to call the police."

Albert's describing for Sonia how the song developed. "We were on our last nerve. There wasn't anything for it but to pray or sing. People say a white man had no business to write that song. I tell them John didn't write it. It came through him."

A wide shot catches Xan shrinking in his chair.

This is the guy who looked me in the eye and said he'd not condemn a kid to college.

"Look at him cowering," Leilani says.

"It's called bashfulness. That happens to people who didn't expect to be lionized. I didn't believe Caitlin before, but I'm convinced. He really *was* John Henry."

"Weakness, if you ask me."

The final question of the evening goes to Xan. "Now that your secret's out, what's next for you?"

"Recuperation," he deadpans. "I've never done an hour of live TV before." Sonia laughs. "And seeing what can be done for Shawna and La-trice."

Caitlin adds, "Your network could investigate the training schools."

Sonia has to leave it there. She's out of time.

"Good job, Caitlin," Wally whoops as Leilani picks up the popcorn bowl. "They did well, didn't they? Let's call and congratulate them after I check messages."

"I'll be in the kitchen."

While she's occupied he activates the wireless camera an

OstarFX tech secreted in his office, stashes his phone in the desk drawer opposite the one containing the burner she discovered, and sneaks back into the family room with his tablet to scroll through texts. The agile methodology for software development doesn't recognize quitting time, particularly in war zones. Chagas's detention this morning by military units and the imposition of martial law must now be supported by the restoration of Brazil's infrastructure. A new enhancement to Whirlwind capabilities is already spinning hydroelectric plants to life there. The power grid and state communications systems should regain nominal function within hours. Wally sends kudos to his guys and gals.

When Leilani reappears he asks her, "Want another drink? I'm having one."

"No, thanks."

"Caitlin's new number is in the phone in my desk drawer. Go ahead and dial. I'll be right with you."

He counts twenty and follows her down the hall. She's at his desk, staring at the burner phone. "This is the disconnected number."

"How'd you find *that*? Mine's in the other drawer."

"You said look in the desk. I did and there it was."

"You saw it inside the printer cartridge box? What makes you think the number's out of service?"

"The automated attendant."

"I didn't give you time for that. I may be a fool, darling, but I'm not clueless. You've used that phone before." The statement is uttered with unemotional certainty. He's pleased with himself.

At first she says nothing. Then her jaw hardens. "I needed her address."

"Not for Christmas. Your boss's number didn't quite get erased."

She slams the phone on the desk, breaking the case.

"That won't damage the SIM card," he tells her. "The data has also been copied. Hank is aware of it, also of your attempts to hack an OstarFX computer. The evidence we've collected is irrefutable."

"I don't have to listen to this." She starts around the desk toward him. He circles too, keeping wood between them, retrieving his regular phone from its drawer.

"No, you don't have to listen," he says. "But you might want to. Techs will be here shortly to sweep for surveillance toys. If there are any ISA isn't prepared to lose, collect them now."

She stops. "You're out of your mind."

"If that's how you want to play it."

"You'll regret this." She snatches the paperweight from the desk.

"I've been regretting it for months." *And now it's your turn, bitch.*

She knocks the rigged laptop to the floor and swings the paperweight at him.

"It won't help, Leilani. There are other recording devices in this room." That's small comfort at the moment. Her youth and talents in martial arts are likely to put him on the short end of any physical altercation. He needs to maintain focus, stay on his toes. There'll be time to admire his performance later.

"I'll report you to 911. This is wife abuse."

"That's not what your paperweight and my devices are picking up. Face it; your cover is blown. You're being offered an opportunity to cut your losses. Think carefully." He speaks her ISA contact number into his phone. "Will your handler answer directly or is there an authorization procedure?"

"Go to hell."

A synthetic voice instructs Wally to identify himself. He does. The voice tells him he's not recognized and disconnects.

"Maybe your 911 idea was better," he says. "Leave now or I'll dial it myself."

While she rages through the house he shuts and locks the office door, stores the broken laptop and phone in his safe and sits tight under the watchful eye of a surveillance camera uploading to an OstarFX cloud. He prays she doesn't break through the door with a weapon and send him to join the data there. For once, he wishes he owned a pistol.

It's not the doorknob that finally moves. The home defense display changes to report an open garage door. He peeks around the window curtain. She's backing her car out of the drive. He watches her speed away. Before bed, and the dreamless sleep of the satisfied, he changes alarm codes. He'll have a locksmith out first thing tomorrow. There are also bank accounts and credit cards to contend with. *Marriage is such a pain in the ass.* He wonders if Barb is licensed in Virginia.

rhythms on a flaming drum

dr. wachowski

Simple as that? Huskins pulls the plug and walks away? The announcement that Palomar is shutting down doesn't bring the sense of triumph Caitlin imagined. Nor is there a sense of vindication in her dad's marital separation. She wishes she had the emotional reserves to be there for him but she's stretched too thin. The Memphis Interfaith Council may relieve her of responsibility for organizing around Shawna and La-trice Griles; that hand-off can't occur soon enough. Xan's in a tailspin. His nightmares make it dangerous to sleep together; she has the bruises to prove it. He's seeing Izzy for post-traumatic stress but remains as obsessed with his feeling of violation as a rape victim impregnated by her attacker.

He'd probably try to cut the GPS out himself if not for Dr. Wachowski. Caitlin's experience as a support person for women in need gives her the utmost confidence in Wachowski's skills. His patients don't get infections and law enforcement agencies leave him alone. If it takes an operation to put Xan on the road to recovery, the vet is the man to do it.

He has a rule. Human clients must be accompanied by a pet, establishing a plausible rationale for the appointment. Caitlin shanghais Gertrude for the role. The big galumph is delighted to go for a ride, less so to discover where it ends. Sweet talk doesn't convince her to jump down from the van. Xan has to push from behind to dislodge her.

A basset hound with a shaved leg and Elizabethan collar alerts everyone in the lobby to the arrival of the monstrous new beast. The lady with the pet pig calms it with a forehead rub. Whatever's in the animal carrier stays quiet, out of sight. Gertrude responds to the receptionist's personal greeting with the vaguest of wags and sprawls immovably at the earliest opportunity.

Caitlin's surprised that the dog obeys when they're called to the treatment area. Wachowski welcomes them into his office with the grandfatherly manner that rapidly wins the trust of his patients—the freshly-ironed lab coat is a touch reserved for the two-legged variety. He congratulates Caitlin on the Palomar closure. "I hadn't heard of your interest in water pollution. Is there a worthy cause you're *not* involved with? Please folks, have seats."

Gertrude isn't listening. "Sit," Caitlin tells her. "Good girl."

Three pairs of eyes regard the doctor across the desk. He pulls up a digital image of Xan's X-rays. The bug is rectangular, the size of a tube of lipstick, with a dense object and wispy threads inside. Wachowski says, "One end may be attached to the abdominal wall. See how it projects at a right angle? If tonight's films show the same position, local anesthetic and light IV sedation should be sufficient."

He reviews the post-operative plan. Xan will protect the anonymity of the visiting wound-care nurse by boarding with the Steins. He's to wear the GPS around the clock for a minimum of a month before disposing of it, bearing in mind that any physical separation between him and the signal is bound to be detected. The consequences of discovery could be extreme and widespread.

"This procedure is expensive; I don't apologize for that," Wachowski says. "But *no* surgical fee is worth the risk to me, my family or the practice. I wouldn't touch this case if the two of you weren't who you are. You understand what it means to put yourselves on the line. Consider this my thanks for your community service."

"I'm grateful to you," Xan says.

"In the event of complications, antibiotics can be arranged. Pain control is another matter. Do you have it covered?"

Xan produces a pill bottle. "These are left over from my hand injury."

"Do you tolerate discomfort well?"

"I used to think so."

"He'll be okay. If he needs more, we have friends."

"Good," the vet replies. "And the fee we discussed?"

The $5000 in the envelope Xan slides across the desk nearly wipes out his savings but he wouldn't allow Caitlin to pay.

Wachowski deposits the envelope in his white coat. "Well then, follow your pre-op instructions and I'll see you this evening. Gertrude, how about a treat?"

rhythms on a flaming drum

a procedure

Xan can't live with a GPS in his gut. Maybe not without it either. Dying on the operating table might be best. End of story. He insists on driving to the clinic so Caitlin won't blame herself in the event of lights out. Gertrude is again bummed by the destination. The woman who lets them in conceals her identity with a hairnet and surgical mask.

"Did you shave your abdomen?" she asks, closing the window blinds. "When did you last eat? Any allergies or sensitivities you forgot to mention?"

Satisfied with his responses, she tells Caitlin, "We can't break sterile procedure for progress reports. Expect at least an hour. Do you want to watch TV?"

Caitlin shakes her head.

The woman disappears into the treatment area, saying she'll soon fetch him for X-rays. This is when it gets real. The stitches last summer are as close as he's been to an operation. At Urgent Care, spotless housekeeping bolsters illusions of confidence for those on the public side of the façade. Here they use claw-proof chairs, linoleum and wall panels resistant to industrial strength disinfectant. *Is there an incinerator in back? Do you realize you're dying when anesthetized?*

Caitlin wears a brave face: head high, fixed smile. He shows the same, memorizes as much of her as possible.

"Hey," he says, "this guy doesn't lose patients, remember?"

Her voice wavers. "I'll try to."

"Will you be able to load me in and out the van by yourself?"

"If you're wearing an Elizabethan collar I'll send for reinforcements. Otherwise, I think I can manage."

The door to the treatment rooms swings open. He pecks her cheek. "Wish me luck."

worker bots

Stripped and strapped, arms outspread on a queasy carousel under a merciless sun. Worker bots in facemasks and lunch-lady hairnets peer through bean-slot gaps. One stabs the crook of his arm. The Texan orders him to hold still. He struggles to no effect. Haitians in dirty t-shirts burst through the door. Tongues of flame slam his father against the chalkboard. He fights, falling, dizzy, dissolving in a red smear.

rhythms on a flaming drum

He's worried he'll die and thinks I don't notice. Well, fuck you, Xan. But it's too late to argue when the nurse appears at the treatment room door. Caitlin numbly watches him drop his coat on a chair. His flannel shirt is bunched and bagging. She's surprised his jeans stay up. *He can't go like this.* But he has. Her fingers reach for the charm under her blouse—his; they traded in Charlotte. *Is he wearing mine?* The prayer she sends him through it reminds her of standing on a chair, stirring the soups she and her mom created a long, long time ago. According to Maeve, proper soup can't be made from a can or cookbook; it's the casting of a spell. Cayenne for fire, sugar for sweetness, carrot for an interesting sight, bitter rue for regret. Every bowl a special blend, appropriate to the day. Caitlin's plea to Xan is complicated, tinged with rue.

The amulets. Maeve's magick pouches are still in the travel case where they've been since Toronto. *He should have his.* "Tomorrow. I'll put it on him tomorrow. I promise."

Gertrude lifts her head, uncomprehending.

"May as well lie down," she tells the dog. She sits beside Xan's coat. Gertrude does an impersonation of a bearskin rug. Caitlin would snuggle with her if it wasn't so pathetic. The magazines on the tables are unappealing collages of cute pets, babies and travel destinations. Consumerist fare. She scrolls through text messages—with Xan already under surveillance, why not bring the phone? Barb DeShazer asks if she's willing to answer media questions on the Palomar announcement; talking with selected outlets could be advantageous.

Caitlin thumbs a reply. "Depends. Phone is best but maybe an interview at News2." She pulls up the station's webpage. Palomar coverage consists of unexamined claims of job losses and danger to national security set against praise for the closure on grounds of public health. Given the NewsStooge history as corporate tool, this brainless balancing act represents progress. A news crawl says two Lumet County deputies have been shot. Trade talks with the newly installed junta in Venezuela are underway. *The free-marketeers can't even wait for the blood to dry.* She returns to texting.

The phone rings. A male caller leaves a voicemail asking her to contact News2. The shootings and standoff at Lake Hollister involve a suspect in Mari's murder.

She dials the callback number.

"Ms. Schmidt?"

"Speaking."

"Yes, ma'am. In case you haven't been following the news, an arrest was made in connection with Ms. Errandonea's death. A second suspect barricaded himself in a residence near the lake."

"This is the first I've heard."

"The suspect in custody is Thomas E. "Tigger" Henshaw. Are you familiar with him?"

"What does he look like?"

"Big man. Heavy build. Blond."

Gertrude alerts at the sound of the swinging door. It's Dr. Wachowski.

Caitlin's heart freezes. *It hasn't been an hour.* She hangs up. The vet is holding a sandwich bag as if it contains a dead mouse.

"The procedure went well," he says, handing Caitlin the bag. The GPS is black, tubular. A white ring around the middle has numbers printed on it. "Don't twist the barrel," he warns. "That could be the On-Off."

"How is he?"

"Regaining consciousness. We had a tussle with the anesthetic but he'll be fine."

Her phone rings. She switches it to vibrate.

"See this?" he asks, showing her eyelets at the ends of the tube. "They anchored the device with one of these. If they'd left the stitch loose the unit could have floated in the cavity. Instead it was cinched tight to the musculature and impaired bowel motility. The idiot who implanted it should have his license revoked. But he made my job easy."

"Xan's okay?"

"The prognosis is excellent."

The phone stops buzzing. "Can I see him?"

"Let him wake up first. We'll bring him out. He'll have a compression wrap over the dressing. Leave it in place until he's in bed. There's to be no stress on the suture line. He should use a pillow if he's nauseated or needs to cough. Start clear liquids in the morning."

"Chicken broth for mother love."

"Excuse me?"

"I'm the daughter of a soup witch. He'll have chicken broth for mother love. Ginger for a tummy ache. Garlic to ward off infection. Barley for renewal." *I can't believe I remember this.*

Evidently Maeve's remedies are outside the vet's scope of practice. "Try the broth alone first," he says. "Add barley as tolerated. Anything else?"

"I'm sure, but I can't think of it. Thank you again, so much."

"It's an honor to be of assistance. The sedation is short-acting. We'll have him ready in half an hour, give or take."

Caitlin zings with relief as he and the bag return to the treatment area. Her phone buzzes again.

"Ms. Schmidt?" the man from News2 says. "We were disconnected."

"Sorry, there was a small domestic emergency."

"No problem. About the suspect in custody, Tigger Henshaw? I was wondering—"

"One of Mari's attackers was big and blond. I'd need a picture."

"Does the name Dewayne Mark Bowman ring any bells? He's the suspect in the standoff."

"Josh was the only name I heard."

"When photographs are available, may I send them to you?"

"I should consult my attorney first."

"It would be great if you could identify these guys."

"Maybe, after speaking with my lawyer."

"Great. I'll pass this on to Francine. Do you have any comment at this time?"

"No. Things are hectic right now."

She's too keyed up to sit and shaking too hard to text. Gertrude paces with her at first, then tires of it and lies down. The magazines are boring. The television remote isn't on the receptionist's desk. It would be totally inappropriate to open drawers, but she's almost reduced to it when the nurses roll Xan out in a wheelchair. He's loopy. A finger on his shoulder keeps him seated.

"Hi, babe," he says. "You should drive."

what goes without saying

Drumming is as natural to Xan as the sound of thought. Fingers and feet, the instrument of breath, tongue-tapped rhythms. Since the surgery he has spent his days listening to them. They tell him he's a broken record of a junk song, and not because of his stomach. He has gained six pounds. His guts didn't spill when the stitches were removed. He eats without pain but the fear of it abides. Like the nightmares. Like the cringing.

Tijon and The Blownglass Trio were stoked for band practice tonight. Caitlin and Janet had to meet anyway to tackle the collective's financial ills. If nothing else the theater trip was a welcome change of scene. He shouldn't have come. The beer and weed hit him hard but that's not why his performance sucked. Prison World did a worse number on him than he realized. Music should be a Free Territory. It isn't. Scamp tells him not to stress; he did okay. Xan acknowledges the polite lie, continues breaking down equipment. The stage must be cleaned and swept. Joyce rented the space for an eldercare training tomorrow.

As with many things in this looking-glass version of Calhoun, his lack of a future in it goes without saying. He can't tell people he's a Judas Rat. Those who are aware of it can't say so without declaring themselves Diggers. Caitlin surely realizes he'll have to vanish when he loses the GPS. He can't discuss this with Izzy, who'd tell Caitlin, who'd have a fit. What's she supposed to do, abandon her socially responsible life to skulk the back roads with a mental case? No sense belaboring the obvious. Or aggravating her frayed nerves by mentioning the pistol he bought for self-defense. He'll endure no more Texans or shock belts. But he won't go out in a delusional blaze of glory either. Camo Man got his wife and kid slaughtered alongside him at the lake.

In any event Lightning thinks it's stupid to act before fulfilling the contract for the John Henry story. The quickie TV movie deal minimized demands on him. The writer is a tedious sort but she already has enough to spin into a salable lie. He hates leeching off Caitlin. He also hates her hovering, the healing concoctions, her solicitude. He hates that they can't sleep together. Breathe in. Breathe out. Cleansing breaths. In. Out. The technique is usually effective—for a few minutes.

He scoots his gig bag toward the stage wing.

Scamp asks, "Throw your back out?"

"Sledgehammers get heavy." This isn't Tijon's first dig at John Henry tonight.

"I tried to put it down but they wouldn't let me."

"Tijon," Scamp says, "anybody ever tell you you're a dick?"

"Fellas say that to me all the time."

Scamp's no stranger to prison industries. "Save the bragging until you build a year or two in the joint."

"Thanks," Xan says when Scamp takes the bag. The doctor's prohibition on lifting is another thing that shouldn't be revealed. "I overdid it today. Winter brought down a lot of limbs where we're staying."

"The box saps your strength. I'd rather pick strawberries for Correctional Rehab than sit in a godforsaken hole."

The girls appear at the rear of the house. "Finished for the night?" Caitlin asks.

"We wore him plumb out," Scamp says. "Take him home."

Caitlin drives. They're on the two-lane north to Laurel Ridge before she brings up band practice. "It sounded good," she says.

"I stank."

"Don't be hard on yourself."

"I played better in high school."

"Maybe you had too much to drink."

"Beer calms my nerves."

"Izzy told you drinking is bad for post-traumatic stress. The internet agrees with him."

"I'll write that down. Got a pencil?" He lowers his windshield visor to block a line of approaching headlights.

"You have to do your part."

He stares into the dark oval of the visor. "All is lost. Isn't that what they say?"

"Why must you do this to yourself? I want us to be good again, like we were. Please?"

The passenger wheels wander across the rumble strip onto the shoulder of the road. She overcorrects. Luckily there's no oncoming traffic.

"Want me to take the wheel?"

"Can you imagine how it hurts to watch you flounder?" Her voice cracks. "It's like you're trying to slip through my fingers. But I won't let you. I won't." She pounds the steering wheel in frustration.

"Things happen."

Now she's mad. "Listen to me. You're turning the corner, gaining weight. Izzy says you're making progress. Another few months and you'll be well. You can't give up."

"Aren't we forgetting the bug?"

"My sources say the battery life is six to nine months. Some of that has expired."

"Third hand information."

"That's for our protection and you know it. ISA can't catch us researching GPS units used in marine fish."

"So what happens when the battery dies? Do they reel me in again? What if a blue shirt frisks me at a checkpoint? You'd be busted too. I don't want that on my conscience."

"We can't worry about 'what ifs.' We do today what we can do today."

Such as vanish. He doesn't say that aloud. She's driving.

Take him to a doctor. Check him into the hospital." Wally tries not to shout into his headset. The shopping mall reverberates with canned music, talking ads on vid screens and shoppers hollering at each other above the racket.

"It isn't that simple," she complains.

What did I miss? Her boyfriend has a traumatized psyche, hardly surprising. "Why not?" The response is dead air. "Caitlin?"

"I'm here. He's *in* counseling, and has been since coming home. A hospital would be like prison."

"Then, keep him busy landscaping at the house."

"He is, but he's still weak."

"Is there something you want me to do?" This is his second circuit of the ground floor. The doggy Easter outfits in the window display are no cuter on this pass. He recognizes a gaggle of roving teens—none of the girls in hoop earrings is old enough for the trash she's wearing. He had forgotten how much he detests shopping.

"I don't need you to *do* anything. It was nice of you to loan us the house. He'd go crazy if we were cooped up in the apartment."

"Stay as long as you like. No telling when I'll have the chance to visit. How are you doing otherwise?"

"Other than being worried sick, you mean? I'm furious. The

Sheriff's report says nobody but Camo Man attacked us at the lake. He's conveniently dead. Josh Rice was supposedly trying to help Mari when she stabbed him and Henshaw shot her. A tragic misunderstanding, justifiable homicide. They're sweeping murder under the rug and the media is only interested in Palomar going out of business."

"Give yourself credit. That's a lot to be proud of." *The Department of Defense will happily give you credit.*

"Teddy's dead. Mari's dead. Xan's a wreck. Huskins and his creeps dodge criminal charges. Isn't reform wonderful?"

"The world doesn't change in a day."

"It sure can for a person."

He wants to say he's considering a drastic change himself. Computer security wasn't a nasty business when he went into it. There was always a gaming aspect to shielding white hats from black hats, of course, but one guided by righteous motives. Those eroded years ago. The Latin American application of weaponized software has been a bitter revelation. Havoc remotely inflicted by cubicle-dwellers takes the dehumanization of warfare to new levels. Deposed leaders and their supporters are being systematically rounded up and executed but none of that blood spatters the shoes of coders and cyber-ops technicians. *Shouldn't it, to mitigate the victory intoxication?* Wally's ready to kiss goodbye to all that, take early retirement and reacquaint himself with nature on a Vermont mountaintop. If anyone could understand, it's Caitlin. But her plate is already full.

"Have patience, sweetie."

"Mom says the same thing. I haven't told Xan yet but she's flying down to stay with us for a while. If that's a problem, we can put her up at the apartment."

"You're surprising him with Maeve?" The teenyboppers in hoop earrings have picked up an escort of older boys in letter jackets. The girls' parents would not be happy.

"He thinks a lot of her and he accuses me of hovering but I'm afraid to leave him alone."

"Why? What's he doing?"

"Nothing. That's what scares me. It's like he's somewhere else."

rhythms on a flaming drum

storm damage

Xan hasn't worked a full day since his arrest. He piddles at Laurel Ridge, has diddly to show for it. Apathy is more debilitating than lack of stamina. He's tired of everything, especially inertia. With Dr. Wachowski's blessing for moderate activity, he's ready to power through it.

The job is a winter-mutilated landscape planting at a bend in the driveway. He's in pitiful physical condition. His wrist wobbles behind the pruning saw. The side of his thumb reddens as he dismembers gold-tipped junipers. He puts on gloves, which he should have done in the first place. When he's finished this bed will feature azaleas and a pink dogwood.

Maeve's lending a hand. He's annoyed that she's in town to babysit but her steadying influence salves raw nerves. Instead of freaking when he and Caitlin told her about the GPS, she matter-of-factly suggested that they hide it in a building the signal can't penetrate, then flee to Canada. Caitlin disagrees. Her life is here. She wants him to wait out the battery. Neither plan addresses the monster in the room: Xan Hicks. He's unhinged. No one, not even himself, is safe from him, whether in Toronto, the gentleman's jail at Laurel Ridge, or Timbuktu.

But this morning the birds are bonkers with spring. Trout lilies hoist yellow stars above purple-stained leaves. Conifer resin spices the musty, damp soil. He saws. Maeve stacks branches. Caitlin wheelbarrows them to the village road. Her last load was mounded so high her mom bet it wouldn't arrive intact. Loser cooks tonight. Xan wins either way.

He has stripped a contorted Japanese pine of its lower limbs, now drops the splintered crown and strips that. "Physical activity becomes you," Maeve says. "It's good to see the energy flowing. But looks can be deceiving, can't they?"

Because he likes her he deflects the intrusion. "Laying around is harder than people think." And because she's never given him a straight answer on witchcraft, he counters her nosiness by asking again what exactly she's a priestess of.

"A circle of explorers in the magickal arts. Last weekend we gathered to celebrate the Sabbat of Ostara."

He hasn't heard of it.

She deposits an armful of small boughs on the drive. "Ostara is spring equinox. It loaned Easter the eggs and bunnies. Don't let me forget: I brought you and Caitlin ashes from our bonfire."

Ashes? He's transported to the pyre at the lake. *Izzy's breathing exercises. In. Out.*

"Oh, goodness," Maeve says. "The burning. I apologize."

Bizarre comments are not what he needs right now. It's absolutely necessary to change the subject. "So you *are* a witch?"

"Labels cause such confusion, don't you find? I often avoid it by identifying as a life coach. But generic labels are limiting as well. A life coach can't travel to the spirit world for a First Nations member with soul sickness. Only a shaman can recover the missing pieces of a soul. So, when necessary, I'm a strangely pale shaman. Transformation takes so many, many forms, some even joyous," she says, dragging more branches out of the work area.

Xan links his respiration to saw strokes, breathes a kerf into the mangled pine trunk. "Caitlin appreciates what you did for her in Montreal."

"It's better to prevent illness when we can."

The twisted pole loosens in place, binds his saw. Maeve pushes the trunk to open the kerf. He completes his cut. "I'm glad you're here for her," he says as she drags the log toward the asphalt.

"While we await your decision?"

What decision? Damn it, woman, can't you shut up? He trades the saw for a shovel.

"Should you be digging?" she asks, dubious.

"It won't damage the bed as much as jerking the stump with the van."

"Don't hurt yourself."

He drives the shovel blade with leg power only. "We can't replant until the damaged stuff is out."

"Such a shame," she says, "this cult of the unblemished. A life that survives the worst Nature can throw at it has so much more character."

"Sometimes the damage is too severe."

"So much to consider."

He hears the wheelbarrow. Caitlin's running in their direction. "Mom," she shouts, "don't let him do that. Can't I leave him alone for five minutes?"

Maeve tells him, "Why don't you take the next load? She and I can manage this stump."

"Fine with me." He leaves the shovel, goes to meet Caitlin, glad to avoid further prodding. "Ready to switch jobs?" Her face flickers with emotions he's learning too well: fear, resignation, anger, restraint.

"Sure." She almost says more but doesn't.

He saws the pine log into short lengths, fills the wheelbarrow, sets off for the road. He'd like to keep going, walk on out of her life. But that wouldn't stop the Prison World poison from spreading in him, deranging, paralyzing his will. If he trusted the advice of his frazzled brain he'd blow it out.

It occurs to him that an extended trip to the Free Territories, away from all this, might be his solution. Maeve, at least, ought to understand a vision quest. If the answer is suicide he can eliminate the evidence of Dr. Wachowski's work although, without an explanation, Caitlin would take it wrong. He'll deal with that in a letter, and include a blank check on his account. She should have the money. Selling the rights to John Henry was her idea.

That's a nasty thought. This is a nice day. Soak it in.

The empty wheelbarrow has a mind of its own and veers unpredictably on the driveway. Caitlin rounds the bend to the landscape area where they're working. Her mom's dragging a log. Xan's digging a grave.

"Mom," she calls, breaking into a run, "don't let him do that. Can't I leave him alone for five minutes?"

He stops digging.

"Ready to switch jobs?" he asks her a moment later. This morning, for the first time since ISA let him go, his eyes had life in them. It's gone again.

"Sure." *Don't scare me like this.* But her crazy imaginings aren't his fault. She leaves the wheelbarrow and turns so he won't see her cry.

"Mom," she says when he's out of hearing, "what are we going to do?"

"Dig around this stump." Maeve hands her the shovel.

"I meant about helping him. He doesn't let us. You told me you read the cards before coming down. Did they offer any advice?"

"That reading disturbed Geoff enough to quit grumbling about having to cook for himself while I'm gone," Maeve says. "I saw an approach, but the details can't be shared with Xan."

"Why?" Caitlin bounces her weight on the shovel, stopped by

a stubborn root.

Maeve picks up the pruning saw. "Clear away the soil. I'll get that." With the root cut, she says, "We mustn't appear to mother him. That's critical. Distressing as it is, we're to await and respect his judgment."

"What judgment?"

"The judgment of severity. His reading was lousy with fives. Mars is going to war. Destructive power without mercy. Hot oranges and reds. There's Defeat, the Five of Swords, but also a potentially saving Six of Wands. He'll be changed if he pulls through. If not, it's because he didn't believe he could control his fate in any other manner. Power is the crux of his wound. If we try to take it from him, the cards warn of dire consequences. Has he mentioned a guardian angel?"

"He doesn't believe in them."

"Ah, well. Let's dig, show him we're not powerless either."

The stump is waiting on the drive when Xan returns, his sunny mood restored. That doesn't reduce Caitlin's horror at the plan of self-treatment he proposes. *Anything could happen on magic mushrooms. He needs more self-control, not less.* She wants to tell him that, tries to, but nothing comes out. Her mom puts an arm around her shoulders. It wills consent, or silence.

Maeve says, "Xan, do you stand by your vows to Caitlin?"

"Always."

"Then for her benefit and yours as well, I'd like you both to repeat them. Caitlin, go take his hand."

She staggers over to him. His warmth and sweat are so alive. She imagines him tripping, taking a flying leap off the mountain. He wouldn't mean to, but he'd be dead. Her mom can't possibly expect her to approve.

"Caitlin, let's begin with you. Will you cause Xan pain?"

"I did." She clutches him. "I caused terrible pain."

"Was that your intent?"

"No. Not ever. I'd do anything to take it away."

"Anything? Even permit his vision quest?"

This is too much. Don't make me say it. But she forces herself to nod, sobbing, into his shirt.

"Xan, will you cause Caitlin pain?"

"I'm causing it now."

"Is this your intent?"

"That's why—"

"Xan," Maeve says. "I asked if it's your intent to cause her pain."

"No, babe. Whatever happens, it's not."

"Caitlin, do you love him with the wholeness of your being?"

"I do." *Please believe me. Please.*

"Xan, do you love her with the wholeness of your being?"

His hands caress her back. "Never doubt it."

"Then seal it with a kiss," Maeve says, "and let's get busy. There's planting yet to be done."

rhythms on a flaming drum

the gory chalice

Collective Harlequin's revenue stream has dwindled to rental income for the theater space. That barely covers fixed expenses. Last fall's upgrades to building security dented the rainy day fund. Taxes will take another bite. Six members, upset by a lack of paychecks and the risk of reprisals from Palomar allies, want to be bought out. Cash on hand is inadequate to accommodate them and launch a new season. The collective is gathering to resolve the crisis.

Xan's not up to attending but the collective's future is too important for Caitlin to leave to others. Besides, these people are friends; she hasn't seen or spoken with many of them since Canada. From the moment of her arrival until Denny and the Steins flank her like bodyguards in the ring of chairs, she's hugged, pawed, commiserated with and questioned. Tijon innocently continues the pressure by convening the session with a special recognition of her presence and declaring that Mari is a martyr to the cause of social justice. The standing ovation and worshipful gazes bear down with weighty intensity.

What are they doing? "Thank you," she says. "Mari would be honored. Xan too. I'll pass along your good wishes. But let's move on. We have business." Her words are met with another wave of adoration that threatens to suffocate her. She's forced to escape the confines of the circle for the open space at the front of the house.

Backed against the stage apron she begs for quiet. "You're very kind." She shouldn't say what she's about to but can't hold it in. "I appreciate the welcome. I do. But please, don't turn me into something I'm not. Mari and I thought we could sneak past Palomar security in the rain. That was stupid. She had no intention of being a martyr. I ran when they attacked her. That's not courage. And she wasn't beautiful lying in her own blood with a bulging eye and brains in her hair. When I tried to lift her, the hole in her chest burped foam. It was beyond gross."

Denny, who had a sweet spot for Mari, hides his face in his hands. Caitlin wishes she'd sit down but the dam has burst. "And I'm to blame for everything that happened to Xan. I did the things I did afterwards because I owed it to him and Mari. That's all. There wasn't a heavenly guiding light, no surrender to a higher power. It was shame and guilt. Mari and I fucked up, and because of that she and Xan paid a horrible price."

Someone says, "But you won. We never win."

"Don't make it like that. Don't forget the leaked documents. Or Teddy. Or the lawsuit, the protests, Gil's radio show, Dr. Sigurdsdottir. I have to tell myself everything counted. Corporations don't care about dead or damaged people who don't affect the bottom line. And if it really does take the suffering of innocents and blood of martyrs to mobilize public pressure in this country? That's barbaric too. I don't know which value system is worse, blood or money. They're both dehumanizing, atrocities to be outgrown not perpetuated. This is the twenty-first century, not the first."

"Caitlin," Izzy says, "let's not—"

"If human sacrifice is the measuring stick then the Fiery Sword asshole outscored us with his shootout. He took his wife and son with him. Do kids count extra points?"

"No, but—"

"No buts, just no." The faces are uncomprehending. *I should be with Xan.*

His van isn't in the garage. She must have forgotten an errand he planned to do. But her mom's expression confirms the worst.

"He doesn't have the mushrooms yet," Caitlin wheedles. "He was supposed to do it here. Where is he? I don't get to say goodbye?"

Maeve draws her under her wing. "He didn't tell me where he was going. He said it was time to learn whether he's an Egyptian and you'd know what that means. Evidently it has to do with the charms you wear. I believe he has his with him. Silver makes a powerful amulet."

"The Egyptians lost their ships. He'll die! Why didn't you stop him?" Caitlin cries. "How long has he been gone? Where's my phone?"

"He took the van out shortly after you left. His phone's in your bedroom. He asked me to say he loves you and if we don't see him again you'll receive a letter."

"What!" Caitlin struggles, but her mom's right. What would tearing around the county in a car accomplish? Better to think.

"He had the impression you'd appreciate it."

"A goddamned letter?" Caitlin pulls free. "I hate him. How could he do this?"

"Sit down with me." Maeve directs her to the couch.

She collapses into her mom's lap. Soothing fingers stroke her hair as they've done since forever. "I don't really hate him," she says. "But there must be something we can do. What is it?"

"We wait."

"But isn't there a spell? Anything?"

"We've cast several. You and I have been busy."

"When?"

"Right along. He's prepared for this as best he can be. The

forces are strongly aligned to favor his return."

"But will he?"

"It's what he wants, if that matters. A physicist friend tells Geoff and me that spacetime already exists in its entirety from the big bang to the end, if there is one, and that nothing in the universe has the power to change what seems to us to unfold across time. The book's been written. If he's correct—and he says it's a common view among his colleagues—then when I say our spells align the forces I mean we align ourselves and him in a manner consistent with our desired result. It's no huge surprise when a deeply loved person survives an ordeal. The past pushes; the future pulls. Some of us believe we're sensitive to the shape of that pull. But until science validates divination, take me on faith. There is hope."

Xan's open-air terrarium teems with nightlife. Pale blue tourists, yellow skirts immodestly fluttering over their faces, gyrate and chitter along aimless black spans, dropping bags of peanuts to the humans on display in the glowing lava fields below. Too many souls to count. Millions, billions maybe. One. Strapped to a cart, arms outstretched, wriggling, injected by hairnet robots. They wrap him in a shock belt bandage, wheel him off to a cell, lock the door.

Rat-tat-tat in a hellscape school. Arks of blood, two by two, pierce the fiery atmosphere, crash dying at his feet. He picks his mother off the ground. She burns until he drops her. Vanished in the dirt. Lost in brain-scramble eardrum thunder.

Unfazed, the walls of the night breathe in and out. A moment of claustrophobia passes. He can't complain. They've taken away the shock belt and given him regular clothes. As cells go, this is roomy.

He hears laughter, unrecognizable until Lightning speaks. "You white meats is crazier than anybody."

The voice surprises him. "Where were you? I was afraid you went away."

"I got nothing better to do than mind your business?" Lightning's tricked out in his Beale Street best. The gig suit is a questionable choice for Saturday night on the banks of Lake Hollister. He's warming his hands, the satin stripe on his pant leg a snake in the firelight. "Never tried them hippie toadstools, myself. Reefer do for me. What that in your pocket, a .38?"

Xan admits it.

Lightning grunts approval. "Snub nose all right for close work, unless you shoot your fool balls off jerking it out your pants. What the gasoline for? That shit bad to flare up."

Xan explains it as he did in the letter to Caitlin. If this is his night to die he'll stand over the fire, gun in one hand, two gallons of gas in the other. There won't be enough left to raise questions about the GPS. The location and method are purely practical. The condemned was allowed to drag himself kicking and screaming to the foregone collusion: a Texan-sized joke.

The pathetic creatures in the lava fields scurry in their exhibits under the bridges of Mari's roasting limbs. *Les Frères* think they're doing him a favor by hustling him away from the schoolhouse coup. Tonight, lamps gleam from every shanty. *When the poor step out to piss in the gutter do they see me staring?* He kicks the fire, burying them with ashy landslides. Charred bones flatten Cité Soleil. Iridescent beats of purple, blue, green and gold scorch his face with splendor.

New wood, damp from the ground, triggers a wider disturbance. Bullets whizz, snap, pinwheel into space trailing curlicue streamers. The sky is papered with sheets of Warhol stamps— half a papaya and a palm frond—shot through by stardrops. The battle at his feet rages to the music of shrieks, whistles, samba drumming. *Carnival's late this year. Maybe it was the war.* Dancers in regalia parade across the coals.

"Redeem this," he tells them, kicks the fire again.

Lightning is dismayed. "Naw, now. Brazilian womens want to shake they booty? Count your blessings and beat your drum."

Instead he sees himself and Caitlin in the ashes: the Xchange mart and her sea-green eyes, the intertwining of lifelines, his letter fluttering from her hand. He watches himself diverge from her, mail the letter, buy a triple hit of shrooms, fill the gas can, relocate this rutted road. The fire ring was an empty crater, vacuumed of evidence. He collected wood until dusk.

Each moment leads only to another. The clockwork raises a hammer, bangs down. Heartless. Thoughtless. Lightning pinned, extinguished. "A man do what he got to do." Trip hammer today, cog tomorrow, and off to the dump te dump dump dump.

"That was a sorry day I lost my pistol," Lightning says. He has moved to the other side of the undulating bed of fire roses, now one, now many, tall, short, beautifully complex. "You done me right when I was in need. I come this evening to return the favor. You smarter than me, though, carrying your piece where there ain't no losing it. But don't shine me on with no bullcrap. You got your legs. If you laying in your own mess, that your choice. So I be going now. See you around, white meat."

Xan flies across the roses, sweeps the darkness where Lightning stood. Nothing. To his amazement his own shirtsleeves are empty as well. His hands feel normal but they're invisible as the breeze, fused with the air, atomized. His clothing falls in a heap. He disperses across bumpy ground, envelops tree trunks. Has the sensation of rising, flowing into the lake. He drowns unharmed. Movement loses relevance. Only two artifacts of him remain: the Phoenician sea charm and the ISA's ridiculous plastic turd. He laps the shore and peeps the frogs. Squawks a night bird and flaps away.

As his vision adjusts, the markings on the charm take on the character of an Egyptian ankh and pyramid. The lake has the same liquid metal sheen and, across the cove, the bristly ridge is crowned. The ankh rises as a moon slightly past full, dragging tides along the glyphs of living and dying, wheeling signs of an ancient zodiac. Moons turn, and planets, but the unseen star they reflect is Present, undying, perpetual.

He reads his face in the blazing silver surface, sun and planets, presence and change, wide as the universe, particular as a naked man crouched at a campfire. Both together, inseparable. He is free to shoot or not shoot, build, destroy, suffer, exult, regain his strength. Now. All at once. He is *not* an Egyptian. He's free to go home.

At dawn, he will. Until then, he has astral rhythms to study on a flaming drum.

ash people

Caitlin refuses to wake. She never wants to without this feeling of Xan's arm around her. She smells smoke. Alarmed, she rolls over.

"Good morning, babe," he says.

There are no other words.

The clock radio reads 1:17. Past noon. He's quiet beside her. *I should tell Mom.* She throws off her covers but he catches her by the waist. "No kiss?" He's streaky with soot, reeking like sex in a forest fire. For the first time since prison that's the way they'd done it, heedless and all-consuming. She's sticky all over, as grimy now as he.

"Can't sleep?" she asks, kissing him.

"I got a little."

"Littles like that'll get somebody pregnant."

"In the mood for twins?"

At mid-afternoon they're scrubbed and ready for the world. Maeve pretends to take Xan's return in stride. "Hungry?" she asks. "We're having eggplant parmesan for dinner. But that's hours away."

Caitlin breezes into the kitchen on a magick carpet of desire.

"What's in the fridge?"

Leftover stir fry never tasted better. As Xan gathers dishes, Caitlin has a domestic moment. She'll wash them by hand. Her mom sprinkles salt on slices of eggplant and says, "Last night was difficult for us, Xan."

He piles plates in the sink. "If there'd been another way…"

Caitlin starts the hot water. She could grow to like the scent of wood smoke in his hair. But her mom has ruined the daydream. "You weren't actually going to send me a letter."

"I should collect the mail for a few days."

"A letter? Do you have a clue how dismissive that is? I want to see it."

"No, you don't."

"Was it *that* mean?"

"The opposite. If things went a different way, I couldn't have you misunderstand."

"Misunderstand what?"

"What happened. But it didn't and that's over for me."

"You're certain?"

"Totally."

"I still want to read the letter."

Maeve stacks columns of eggplant in a baking dish to sweat. "Isn't it strange," she says, "how much easier it is to entrust loved ones with our lives than with their secrets? Does Xan know what went on at your theater meeting?"

Her mom waits. He waits. They watch her add detergent to the dishwater. The silence becomes awkward. "Tijon called Mari a martyr and it set me off. I mean really. Nobody sacrifices goats anymore; that's cruel and superstitious. But grassroots movements aren't taken seriously until *people* die? That's what it takes to sway public opinion? Human victims sacrificed by psycho priests? Mari wouldn't stand for being remembered like that. She'd want to be mourned, not venerated."

The rumble in his throat might signify agreement, or drug cobwebs.

"They just stared at me, even Reba and Izzy."

Maeve says, "Don't be too hard on them. You went through a hell you wouldn't wish on anyone for that lesson. Whatever else may be true of such experiences, they set apart and draw together. You and Xan forged a bond calamity couldn't break. Are others wrong to be a bit in awe? I'm reminded of the tattered hero of *The Russia House* who tells his lover, 'You are my only country now.' You understand that at a depth closed to the rest of us."

"Am I your only country?" Caitlin asks, passing Xan a dripping plate.

He dries it. "Absolutely. And our kids. And your mom. Maybe even your dad."

"Cheating? Already?" She squeezes sponge water down the nape of his neck. He yelps.

Maeve says, "The ashes I brought may be redundant."

"Again with those ashes." But his body forgets to rebel at the word.

"A remarkable change," she tells him, bowing slightly with her hands in the Indian position of greeting. "Namaste."

"Ashes?" Caitlin asks.

"I'm ready for a child to call me Grandma. Ostara ash aids fertility."

"Are you serious? I'd be afraid of ashes more potent than those he brought home this morning. What do you think, Xan, Ashley? Or Smokey maybe, if it's a boy?" She hands him another plate.

"What I think," he says, "is that you inherited your crude streak from your mother. Not that I'm complaining."

"You'd better not," Caitlin says, threatening him with another sponge bath. "But, Mom, answer me this. You brought us ashes from Canada?"

"That's right."

"When we were such a mess? Are we supposed to believe you knew what would happen?"

"If I were omniscient I'd not have bothered with the ashes. Let's just say I know that you're resilient, resourceful lovers. Who in their right mind bets against that? My grandbaby will be someone to behold. But Caitlin, sweetie, forgive my saying; isn't Ashley a bit overdone?"

black birds

Two months out from surgery Xan's nightmares and panic attacks have abated. The campfire licks he learned spark bright in band practice. He seldom breaks his self-imposed GPS quarantine for other purposes, but the Laurel Ridge grounds are the better for it. He's removing invasive vines from a woodlot when his phone rings.

It's Caitlin. "The gatehouse says ISA is on the way up. I'm calling Barb."

A lawyer in Charlotte won't do us any good. "Find your camcorder. I'll be right there."

He'd caved and shared the suicide letter before Maeve went home. She and Caitlin accepted the contents better than expected, though not his refusal to part with the .38. There's suicide and then there's suicide. He's done with prison. The pistol is in the van, taped beneath the driver's seat. He grabs it, dashes inside.

"Where are you?" he shouts.

She's in the great room. Phone to her ear. Palm-sized video camera at the ready. She sees the pistol. "No! Don't."

He jams it into his hip pocket. "If they go for the handcuffs, run and don't look back."

"Not again. I won't leave you."

The doorbell chimes.

No time for this. "Hide the camera where it can see this room," he tells her. "I'll steer them to the couch."

Instead she follows him, talking into her phone, "It's an emergency. Tell Barb ISA is at my house. Xan has a gun."

"Get back, Caitlin. Now."

The men on the other side of the storm door are bulked up, wearing vests under black blazers. *Head shots, if it comes to it.* One is the grizzled reptile with wire-rim glasses who lorded over the jailhouse questioning and pretended to investigate the theater vandalism. A badge hangs from his jacket pocket. His buddy is younger, plump, sandy hair, badgeless.

"Mr. Hicks," the reptile says, "I'm Special Agent Doak with the Calhoun office of Integrated Security. We met during the homicide mix-up. My associate and I would like to speak with you and Ms. Schmidt if she's available."

"About what?"

Doak spots Caitlin and grins. "Oh, Ms. Schmidt, glad to catch you in. Filming? That won't be necessary. We just dropped by for a chat."

"Please," Caitlin says to whoever she's speaking with. "This can't wait."

"Cooperation is strictly voluntary but we have a proposal you'll be interested in. May we enter?"

Xan blocks the door. "You're fine right there."

"If you'd be more comfortable," Doak says.

"What would make me comfortable is you losing your jackets and weapons. Guns make me nervous. Maybe you too." He turns his hip, flashing the butt of the pocketed pistol. "If you want to talk, do it without hardware."

Doak raises his hands as if his intentions are being misconstrued. "That's against policy, Mr. Hicks."

"Then goodbye."

"You can't expect us to enter unarmed."

"Then don't."

Doak talks past him. "Ms. Schmidt, are you aware of the investigation involving your father? He might be retiring to Leavenworth instead of Vermont. If we can come in I'll explain."

Xan and Doak negotiate an unarmed, outdoor sit-down. His chubby partner readily reveals the taser and handcuffs on his belt but doesn't show the semi-auto strapped to his ankle until specifically asked to hike his pant legs. Xan watches him and Doak lock their jackets and paraphernalia in the car. Only then does he direct them around the garage to the deck steps. He leaves his pistol on a hassock in the great room where it'll be visible through the sliding doors.

He shows his hands and empty pockets at the top of the stairs, tells the agents where his gun is. They verify it when they're up, but fail to notice Caitlin's camcorder peeking from a planter. She tracks their movements with her phone.

Doak tells her to shut it off. "This isn't a conversation you'll want to publicize. Nice to see you again, by the way. Did you hear we got the arsonist who tried to torch your theater?"

"Who was it?" Caitlin says.

"That fisherman who assaulted Miss Errandonea. Too bad he wasn't apprehended alive. Pity about the wife and boy."

Caitlin lays her phone on the deck's serving table and scoots a chair to it. "We'll have room here," she says. "Bring your own seats."

And smile for the camcorder. Xan takes the end of the table nearest the sliding doors. The agents opt for the side close to the stairs.

Doak's knees crack as he sits. "What a view," he says. "Must give a man a sense of power to have the whole valley laid before him."

"You didn't drive up here for the view," Xan says.

"Actually I did, in part. But you're right. We're here to remind you that this country has laws against abetting enemies of the state and conspiring to obstruct justice. You're cognizant of your father's work, Ms. Schmidt?"

"It's classified. We don't discuss it."

"But you did operate as a member of the Digger resistance and established an irregular line of communication with him while on foreign soil, did you not?"

Caitlin snatches up her phone. "I'm contacting our attorney."

The young agent also produces a phone and says, "I'm disappointed, Xan. You haven't told her we're not encumbered by criminal statutes?" He speaks with a chillingly familiar drawl.

This doughboy? The Texan taps his phone screen. Xan flinches at the shock tone throb.

"They're asking us questions," Caitlin says. "Can't you get her for me?" She hangs up in frustration.

The distraction allows Xan to regroup—he's improving at Izzy's exercises. "Babe, I should introduce someone. Remember the prison interrogator, the Texan? That's him across the table. Looks nothing like I thought. Maybe he'll tell us his real name."

"Pleasure, ma'am." The man tips an imaginary hat. "Posh spread you have here, Xan. Sweet. Hope you're around to enjoy it."

The remark further incenses Caitlin. "You tried to kill him."

The Texan smirks. "ISA pays my firm to add value, not destroy it. We asked him to lead us to you and here you are."

"I have immunity. You can't touch me."

"Don't kid yourself."

Doak serves his offer on ice. "You have no deal with me, Ms. Schmidt. But you could. That matter of your father conspiring with the Digger resistance? I can make it go away. He'd be allowed to retire in peace. Your boyfriend could get off this mountain and reap the rewards of being John Henry. All I require is cooperation."

Caitlin is speechless.

Go on, Xan thinks. "What sort of cooperation?"

"Two primary things," Doak says. "I'll need the encryption key to the laptop impounded from your apartment."

"And names," the Texan says, drawing out the word. "Digger names. We could begin with Wraith. Who is he?"

"Get off this property," Caitlin says.

The shock tone doesn't surprise Xan this time. His cower is pretense. Unfortunately Caitlin buys it, springs from her seat, throws protective arms around him. "I said get out!"

He caresses her arms. "It's okay, babe. Calm down."

The Texan switches off the tone.

"Listen to him, Ms. Schmidt," Doak says, raising a cautionary hand. "I don't require an immediate answer. But until you're ready to assist us I'll ask you to surrender your passport. It can be reclaimed at my office."

"Forget it," she hisses.

Xan dares not release her.

Doak shrugs, pats the table, rises. "Have it your way," he says. "The document itself is a symbolic convenience for Customs and Border Protection. I'll flag your profile, like we did your boyfriend's. If you attempt to cross an international border you'll be detained. We might even send a black bird for you. That's what Diggers call our special ops vehicles, isn't it? Black birds?"

The Texan pockets his phone. "Sir, I believe the term is Black Mariah, sir."

"Black Mariah, then. ISA has zero tolerance for unlawful flight. Consider the offer, folks."

rhythms on a flaming drum

flushed

You are my only country now. Doak's threat and two positive pregnancy tests focus Caitlin. She can't afford to reflect on the losses. Collective Harlequin. Orange azaleas blooming wild on Laurel Ridge. The brave little Civic that carried her safely through the Great Memphis Quake—the car and any tracking devices it might harbor have been sold. Bitsy and skittish Mrs. Letourneau. The innumerable nooks and crannies of hometown life, as familiar as second skin. Most of all the alternative community she dedicated herself to in the shadows of the free market, so many friends and colleagues who won't hear her say, "We may not meet again." Goodbyes are security risks and guaranteed meltdowns. *You, Xan, are my only country now.*

They're preparing for Canada behind a façade of business as usual. Boxes of nonessentials dribble toward Toronto from unsuspicious locations. Heavy boxes and percussion equipment wait in the theater prop room. Denny will ship those later. Later is also when he'll post the Doak and Texan video on the darknet. Caitlin did send copies to her parents—minus the weapons negotiation—and new burner phones.

Wally denies being an ISA target. According to him, Doak's claim was a scare tactic. Perhaps. Nevertheless she hasn't informed her dad of the Judas Rat unit or emigration. Later, when he's pissed at being shut out, she'll remind him there's no such thing as an absolutely secure line of communications.

Her mom is a marvelous source of practical information. For a fat price, Canadian sportfishers smuggle refugees across the Niagara River. Interdiction by U.S. Border Protection is less likely on water crossings. Canada can't be bothered to try. Maeve has ferreted out a contact on the American side. But she also warns that a glut of immigration applications from U.S. citizens works against illegal entrants. While permanent status may eventually be granted to refugees with Canadian family members and proof of political persecution, many give up and resettle elsewhere.

It's a chance Caitlin and Xan have to take. Today is departure day. He's trading the van for a used Subaru without cell or satellite features. He'll collect suitcases from her apartment and drive here, to the Medical Center, where the Steins are visiting a sick friend. The goodbye afterwards in the hospital café is the one Caitlin dreads most and won't permit herself to avoid.

But first, she and Xan need to disappear. She'll leave this unisex restroom on the radiology and lab test floor as a matron wearing disposable, eye doctor sunglasses. She reverses her shoulder bag from the beige side to the print and stuffs her sundress into it. The streaky gray wig suits her boonie hat, blouse and chinos. A tinge of unhealthy purple on the lips. *Careful not to overdo.* A dab on the mirror to signal Xan. He'll ditch his coveralls here to play her son, a beardless jock who'll obscure his facial features with wraparound shades and a CHUAAS Engineers cap. She runs water in the sink, dons the flimsy eye protection and is out the door. A nursing assistant transporting a chart in a wheelchair pays her no attention.

The car Xan traded for is clean, has a rebuilt engine. Not flashy, not a rust bucket. It's a ride to bore state troopers on shakedown patrol. License plates are trickier. He and Caitlin agreed that a temp tag beats stealing a plate. Thirty legal days should be plenty. Barring breakdowns they'll reach Niagara Falls tomorrow.

He does a final walkthrough of the apartment in town, unplugging, locking windows. Caitlin will miss her furniture. Some of it holds fond memories for him as well. The Subaru could haul twice what he loads, but they're not counting on unlimited boat space.

It's said that layers of concrete blind GPS satellites. He spirals down into the subterranean levels of the hospital garage. ISA may glimpse him again, briefly, on the short walk between parking deck and hospital entrance. He should be invisible again once inside. Half an hour behind schedule. The café is where Caitlin told him he'd find it. He sees her there, facing away. Reba's wiping her nose.

The third floor toilet is in use. He strolls on to the visitor area where an elderly lady sits knitting. She says her neighbor is having a bone scan. Xan excuses himself the moment the restroom door opens.

Caitlin left him a purple mark on the mirror. Though there's no reason to, he rubs it off. He takes the black curse from its cord, twists the halves of the barrel, hoping to kill the ISA's chances of determining that battery failure didn't cause the prolonged loss of signal. If the GPS is still broadcasting when it arrives at the water treatment plant, ISA could discover the truth within hours. Deactivated or not, the turd is a sinker. He christens its voyage through the sewer system with a hearty piss. Flush. Gone. Wig, sports glasses, ball cap, on. Wet paper towels hide the trashed coveralls. Flush. Double gone.

"Izzy, Reba, what a surprise." *You look like somebody actually died.*

Caitlin turns at the sound of his voice. *These are my dearest friends.*

They've saved him a seat at the table. He thanks the Steins for everything they've done for Caitlin, for him.

Reba strikes a stoic pose. "It's been our privilege."

"I feel like a crasher, taking her away like this."

"A hazard of the work," Izzy tells him. "We had no opportunity to say goodbye to Mari and almost missed it with you. This is much better. Since sacrifice has become a dirty word around here, I'll just say an ungrateful nation is better for your time among us. Reba and I are sorry it's ending so soon."

Caitlin can't endure another minute of imagining a future without him and Reba in it. She totters to her feet. "Ready?" she sighs. *Please.*

"If you are, Mom." *Did you tell them about your test results?*

No.

Tearful hugs all around.

"Be safe. Take care of each other."

"You too."

"Be in touch."

Hurry, before I'm a puddle on the floor.

Wally lowers the burner phone from his ear, closes it and stares at the gray clamshell. Caitlin's in Canada again. This time for keeps. At a narrow, pragmatic level he supposes skipping out made sense. ISA left them few other choices. But why must it have come to this? There were other ways to fight water pollution. They could have campaigned for better filtration systems instead of taking on Bobo Huskins. People are dead. Xan spent tortured months in prison. Now exile. And, at the end of the day, for what? Palomar has closed; jobs were lost but there's no cleanup announced. Calhoun municipal water remains cruddy as ever.

They're starting a new life, she'd said, in a place with a younger heart and a desire to evolve. Countries can become as rigid as some old people. What's *that* supposed to mean? It wasn't meant personally? How the hell else should he take it? He hopes she embellished the story of the border crossing. A rubber dinghy under the nose of the Coast Guard in the dead of a rainy night? But she courts trouble. She didn't used to. She was a happy kid, gifted with every opportunity. She could have been anything. Why an enemy of the state? Was life so boring she had to adopt other people's problems for excitement? That won't be an issue going forward. Immigrants don't have it easy anywhere.

He doesn't accept her excuse for not bringing him into the

loop while alternatives to expatriation existed. Okay, so he's not at liberty to explain the Whirlwind inquiries but surely, when he tells her not to worry he's earned the right to be taken at his word. Maeve wasn't any better. She might have said something during their discussion of the ISA video. He can't help but think the real reason for not seeking his counsel is rejection of what he stands for. Caitlin implied as much with her disparagement of "American values." To her, those are toxic. "Getting ahead in life is an American value, Dad," she said. Since when is that evil? Survival of the fittest has been around since life began. She dreams of a community without ambition, that cultivates feel-good vibes. Supported, no doubt, by the trust fund *American* values secured for her. It's maddening.

She's pregnant. He'll never be able to look into the face of his grandchild without seeing Xan Hicks? Grandpa should rejoice that daddy threw his pistol in the river? A gun? She must be freaking kidding. "This is the father of your baby? Who does he think he is, Clint Eastwood?"

"Guns are America's second language," she'd said. "Xan and I may never forget it but our kids should never learn."

"In what backwater of social engineering?"

"You're moving to Vermont and ask me that?"

Retirement is different. The mountains of his youth, the ponds, the fish are calling him home. She has denied herself those future comforts. And she's denying him the blessing of sharing Vermont with her, his flesh and blood.

"We'd rather be close to you and Mom but if Canada doesn't work, we'll go elsewhere. New Zealand maybe. Denmark. The sun's always shining somewhere."

Denmark? His grandbaby's second language might be *English*? Wally can't begin to come to terms with that. For such a child the United States would be the old country, the birthplace of his parents, as Prussia was for Friedrich Schmidt, fifth son of

Zacharias and Anna Catherine who fled the Pomeranian War. That any real war should have been named after a breed of lapdog once struck Wally as hilarious. Now the factoid is dry in his mouth. History forgot the particulars that drove Zacharias and Anna Catherine overseas. Nor does it record the names of the parents they left behind.

Pisgah Press

Also available from Pisgah Press

Mombie, the Zombie Mom $15.95	Barry A. Burgess
Letting Go: Collected Poems 1983-2003 $14.95	Donna Lisle Burton
Unbelievable: Faith, Reason, & the Search for Truth $16.00	Joseph R. Haun
MacTiernan's Bottle $14.95	Michael Hopping
I Like It Here! Adventures in the Wild & Wonderful World of Theatre $30.00	C. Robert Jones
Lanky Tales, Vol. 1 $9.00	C. Robert Jones
Fragments $16.00	Martin A. Keeley
Oscar & the Royal Avenue Cats $15.00	Martin A. Keeley
RED-state, WHITE-guy BLUES $15.95	Jeff Messer
A Green One for Woody $15.95	Patrick O'Sullivan
Reed's Homophones: a comprehensive book of sound-alike words $10.00	A.D. Reed
Swords in their Hands: George Washington and the Newburgh Conspiracy $24.95	David Richards
Trang Sen: A Novel of Vietnam $19.50	Sarah-Ann Smith

To order:

Pisgah Press, LLC
PO Box 1427, Candler, NC 28715
www.pisgahpress.com